FOREIGN EXCHANGE

This is a collection of new short stories, set in exotic, mysterious and extraordinary locations such as Mexico, Cuba, Greece, Russia, the Solomon Islands and Umbria, and written by such highly-acclaimed writers as Lisa St Aubin de Terán, Michel Déon, Clare Boylan, Colin Thubron, Norman Lewis and Fay Weldon as well as a number of new voices.

FOREIGN EXCHANGE

Edited by Julian Evans

Published in Great Britain simultaneously by
Hamish Hamilton Ltd and Abacus 1985
Abacus are published by Sphere Books Ltd
30–32 Gray's Inn Road, London WC1X 8JL
This collection copyright © 1985 by Julian Evans
Individual stories copyright by the author

This collection copyright © 1985 by Julian Evans
Individual stories copyright by the authors:
Puerto Vallarta copyright © Carlo Gébler 1985
A Weekend in Havana copyright © Norman Lewis 1985
La Plume de Mon Ami copyright © Rose Tremain 1985
The Ear copyright © Colin Thubron 1985
Ionian White and Gold copyright © Anne Spillard 1985
I Never Eat Crabmeat Now copyright © Lisa St Aubin de Terán 1985
Umbrian Afternoon copyright © Éditions Gallimard 1984;
translation copyright © Julian Evans 1985
L'Amour copyright © Clare Boylan 1985
The Blind Man Eats Many Flies copyright © David Profumo 1985
Walkabout copyright © Nicholas Wollaston 1985
Au Pair copyright © Fay Weldon 1985

CONTENTS

INTRODUCTION

These stories arose from a very simple idea. The idea was that all travel writing is fiction. Of course it isn't. Yet even if one ignores the circumstantial evidence that some of its greatest practitioners are novelists, and that much talk about travel writers praises exactly those qualities admired in writers of fiction – their lyrical powers of description, their set-pieces and extended jokes, their appetite for telling stories – the experience of reading Robert Byron's *Road to Oxiana* or Norman Lewis's *A Dragon Apparent* or Patrick Leigh Fermor's *Roumeli* is very akin to reading a novel. (And it would have to be an outstanding one.)

Travel books are romances, just as novels are journeys. They have to be good escapist stuff. If that kind of escape is not required, then why hasn't there been a sudden vogue for reading atlases, far-flung histories or thick volumes on Islamic architecture, instead of reprints of every writer, good and less good, who ever went further south than Issy-les-Moulineaux?

The mechanism by which a travel book works seems to me to be an interesting, and potentially precarious, one. There is a definite conspiracy at work, one in which the reader periodically allows his eyes to have the wool pulled over them, feigning not to notice, in order to see a greater truth. He knows the writer selects what he wants to tell him. From selection to invention is no distance at all. From a lie of omission to an encounter with myth, only a bit further. Is it possible that what might have happened is more important than what did, and is inserted in its place? For anyone who travels alone, the lack of witnesses must be a constant temptation. But the terms of the conspiracy are that as long as the imagination doesn't fail along with the landscape, the reader will not mind.

The first thought was that *Foreign Exchange* would merely relieve its contributors of any necessity to tell the truth, and then to see what happened. The stories are not really meant to propose the motion that all travel writing is fiction, if only because no short story was ever written for the sake of an editor's thesis. For example, even when the characters are not themselves central – as they are in Clare Boylan's and Fay Weldon's stories – there is an emphasis on the centrality of character which is absent in travel writing. Nicholas Wollaston's story, too, might have to abstain from the debate if there was one, since it features a narrator by the name of – Nicholas Wollaston.

Yet one of the great assets of short pieces of fiction is their suggestiveness, and the second thought which emerged was the way in which a sense of place determines people's actions, however unvoiced or intangible. In different guises, Michel Déon's young Frenchman in Umbria, Colin Thubron's English visitor to Leningrad, Norman Lewis's US President in Havana, the two Ionian stories by David Profumo and Anne Spillard, and Carlo Gébler's and Rose Tremain's young men in Mexico and Corsica all contain that relationship. Finally, there is Lisa St Aubin de Terán's Normandy beach, a nightmarish territory which reminds us that the places where people find themselves are often the landscape mirror-images of their own minds.

By the end I began to feel that there was a case to be made in both directions, that perhaps fiction writers are travel writers, just as travel writers are fiction writers: both of them masters and mistresses of description and deception. But this is loose talk. I can advance no proof of any such incestuous relationship, and in any event the only important thing is that the stories in *Foreign Exchange* should entertain. Yet – one last tug at the question – I can advance a precedent. Over 250 years ago, in a Preface to his first prose work, the translation of a travel book entitled *Voyage to Abyssinia* by a Portuguese Jesuit named Lobo, Samuel Johnson wrote:

> The Portuguese traveller... has amused his reader with no romantick absurdity, or incredible fictions; whatever he relates, whether true or not, is at least probable; and he who tells nothing beyond the bounds of probability has a right to demand that they should believe him who cannot contradict him.

Julian Evans

PUERTO VALLARTA

by

Carlo Gébler

My mother recently announced that she was selling our house in Richmond. I still had a room in the place, although I had not slept in it for years. In the course of removing my remaining possessions I came across a Fortnum and Mason's Christmas Pudding Box labelled 'Mexico'. It contained shells and stones; a terrifying picture of Jesus racked on the cross which I had cut out from a religious magazine I had found out there; photographs naturally; a half-consumed bottle of quinine tablets; TWA coaster mats advertising Canada Dry Ginger Ale; and a paper umbrella which had been served with some exotic drink in some long-forgotten exotic nightspot. Like an old magnet found in a drawer, these objects had not lost their power. As I continued packing, long-forgotten memories came flooding back. I could not get Mexico out of my mind. I could see it and I could smell it. I left my mother's early, making excuses, and went to a coffee shop. There, amidst school children smoking cigarettes with their satchels hanging over the backs of their chairs, I pored over the objects, particulary the photographs, and began to write down the story as I remembered it.

I was sixteen when they sent us. It was just at the time of my parents' divorce and they were trying to atone in the way they always did, which was by giving us something. When I say 'us' I mean myself and my half-sister Laura. She was eighteen. Laura's surname was Henson. My surname is Greene. After her marriage to Laura's father ended, my mother re-married my father who is called Greene. It was always complicated being introduced to strangers when we were children. The Mexican summer, as I like to think of it, it was my parents – the Greenes – who were separating, Laura's father being long dead.

The man we were sent to stay with in Mexico was Laura's grandfather. He was a rich old American who had made his money in the forties. I think he owned a small passenger airline that was bought out. I can clearly remember his visits to our house in

3

Richmond when I was a child. He was a very tall man with a long face and rather small eyes set close together. He smoked cigars and carried a cigar-cutter on a gold chain in his waistcoat pocket. I was always intrigued by the lengths of ash he tipped from the ends of his Havanas, so like pumice stone to my childish way of seeing things. He was a generous man; his presents were always lavish; and he always treated me on equal terms with Laura. But I was not particularly friendly with him. None of us was. He was not 'family' you see. His son, who was Laura's father, committed suicide only a couple of months after marrying my mother and so there was never an opportunity for proper family links to develop. We never called him grandfather. He was simply Old Man Henson.

We arrived in Puerto Vallarta at midday. Los Angeles, where we had stayed overnight on the way, had been hot but nothing could have prepared me for my first encounter with tropical heat. When I stepped through the door onto the stairway it was like plunging into a molten sea. Lush green trees hovered on the horizon, suggestive of the jungle. Men with walnut-coloured skins lounged on a luggage trolley. Spanish voices muttered darkly below. It was my first real taste of abroad and I believe I felt more excited than I had ever felt in my lifetime before.

We went to the baggage room. Everyone's suitcases were being thrown through a hole in the wall and porters were slamming them onto metal counters. Laura feared her scent bottle would break. A man with a large gold badge pinned to a faded blue serge uniform chalked X's on our bags. Through a small side door I noticed a woman staring at us closely. As we went towards the door she smiled as strangers meeting strangers always have to.

'Are you Johnnie and Laura?' she asked.

We said we were.

She introduced herself as Mary Hughes. She was Old Man Henson's secretary. 'I'm afraid he couldn't come in person,' she explained. 'We've had something unfortunate happen.'

We shook hands. Her skin was creased from years of sun-tanning; a pair of large sunglasses rested on top of her hair; and her eyes were rimmed red as if she had been crying.

We crammed into a tiny Fiat and began to bump towards the town. Fields stretched on either side, green like spinach. The earth

4

where it was exposed was the colour of terracotta. Everywhere cork trees grew like giant mushrooms.

'What was the unfortunate thing that happened?' I asked.

'Two of our workmen were on the roof with a metal ladder,' she began. 'Somehow they touched one of the high wires that bring in the town's electricity. The cables run right above the houses. The voltage was so strong all their flesh was burnt away where the ladder touched them, right down to the bone. The local hospital here wouldn't take them. Their National Insurance contributions weren't up to date or something stupid like that. We flew them to Guadalajara. The hospitals there wouldn't take them either. Twelve hours I was with these two guys going from hospital to hospital in this boiling heat. The Red Cross took them finally. We buried what was left of them yesterday...'

I took it all in without feeling very much. I have to be immersed in a world before I can begin to respond. The indicator flashed and we pulled into a garage, stopping in front of a grimy pump. I heard an engine rumbling somewhere and a moment later a jeep braked sharply in front of us. Four soldiers with shiny boots were sitting in the back. They were short-haired and utterly still like shop mannequins. In one effortless movement the pot-bellied attendant, who had been walking towards us with the hose, turned away and bent towards the jeep.

'But we were first,' protested Laura.

Mary took off her sun-glasses and put them on the dash-board. 'No. In Mexico the National Guard are always first,' she said.

We arrived in Puerto Vallarta. Peeling walls; women walking slowly, loads balanced on their heads; early afternoon buses with workers clinging to the sides glided past our windows. We turned off a busy square into a residential area. The streets fell silent. Suddenly Mary began to accelerate towards a blind corner. I gripped the seat and I could see Laura looking dismayed.

'Let's hope we don't meet anything coming the other way,' muttered Mary. Abroad we trust ourselves to madness as we never would at home.

I went round the bend with my eyes shut, my body crushing against the side. As soon as we were around, I heard the engine screaming and sensed that we were slowing up. I opened my eyes and saw that we were climbing an extremely steep hill with a pit in the middle of the road large enough to have swallowed our car. We swerved up the cobbles, negotiating this danger and finally turned with relief onto a flat road. 'That's the only way to do it,' exclaimed Mary, settling back in her seat. 'Go for it blind . . .' A line of villas stretched away from us, a bridge connecting two of them at the far end of the street. We pulled up in front of a large white building. The children playing on the steps vanished like minnows. Over the door was a granite keystone with a coat of arms. This was Casa Bianco, our home for the month ahead.

I climbed out of the car and looked up without thinking about it. A thick metal cable stretched above me, attached by wooden arms to the gables of the houses as it ran down the street. Standing on any roof I could have easily reached out and grasped it, the town's electricity supply.

'Why don't they insulate it?' I asked.

'I don't know. This is Mexico. Nobody cares. The government can't afford to.'

'And do people electrocute themselves all the time?'

'All the time, honey.'

A man came out who was introduced to us as Luiz, the houseman. He was small like a jockey, wiry and capable. We said that we could manage but he pushed us aside, took possession of our luggage and pointed towards the door.

Inside the hall was large and spacious. A nineteenth-century child's wooden horse hung from a wall and a carved Virgin Mary stood in the corner. We followed Mary up a sloping ramp set with stones that pressed into our feet and found ourselves in the living room.

Old Man Henson was sitting on a chair by the balcony, looking exactly as I remembered him, staring at the jungle-covered hills beyond the town. Suddenly I felt I had blundered into a house of mourning – and I wished that I could have turned around and tip-toed out.

Mary called his name.

'Leo' turned in his seat and looked at us blankly. Then his face changed like a slowly developing picture.

'Well, well, well,' he said, the words rising and falling musically.

He rose from his creaking cane chair and came forward wheezing slightly. He was a tall man with a slight stoop and an old face like a monkey's.

'How do you do ... You are very welcome.'

He embraced Laura then squeezed my hand.

'Well, well, well. Laura a woman and you, Johnnie, a man!'

He held us at arm's length and looked us over from head to toe.

'Come and meet our guests, honey,' he called coaxingly across the room.

I heard their bedroom door opening and round the corner came a youngish woman with a dark brown dog at her side. The woman was small with a wide face. The dog was snub-nosed and enormous. He was as big as a St Bernard. Underneath his short pelt I could see powerful muscles moving. Fears that I had not known since childhood began to stir.

'This is Ana-Rita,' said the old man, 'my wife.'

Her bracelets jingled as we shook hands. I felt the dog was watching us. Laura and her step-grandmother began to talk about the flight and other trivial matters.

'What kind of a dog is he?' I asked.

'A Rottweiler. They're a Russian breed, bred for sledging and fighting. Marvellously loyal.'

Henson took the dog by the ears and began to move its head from side to side.

'Once they bite they don't let go,' he continued. 'The last one I had took six bullets in the chest and he still held on. That was two years ago when a gang of thieves broke in.'

'What's he called?'

He looked up at me, more monkey-like than ever.

'Prince is his name and he's a prince among canines ... Aren't you Prince?'

'Hey Prince,' I called and slapped my thighs to attract his attention. I was acting on the principle that it is always better to jump into a cold swimming pool than to descend slowly by the steps.

Prince bristled and curled his lips. Henson gripped his collar.

'Don't call him, Johnnie,' he said, 'don't call him. Just let him be. He'll come to you when he's ready.'

'And in the meantime,' added Ana-Rita, 'don't run when he's around and never touch him. He's not used to strangers. But he's quite safe.'

We must have looked very worried for she continued: 'He lives in the basement with Luiz most of the time so you shouldn't be bothered by him. Now, how about some refreshments?'

We drank pina coladas for an hour – it was the first time I had ever had them – whilst Prince lay at Henson's feet, his chest rising and falling as the old man twirled the ice-cubes in the bottom of his gin glass. Finally, Ana-Rita asked us if we wanted to see our rooms.

Yes, we said, and followed her towards the ramp.

'This house is like a ship,' she announced. 'You will live at the top and sleep at the bottom.'

We agreed it had that sort of feel.

My bedroom was the one closest to the bottom of the ramp. I went in and shut the door quickly. I wanted to put a barrier between myself and Prince even though I knew that at that moment I was safe. The room was long and narrow with white plastered walls shedding on the black marble floor. The bed stood at the far end on a dais, a battered fan overhead. I found the switch and the cream-coloured blades started to turn, slowly at first then faster and faster. The air began to move, pleasing and cool.

Beyond the bed flimsy doors of wicker opened out onto a private balcony. I went outside and saw Puerto Vallarta stretched below, a patchwork of tiled roofs. Everything was one hue, a reddy-yellow colour, except around the chimney holes where the tiles were black with soot. Behind her wicker partition I heard Laura singing in her bedroom. I crept up to her door and burst in baying like the hound of the Baskervilles.

'Oh you little horror,' she screamed, and collapsed onto the bed laughing. 'Did you see the way that horrible dog was watching us? He's got the most horrible eyes. If his master and mistress hadn't been there I'm sure he'd have taken a huge chunk out of each of us. I hope they really do keep him locked up.'

'I'm sure they do.'

I took her arm, pretending to bite it, and we went out onto the balcony laughing. It began to get dark, the darkness falling suddenly like a curtain. Cars flitted in distant streets, their headlamps sending out tunnels of light. The roofs below us merged into a single shape. One after another lights came on in the town and started to twinkle. I said it was just like a scene from a Somerset Maugham story. 'Typical,' said Laura. A mariachi trumpet sounded like a call to pleasure. Laura put her arm around me and we both felt sentimental.

'It's so nice to be in paradise with my kid brother,' she said and kissed me chastely on the temple.

My first night in the tropics I fell asleep to the sound of Prince moaning in the basement, sounding like wind howling in a chimney flue. The next morning after breakfast we put some belongings into a string bag and set off on our first excursion. Outside the streets were still and hot. We photographed each other underneath a tattered poster with the initials PSD on it. A mule clattered by, led by a brown child, a gleaming machete hanging from the filthy grey saddle. We descended by a set of buckled steps with a cock tethered halfway down, his red comb shivering as he pecked the dry earth under a walnut tree. At the bottom stood an enormous church, a black hearse outside filled with bright plastic flowers. The sound of the service amplified over loudspeakers echoed within. A man sat fanning himself, sweat marks under the arms of his brown shirt.

We wandered through the town trying to remember Ana-Rita's instructions. On the corners vendors stood with huge jars of iced cordial. Large black insects with heavy drooping legs swarmed in clouds everywhere, bumping into us like slow-moving pellets. Refuse stank in the gutters. At last we found ourselves on a main road and recognised the Malecon as Ana-Rita had described it. The ocean stretched blue in front of us. There was a post office with a blind man sitting outside the door blowing breathlessly and tunelessly into a kazoo and feebly banging cymbals. He seemed barely alive. A sickly-faced girl in a filthy dress was collecting money from passers-by. We dropped some coins into her hat. She lifted her lips in a smile and revealed purple gums and no teeth. We crossed a bridge. Young boys cavorted in the shallow water underneath, their skin shining like wet rubber. Women were

9

washing clothes on the rocks, islands of suds slipping seawards away from them. The sun rose high in the sky. We grew fractious, thinking we would never find it, and then suddenly there it was in front of us.

'Our first Pacific beach,' cried Laura. We spread our towels on the hot sand and collapsed. 'De, de, de, de . . .' sang Laura, imitating the music of striptease as she removed her yellow shift.

'Last one in the water is a cissy,' she said.

'No, you go on ahead.'

She trod painfully over the hot sand and stopped at the ocean's edge to splash her limbs. She was wearing a bikini and I could see the outline of her body.

'It's lovely and warm,' she called.

'Go on then,' I shouted.

I come from a generation from whom few facts have been kept. But at sixteen knowledge was no substitute for experience. If anything it sharpened one's sense of non-achievement. I had kissed girls in my time. I had even touched their breasts and between their legs in dark rooms at adolescent parties. The vision of Laura was a challenge to my lack of experience and left me annoyed and a little morose.

On the morning we had agreed to play tennis, Mary appeared in our kitchen, immaculate in a set of whites, her Ray-Bans resting on top of her head.

'OK you guys. Get your things. Let's go.' She was bursting with desperate energy.

We picked up our tennis rackets with their strings of slack yellow gut which Luiz had dug out for us the night before and trudged down the ramp after her. When she reached the bottom she put her head over the stairway that led down to the basement.

'Come on, Prince,' she called. 'There's a good boy.'

Laura and I looked at one another.

There was a scampering sound on the stairs and a moment later the enormous vicious shape of Prince bounded into the hall on legs as thick as banisters. He was holding his play-bone, a piece of thick leather knotted at either end and as long as my forearm.

'Would little Prince like to come for a ride this morning?' she asked, stroking his dark cranium. He arched his neck, clearly enjoying the attention. His saliva-covered bone lay forsaken on the marble floor like a cannibal's relic.

'Do we need to bring Prince to the tennis court?' enquired Laura innocently.

'Oh yes,' exclaimed Mary. 'Poor Prince. Cooped up in the house all day. He likes to be taken out now and again. Don't you Prince . . . Besides, I promised Ana-Rita I would . . . Yes, who's a good boy . . .'

She tried to move his head from side to side but Prince remained solid. Her white skirt had risen up her thighs and underneath I saw she was wearing knickers with a picture of Snoopy on the seat.

'Come on then. The court's booked for eleven.' She straightened up and strutted towards the door, Prince going with her.

We followed after them, holding our tennis rackets protectively in front of our bare legs.

Outside the Fiat stood with both it doors hanging open. It was already beginning to get warm. We climbed in, Laura and I in the back, Mary and Prince in the front, and lurched away along the road, the cinquecento squeaking and bumping on the cobbles. As we turned down the hill I saw there were children playing in the pit which we had passed on our first day. We rattled past and they waved at us but I did not wave back.

'When are they going to mend the hole?' I asked stupidly.

'Oh they'll get around to it some year,' replied Mary. Then she added in a fake Mexican accent: 'Mañana, mañana . . .'

A moment later she swung into a side street and pulled up abruptly in front of an apothecary's.

'I hope you don't mind, kids,' she said. 'I've just got to get something. I won't be a mo,' and before we could say anything she was gone and we were left alone in the back of a two-door Fiat with Prince sitting in the front.

'This is unbelievable,' murmured Laura.

'My heart's beating, is yours?'

'Do you think he's safe?'

Prince sat on his haunches staring into the sunny street.

'Remember what father said – If you see a mad dog don't panic.

11

Just stand absolutely still.' My voice trembled as I spoke and my knees were shaking.

'I feel sick,' whispered Laura.

Prince yawned, turned around and lay down. Our feeling of entrapment was complete.

'Good Prince,' I said quietly and gently pushed the seat. My plan was to make him sit up before he fell asleep and then to open the door and escape. I heard a low growl and a moment later we were staring at one another. His lips were curled, revealing rows of strong white teeth.

'Don't,' hissed Laura. 'It's not worth it.'

I retreated back into my seat. Prince growled again and lowered his head. Sweat trickled over my ribs. Laura took my hand. I turned and looked out of the window. A swarm of hornets hovered above the pavement. Two men struggled by with a swordfish, its slippery skin the colour of gun-metal. I noticed a doorway and a young boy sitting outside on a chair. In the room beyond him I could see furnaces filled with flames and a conveyor belt of tortillas moving like pale moons. I could also make out the dark bodies of the tortilla-makers, their bodies glistening with sweat as they worked with long wooden spatulas. Out of a sooty hole in the roof overhead, blue smoke curled into the air. I sat watching for what felt like hours, although it was only minutes. To this day, the glowing coals of the furnace, the gliding tortillas, and the boy on the string-backed chair summon up the spirit of Mexico for me more than any other single memory.

At last Mary returned with a small white package. 'Budge up, Prince,' she called through the window. He heaved himself onto his haunches and she sprang into her seat. Suddenly I felt we were the terrified children of a fairy tale and she was the wood-cutter who always comes to the rescue at the last moment.

We drove through the town and turned onto a highway. Petrol stations and factories spread out on either side of us. Rusty American cars hurtled by filled with brown, staring faces. After a couple of miles a buckled sign appeared with the words 'Tennis Club' on it and we turned through a gate.

We pulled up in front of an unfinished building with pebble-dash walls and columns clad with crazy paving.

12

'Our tennis club – toast of the province,' exclaimed Mary, tipping the seat back. We scrambled out as fast as we decently could. Two boys stared at us as they wheeled by a cart loaded with beach umbrellas.

'Now you stay here,' continued Mary, slamming the door. 'Prince, stay here and mind the car... This way for the courts, gang. Follow the racket.'

She held it over her head like a guide and sped towards the entrance. We followed her across the tarmac hanging back a little. When she disappeared Laura took my arm.

'What is it?' I asked.

She started to laugh uncontrollably. Sometimes she would get like that. She would want to tell you something funny but before she could get the words out she would start to laugh.

'You know when you said what father said about staying still in the car just now...' she spluttered.

'Yes.'

'... well, when you said it, I thought, "This dog would kill a tree if he took exception to it" and I so wanted to laugh only I didn't dare.'

We looked over our shoulders. Prince was watching us through the side window.

'Come on,' urged Laura and we hurried through the door.

We passed through Reception and came out under a verandah covered with palm fronds. In front of us several courts, all of them empty, stretched towards the sea.

'Come and meet my partner Midge,' called Mary. She had donned the wrist-bands of a professional.

We went over and shook hands. Midge was not alone. Her husband and two sons had come with her. The boys wore silver braces on their white teeth and the husband was well-tanned and big.

We stepped out onto the court. The tarmac was sizzling. The white tramlines danced before my eyes.

'This is a nightmare,' whispered Laura.

On the other side of the net Mary and Midge were sporting sun visors which cast a pallid green hue over their faces, and holding steel rackets. It was like a scene from an old-fashioned comic book.

13

The toffs who had all the money were playing the townies who had nothing. This was not the game Mary had promised.

'We'll start with a knock-up,' she shouted and sent a yellow ball whizzing towards me. I held out my racket. The ball hit the gut and fizzled into the net.

'Sorry,' I apologised and lobbed back the ball that I was holding.

It disappeared into the blue sky. 'Kill it Midge,' I heard Bob shouting. Midge stepped forward and sliced the ball. It came back like a bullet and hit the base line. Applause drifted across the court. I glanced towrds the verandah. Deep in the shade sat Bob and the boys, all in baseball hats and sipping Coca-Cola.

We agreed to a game, gritted our teeth and determined we would not be slaughtered. For their part Mary and Midge discovered that our lack of skill badly spoilt their game. An hour later they were in the lead – but only just – and Bob was hoarse from shouting at Midge to pull her socks up.

The time came to change ends and Laura suggested that we might rest for a while.

'Yes, siree,' agreed Midge.

Underneath the verandah it was cool. The women sank onto a bench and began to towel their faces. Wet stains had spread down their backs.

'I bet it sure is hot out there,' observed Bob and the boys.

I nodded and noticed with dismay that their Coca-Cola bottles were empty.

'Where did you get them?' I asked.

'We brought our own but there's a fridge full of 'em behind. Just help yourself.'

He jerked his thumb towards a rusting cabinet with the glorious words Coca-Cola written on the side.

'It must be over a hundred out there,' he said to Laura as I walked away. 'But if you think this is hot you should be here in August. Oh boy, I'm telling you, August is a killer.'

I lifted the plastic lid. An unpleasant smell of old rubber drifted up. The bottles were lying submerged in brown murky water. Floating in the corner, belly upwards, was a large dead lizard.

I shut the lid. 'I don't think we can have this Coca-Cola,' I said.

'Oh honey, of course not,' called Mary. 'I bought some cold

14

drinks for us. They're in the picnic box in the car. Lovely lime juice and guava juice. Would you be a love and get them for me?'

'What about Prince?'

'Don't mind Prince. Just open the door and get it out. He knows you. You've been around him for long enough.'

I walked smartly to the Fiat and found Prince stretched across the front seats fast asleep.

'Hullo, Prince,' I said amiably. He raised his head and growled. 'Johnnie's just going to get the picnic box out.' I reached towards the door handle. Prince rose up on his legs like a monster coming out of the sea and bared his teeth. 'Come on, Prince. Let me open the door?' I coaxed. The hairs on his neck began to bristle. The situation could not have been clearer. I retraced my steps.

'What happened?' asked Mary.

'He started growling and bristling. I couldn't get it out.'

'I don't think Prince likes us,' added Laura. 'When you left him in the car this morning, he was awfully funny with us.'

'You're making a mountain out of a molehill. He's just not used to you...' replied Mary.

I followed her out to the car park, hoping for proof to back up my story, proof which would restore my honour.

Prince was sitting at the window, staring out. As Mary approached he bristled and growled. 'Prince,' she said, 'this is Mary. Remember me? I held you as a puppy.' His growling dropped to a low rumble and his lips slipped back over his teeth. Mary opened the door and pushed him back onto the other seat. In case of attack I made a note that there were some pieces of wood stacked at the side of the club house. Mary ducked down and put her head inside. A moment later she withdrew herself, the white picnic box swinging from her arm.

'Now you be a good guard dog,' she said and slammed the door.

I took the plastic box from her as we walked away.

'You know,' she said, 'that Prince sometimes worries me...'

Then she told me a long story... Prince as a puppy tormented by children, Prince coming to Casa Bianco and everyone having great trouble making friends with him, Prince going to dog-training school in Arizona and being sent home after three days because he was too temperamental for the trainers.

'You'll probably think this is ridiculous,' she continued, 'but after the accident with the electric cable I had to bring the police onto the roof. This is what worries me. Prince was there and he was sniffing the blood and I think he may have been licking it.'

We were standing in Reception surrounded by ancient Coca-Cola vending machines like upstanding coffins.

'Maybe I'm being over-dramatic,' I heard her say. 'Maybe I shouldn't have told you that. Just forget I ever said it to you.'

A minute or so later, when I handed Laura a glass of lime juice, she looked up at me and said, 'You look as white as a sheet.'

The town ran out of water and the sewage could no longer be refined. Excrement began to float in on the tides. From a distance it looked like shoals of corks but close up there was no mistaking it.

At the end of our street there were two houses joined by a bridge. They were owned by American film stars who were not in town. In one of the villas there was a swimming pool kept in a permanent state of readiness in case they should suddenly arrive. The houseman minding the properties was a relative of Luiz's. Ana-Rita gave him some money and told us to leave the beaches for a few days and to swim there. So off we went for the first time...

The house was large like all the houses in the street, with a few barred windows set high. We tugged the handle by the door shaped like an old-fashioned communication chord. A bell tinkled far away. We heard footsteps inside and a few moments later, after much unbarring and unlocking, the houseman admitted us. We nodded a greeting. In the hallway stood a set of huge papier-mâché dolls in traditional Mexican costume. He led us to a secluded pool surrounded by vegetation with thick rubbery leaves. We swam straightaway. The water was cold and chlorinated, reminding us of England. Afterwards we found a watering can in the corner, wrote the names of the film stars in water on the dry stones around the pool, and took each other's photographs from above.

The heat and the activity made us tired. Laura lay in the sun. She was reading a thriller called *Blood of Lucifer* and she kept looking up and saying, 'Ugg! This is really horrible!' and then describing what it was that was really horrible.

Towards midday I said, 'There's something pretty horrible up there!'

She looked up and shrieked. A huge iguana was perched on the roof overhead. It was about four foot long with skin that reminded me of stone. Its tongue snaked deftly through the air.

Although we knew it was harmless the iguana made us uneasy. We decided to leave.

We wandered back through room after shuttered room filled with furniture shrouded in white sheets, calling for the houseman.

'It's like Miss Haversham's wedding feast,' said Laura.

At last we found him. He was fast asleep at the kitchen table, his head resting on his arms. Flies buzzed around half-eaten plates of rice and aubergine. He awoke with a start and apologised in Spanish.

It did not matter, we assured him in English. All the way to the door he continued his apologies.

We said our goodbyes and he watched as we wandered down the street. The door finally scraped shut.

'God, it was depressing,' said Laura, looking up at the bridge which spanned the road. A group of tourists in a nearby jeep were pointing their cameras at it and clicking away furiously.

'This is the famous bridge of love,' the guide explained, 'one of Puerto Vallarta's most famous sites. When the film stars want to see one another they cross over by it . . .'

'Well, we've swum in their pool and you haven't, so there!' said Laura behind their backs, and we went down the street laughing.

Outside our house the little boys from Juarez's shop at the end of the street were playing with a scrawny kitten. Their heads had been shaved and their brown, near-naked bodies had been dusted with white disinfectant powder. As we approached they reminded me of tribesmen I had once gazed at in my National Geographics.

'Money, money,' they called, running towards us.

'No money today,' we said. 'Maybe tomorrow.'

We went up the steps of Casa Bianco and found Luiz inside. He was watering the plants in the hall with buckets of precious water which he had filled from our still-water tank in the kitchen.

I went into my bedroom and changed into dry clothes. Outside I could hear the Juarez boys calling nervously in piping Spanish. I went out to see what was happening. The little kitten had run into the middle of the hall. Suddenly I saw Prince was standing at the top of the stairs leading up from the basement. I shouted at the boy but it was too late. He saw Prince, panicked and scuttled towards the kitten. The dog leapt forward, opened his mouth and swallowed one side of the little boy's head. There was a horrible scream and the kitten started to screech as Prince trod it underfoot. I picked up a large potted plant and threw it across the hall. It struck Prince on the ribs, bounced off and smashed on the marble floor. Luiz ran down the ramp with a dripping pail and threw the water in it with all his force at Prince. The dog let go and Luiz grabbed him by his collar. The younger Juarez boy was in the doorway screaming with his elder brother. The victim lay in a heap with red earth all over his body. There was blood everywhere.

'What happened?' Henson shouted from the top of the ramp.

Luiz said something in Spanish and dragged Prince towards the stairs. Laura came out of her room and ran over to the Juarez boy and picked him up without thinking. I remember the wet earth fell off his body in lumps.

The Juarez boy needed fifty-six stitches. The doctor said he was lucky not to lose an eye.

During the conversations in the house that followed we learnt that Prince had managed to slip through the rope by which he was secured. His attack, the Hensons said, was only natural. As a guard dog of course he would bite a stranger in the house...

And Mexico, they continued, was a violent place. Gangs of thieves descended nightly on the houses of the rich. Prince was their best protection.

In the late afternoon I went for a walk. From the suicide of the son through the two workmen to the present moment, there seemed to be an unbroken continuity of disaster. The large church at the bottom of the hill was empty. I put money in the collection box, lit a small candle and prayed to God to take Prince away.

Maria-Teresa, our hostess, opened the door to us. She was a young dark-skinned woman in a halter dress of the most unbelievably bright colours.

18

'Come in darlings, come in,' she called, pulling us through the door. 'Mary's already here. But where's Leo and Ana-Rita?'

'They send their apologies but they can't come,' explained Laura.

'That was a terrible business with the dog and the little boy,' observed Maria-Teresa. 'Ana-Rita – as you know she's my best friend – she was in the beauty salon two days after – red eyes – bad skin – looking terrible. I said to her, "You've really got to look after yourself, you know! You can't take these things to heart," I said.'

Maria-Teresa pouted her lower lip and shook her head seriously.

'Yes,' we agreed. The business with the dog had taken a terrible toll on both of them.

'But let's not think of sad things. This is a party.'

She dragged us into the lounge and thrust drinks into our hands. The room was filled with businessmen and their wives. On one side a wall of glass looked down to the sea. A pale moon glimmered in the sky and the ocean shone like metal.

I was introduced to the host, husband of Maria-Teresa, a large American called Fred in a blue shirt and red bermuda shorts.

He began to tell me about Rosicrucianism of which he was making a serious study.

I listened, moving my head mechanically until Laura caught my eye across the room and nodded towards a door.

I followed her over and found myself in a bedroom. Maria-Teresa was sitting on the bed mixing grass and tobacco in a pestle.

'We thought you needed a smoke,' she said. 'Was my husband talking about Rosicrucianism?'

'Yes.'

'Did he bore the pants off you?'

'No,' I lied.

'He didn't bore you. Amazing.'

She lit the end of the joint and lay back on the bed. Through the open windows drifted the sound of the sea. The night was warm and still.

'You know,' said Maria-Teresa, 'I'd like to retire to a desert island and smoke my head off for the rest of my life.'

She handed me the joint. I inhaled deeply, scorching the back of my throat.

'Listen,' she continued, standing up, 'I've got a party to look after. So just enjoy yourselves and don't bring it outside, okay. You never know but somebody might have a line to the Feds.'

'Yes,' we called as she went out of the door.

'Have you seen the three Mexican beauties?' asked Laura as I handed her the grass cigarette.

I thought back to the room. All I could remember was my empty glass and Rosicrucianism.

'No,' I said.

'Well they've certainly seen you. They want to meet you. Maria-Teresa told me.'

Ten minutes later I was back at the party. I located the beauties. They were sitting in a demure row as in a dance hall. I found the one in the middle particularly attractive with her bare knees and her glowing shins.

The grass had given me confidence but I needed something to make me talkative. I went into the kitchen and found Fred mixing a fruit cup.

'Have some of this,' he said.

I drank some down and my lips began to burn.

'What is it?' I asked.

He opened the cupboard and took out a vodka bottle without a label full of clear liquid. 'Local hooch,' he said. 'Kick of a mule. Makes you see pretty pictures.'

Returning to the lounge I saw Mary wafting towards me swathed in purple cheese-cloth. Her eyes were shining and the glass of scotch which she held was slopping over the edges.

'I was just coming to find you. I want you to meet someone,' she said.

'Could I meet them later?'

Mary arched her eyebrows. 'First you meet Sherri. She's dynamite.' She squeezed my arm conspiratorially. There was no escape.

Sherri was a tanned American clutching a bottle of Marques de Riscal.

'Would you like some?' she asked. 'It's French.'

I shook my head and her words began gyrating in the air like planets.

20

Mary drank from the bottle and a purple-coloured spot fell onto her chest.

The planets vanished.

'Listen you guys...' said Sherri, reclaiming her bottle.

I was normal again.

'... I have this problem. Maybe you can help me.'

'Anything,' slurred Mary, winking lasciviously at me.

'I'm in the swimwear business. I need a name. I just want you to tell me off the top of your head what you think. Okay, here it is. High Wire.'

'What?' asked Mary.

'High Wire,' repeated Sherri emphatically. 'Like the high wires that carry electricity everywhere. That's our image. Touch someone in one of our swimsuits and you get a shock like touching a high wire. Are you all right?'

'I wish you hadn't said that. I wish you hadn't.' Mary started to sob and I noticed heads turning.

'Did I say anything wrong?' Sherri tugged my arm.

'Not at all,' I assured her blandly.

I led Mary into the bedroom filled with the sweet smell of marijuana and found her a tissue. When I returned to the party again I found the sofa was empty. For a moment I was disappointed. The guests had begun to eat. I went over to the table. Red tropical flowers floated in bowls between the food, petals the colour of fuchsia. The brightness of a flashbulb lit up the room for a second. Somebody laughed. I picked up my plate.

'Hullo,' said a voice at my side.

I turned round and saw that I was being greeted by the girl I had admired. She was short with a round face that had something of a blackberry about it. Her looks were elfin. She told me her name was Angela-Maria.

A few moments later I was seated outside on the terrace with her friends Carmen and Luzia and the four of us were all talking very quickly and excitedly. Their faces shone, I remember, their brown eyes were inviting and at the same time inpenetrable, and the starched white napkins crinkled as they spread them on their laps. When the time came to leave, my feelings were soaring.

Laura drove us home through the dark streets in the little Fiat. I

21

lay back in my seat and looked up through the window. The sky was black as pitch, the stars were brighter and larger than I had ever seen them in my own hemisphere, and the moon was a huge benign presence that I could almost have reached out and touched. I was drunk and I was in love.

I fell into bed under the clanging fan. Prince was moaning eerily in the bowels of the house. I settled myself on the pillow and closed my eyes. A picture of Angela-Maria's face immediately appeared before me. I remembered the way she had squeezed my knee and laughed when the conversation had foundered for a moment. For the first time on that holiday as I drifted towards sleep, I did not once find myself listening involuntarily to Prince.

The water supply was back and Laura and I went to the beach the following day. It was overcast and humid and big shiny bluebottles buzzed around our heads all day. We quarrelled and went back to the house early. I went to my room and fell into a depressed sleep. In the early evening Laura woke me and suggested going out as the Hensons were playing bridge in a house down the coast. I got dressed and we wandered into town. Every time I saw a dark-skinned girl I thought she was Angela-Maria. She hovered before my eyes. Laura must have sensed it but said nothing.

We found a small restaurant. It was filled with middle-aged American women and younger Mexican men. Every year, we had been told, professional American women used to flock to the town in search of the masculine that had vanished from their everyday lives. In Puerto Vallarta they found it, and for the price of a shirt or a cigarette lighter they were able to enjoy sexual favours in the same way they said men had always done. As neither Laura or I believed that even-handedness in inequality was progress we selected a table outside, a wrought-iron one under a red and white striped awning.

The waiter came and took our orders. We did not say much to each other. Pizzas arrived, enormous and swollen. The air was sticky and heavy. I ate the mozzarella off the top of mine and pushed the plate away.

'I'm not hungry either,' said Laura. 'It's too hot to eat.'

22

I ordered tequilas, a dish of salt and limes. We drank a couple and began to cheer up. The air was suddenly very still, like a forest immediately after a gunshot has silenced all bird-song. Thunder rumbled in the distance and a slow insistent needling began on the awning overhead. It was the start of the long-expected storm. Within seconds the noise above was deafening. Water started to pour down on all sides forming sheets like waterfalls. The waiters pulled our table into the restaurant. The electric lights wavered, everyone went 'Ohh' and we plunged into darkness. Beyond the tiny barred windows sheet lightning rolled around the night sky. Candles were lit and the proprietor offered everyone free drinks. A man ran in with a newspaper over his head which disintegrated when he lifted it away. Brown and white arms entwined lovingly in the semi-darkness. Laura and I drank more tequilas. The water pouring over the edge of the awning diminished to a trickle. Those who had taken shelter tested the rainfall with outstretched hands and drifted off. Laura said she was tired and we paid our bill.

Outside the street was flooded with two feet of rain water, dark and swiftly flowing. Suddenly we understood why the pavements were set so high above the roads. A dwarf whom we had noticed begging around the town stood in a doorway. All the street lamps were dead.

We began to pick our way home. Our shoes squelched on the wet cobbles. We turned up the last hill for home. There was something in the pit, sticking out like the prow of a half-sunken ship. We walked up and saw it was an abandoned car. Thunder started to boom above our heads again. That was the way with Mexican storms. They came and went and then they came back again...

I took Laura by the hand and we began to run. The raindrops were as big as two-and-sixes and I could feel all my clothes sticking to my body. Reaching our front door we unlocked it and rushed in. The hall was completely dark. The power cut was total. I knew that Luiz and his family would be cowering in the basement as they always did when there was a storm. Suddenly our feelings of relief to be at home gave way to fear of the darkness and the unknown.

'There's matches and a candle on the hall table,' whispered Laura.

Leaving the front door swinging open, we groped across the hall.

23

Inadvertently I knocked the candle to the floor. Laura found the matches and by the tiny flame of a waxy Mexican match we retrieved the candle and lit the wick. We shut the front door. Upstairs there was an ominous banging, along with another noise.

'There's someone there,' said Laura. She linked her arm through mine and followed me up the ramp. We rounded the bend and the kitchen glimmered in front of us. Rain was drumming on the roof tiles like peas rattling on tin. Sheet lightning flared and for a moment everything was vividly clear: the enormous American refrigerator with rounded edges, the door hanging open and food lying on the floor around it; the magnetic knife rack with glinting blades stuck to it; and the potted plants dotted everywhere with their monstrous rubber leaves stretching like hands towards us.

'Is there anybody there?' we called.

Pitter-patter, came a noise from the far end that was tucked around a corner. That was where the Hensons slept.

'Is there anybody there?' called Laura with all her might.

Pitter-patter, it came again. We walked forward, announcing our presence with heavy footfalls. We passed the linen chest covered with a striped Mexican blanket. The life-size painting of an Indian holding a lily looked down on us from the wall. We rounded the corner and a gust of rain spattered into our faces. The flame of the candle wavered. There was rubble and debris underfoot. We looked up. A huge hole stretched along the side of the house from the balcony to the front. The roof had collapsed in the storm. Sheet lightning rolled across the sky once more and it was then that we saw him, Prince. He was lying on the sodden master bed, surrounded by tiles and splintered rafters, a length of metal gutter beside him stretching up into the darkness. We stood transfixed with terror for minutes, us watching him and he, as we thought, watching us. The storm passed over, it began to grow quiet and it was then that we realised, from his absolute stillness, that it was not Prince we were looking at but his corpse.

'He's dead,' whispered Laura.

We retreated around the corner and sat at the kitchen table in darkness, huddled over our candle. I remembered there was scotch in the kitchen cupboard. I fetched it out and we drank from the bottle. It was old and it tasted musty but it still burnt when it hit the

24

back of the throat. The storm continued to die down and this time we knew it was for good.

'Señor Johnnie. Señorita Laura,' we heard Luiz calling. He appeared at the top of the ramp carrying an enormous flashlamp.

'There's been an accident, Luiz,' we said and solemnly led him to the master bedroom.

In the torchlight we saw everything. Prince's eyes were wide open and his big red tongue was covered with froth like egg-white. The carcass of the chicken which he had taken from the refrigerator lay nearby covered with tile dust. His left shoulder was a mass of bloody tissue and the piece of gutter was covered with blood.

We climbed out onto the roof and there the picture became clearer. The high wire had blown off its wooden arms and got wrapped around the gutter. The two were welded together. When the roof had collapsed the gutter had fallen with it and hit Prince on the bed. He had died of electric shock.

All around us on adjacent roofs there were figures speaking darkly in Spanish. Nearly every house had been damaged in some way in the storm. Luiz called out to those nearest. I did not understand what he said but I thought I caught the word 'Prince' in the darkness. The reply from our neighbours was a whoop of joy and it was soon echoed by other whoops on other roofs spreading away from us like ripples on a pond.

'Prince is dead,' I said.

'Prince is dead,' agreed Luiz, nodding his head and smiling to himself.

Next morning I went out onto my balcony covered with puddles of cold rainwater from the night before. I looked down into the garden below. It was green and lush and in the far corner Luiz was digging a hole.

'Good morning Luiz. *Buenos dias.*'

He turned round and waved. '*Buenos dias*, Señor Johnnie.'

Luiz disappeared into his quarters through the door that led from the garden. I sat down to wait. The canvas chair was damp. It grew hot and the puddles of rainwater began to steam. Luiz and some

Mexicans I did not recognise struggled outside carrying the corpse of Prince on a door.

Old Man Henson and Ana-Rita followed behind. Henson was tall and stooping and impressive in his large hat and white linen suit. Ana-Rita was small, tight and immaculate. The men tipped Prince into the hole and he landed on his back with feet pointing upwards. Terrifying in life, he was comical in death. There was a moment's silence. I presumed prayers were said. Ana-Rita began to cry, her sobs fluttering upwards with the rising wreaths of steam. Henson covered his eyes with his hands.

The men set to, spading in the earth quickly until a ruddy-brown mound covered the hole. A crude wooden cross was put at the head. Everyone turned and went in through Luiz's door.

A few minutes later I heard the Hensons above me, moving about the living room and talking.

'It'll be alright, honey,' soothed Henson. 'We'll get another. Just the same as the great Prince.'

I tip-toed along the balcony and peeped through the wicker screen. Laura's blonde head lay on the pillow. Overhead the fan creaked round and round.

'Laura,' I whispered. She did not stir.

I slipped out of the front door and began to wander down the cobbled street. The fish-man was coming the other way, prickly red mullet hanging from a piece of scaffolding stretched across his shoulders. To bring women out of their houses he was striking the scaffolding with a metal bar, producing a sound that was exquisitely sweet and melancholy. I drew level with Juarez's shop at the end. Prince's victim watched me from the doorway. From the top of his shaven head over his eye and down the side of his face stretched a lumpy white dressing. Below it lay his fifty-six stitches.

I turned around and made my way back to Casa Bianco. Angela-Maria was coming up the steps at the side. I stopped to wait for her, excitement mounting. She reached the last step breathless. She banged her chest and we shook hands. Her fingernails were pale, almost translucent. 'I have come,' she said shyly, 'to invite you and your sister to come out . . .' After that we saw each other every day. I fell deeply in love, of course. But I said nothing.

★

On my last day I was waiting for her in a small square. Shoe-shine boys with lithe bodies and soft blue-black hair were at work nearby, chirping away to each other as they polished the exotic, cuban-heeled boots of a shabbily dressed policeman. A carbine lay across his lap. Angela-Maria appeared at my side, looking sad. Without thinking about it I put my arms around her and kissed her clumsily on her lips. I was more surprised than anyone at what I did. The shoe-shine boys whistled and we broke off our embrace. Red-faced, we walked away arm in arm.

That night, by arrangement, Angela-Maria came to Casa Bianco at eleven. I admitted her quietly and brought her straight to my room. It was warm and balmy. I felt strangely calm, just as I had in the square. We stood on the balcony and drank beer. The town twinkled below us. She was still wearing her black bathing costume which she had worn at the beach where we had spent the afternoon. I undid the halter and lowered the front. Her breasts were pale, almost white. Her skin tasted of salt and her lips smelt sweetly of lipstick. Later we climbed into bed and I made love for the first time in my life. All that I can remember of it is the softness of her skin and the fan clanging overhead.

The next morning we said goodbye a little formally. Then she went off to the shop where she worked and I caught our flight back to England . . .

A few weeks after I had written this down I went to a party given by Laura. She is married and lives in the ground floor flat of a huge stucco mansion overlooking Regent's Park. Not knowing very many of the people who were there, I wandered around, poking into all the corners. I was struck particularly by the large wooden propeller which hung over the mantelpiece and a life-sized figure swathed entirely in bandages.

I sought Laura out in the kitchen.

'Do you ever think about our holiday in Me-hi-co?' I asked.

She was busy extracting baked potatoes from the oven.

'Oh yes, that was where Johnnie first did it, wasn't it?' she said to the assembled women who had gathered to help her.

27

Everyone smiled. Even I did. It was not meant maliciously. It was just somehow Laura's way to come out with such statements.

Later, in the early hours, I asked her the question again. She told me that she remembered swimming in the film stars' pool, the iguana and the nightmare tennis match. That was the sum of it.

I walked through the park as it was getting light. The sky overhead was like mother-of-pearl, and in the chestnut trees with their vivid green leaves, the birds were beginning their dawn chorus. Our life is made up of discreet demarcations when we cross from one state of existence to another. But who knows we are making the passage? Who is there to share it with?

At St John's Wood roundabout I bought all the Sunday newspapers and quickened my pace towards home.

A WEEKEND IN HAVANA

by

Norman Lewis

Norman Lewis has written twelve novels and six non-fiction works. A Dragon Apparent *and* Golden Earth, *both recently reissued, are considered classics of travel, and* Naples '44 *has been described as one of the ten outstanding books about World War Two.* Voices of the Old Sea, *about the three years he spent at the end of the 1940s in a now-vanished Catalan fishing community, was published last year by Hamish Hamilton to widespread critical praise. Lewis himself regards as his principal achievement the world reaction to an article he wrote entitled 'Genocide in Brazil' published by the* Sunday Times *in 1968, which led to a change in the Brazilian law relating to the treatment of Indians and to the formation of Survival International, dedicated to the protection of aboriginal people.*

'A Weekend in Havana' is a revised version of an episode cut from Lewis's novel The Sicilian Specialist *by his American publisher, who found it too offensive.*

The President rang Petcher from Florida where he was officially on holiday recuperating from a recurrence of the usual back trouble.

'Steve,' he said, 'this is James. I'd like to come over and see you tomorrow. Would that be feasible?'

'Absolutely,' Petcher told him. 'My, this is a surprise.'

'It'll be the Beechcroft. Likely to be any hold-ups with immigration?'

'Why should there be?'

'I plan to land at Rancho Boyeros at 1500 hours. Maybe you could find me somewhere to stay for a couple of days?'

'No problem about that either.'

'Strictly a personal visit, eh?'

'Of course,' Petcher said. 'You don't want to meet anybody?'

'We'll talk about that later,' the President said.

'See you tomorrow then, James. And have a nice trip.'

The place touched down on time, and minutes later Petcher saw the President followed by what he supposed to be three secret-service men pass through Customs. At this time the Cubans welcomed visitors with glasses of rum punch, which the President waved aside smilingly. He had changed his hair style slightly and wore dark glasses, but the most successful component of his disguise was a Borsalino hat. The President had never before in his life worn a hat and the change in his appearance was dramatic. Petcher knew that he would be carrying a passport in the name of James Kilmichael, a sales consultant. They shook hands and the President introduced the three men who were with him, Howard Springfield, a young police lawyer from outside the establishment who had risen in meteoric fashion to become the power behind the throne, Teller, a trusted secret-service man, and his assistant, Katz. The five men

31

then got into Petcher's car waiting at the main *llegados* door where only top government officials were normally allowed to park, and Petcher drove them to the house in the Vedado suburb which had instantly been provided.

Springfield and Teller discreetly excused themselves and Petcher and the President settled for a drink on the balcony overlooking the sea.

'Do I look like a Cuban?' the President asked. He had gone to the unnecessary trouble of wearing a guanabera shirt with innumerable buttons and pleats.

Petcher laughed. 'Aren't those Texan boots you have there? They don't need high heels in this country.'

'Should I change them?'

'What does it matter? There's no objection here to looking like an American if you want. They don't bear us any grudge.'

'Well, that's certainly good to know.'

The President tasted the rum with a faint, appreciative smack of the lips.

'Carta D'Oro,' Petcher said. 'Your favourite. Nothing quite like it, is there?'

'Very smooth. It matches the climate.'

The President was in excellent spirits; happy to be back in Havana, where as a senator he had spent so many pleasantly indulgent weekends. The villa had belonged to a sugar baron of extreme wealth and the wildest fancies, who had become in the end the sport of his uncontrollable wealth, and they looked down from a balcony inspired by the decorations of a traditional Cuban wedding cake over the great blue scallop of the bay, scrubbed bright by the norther which reached them in the form of a marine-scented breeze. Negro boys in yellow hats were balancing competitively on the length of two enormously long eighteenth-century cannons pointing vaguely at a patch of ocean where in the old days a French or British privateer, rounding the headland of the Morro Castle, would come first into sight. Laughing girls of all shades of colour and blatantly provocative dresses appeared, then disappeared through the palm fronds as they strolled beneath. The President was pleasantly astonished to note that one of them was smoking a cigar. He sipped his rum again. 'Right now,' he said, 'I'm having traction in a clinic in Coral Gables.' Both men laughed heartily.

'The reason I'm here,' the President said, 'is I wanted to see this place again with my own eyes. They try to spoon-feed me all the time. They feed me crap. I decided to see what was going on for myself.'

'It does you credit, Mr President,' Petcher said. He mouthed the formal mode of address for the first time. A few minutes earlier, in commenting on the girls passing below, he had made a bawdy remark, and where in the past the President would have guffawed, now he did not. He had felt chided by the silence, a Falstaff in the presence of a newly-crowned king.

Petcher, a fat, brutal but sensitive man verging on grossness concealed calculation behind a constant claim that he lived only for the pleasures of the flesh. 'I came here for the pussy and the booze,' he would say, and it was a fact that he collected women like objects for display in a cabinet. He rarely slept, gambled at night when not fornicating, knew, manipulated and got on well with almost everyone in the country, including a number of the long-haired tousle-bearded men who one day in mid-winter had suddenly poured down out of the hills to take Havana by storm. Quietly, without display or fuss, he had become a capitalist, holding a quarter of the equity of the national airline. Now he was a little worried by the suspicion that the President might have slipped beyond his reach, for the business he had with him was of the greatest moment. Was the famous Achilles heel, he wondered, a thing of the past?

'Would you describe this as a free country?' the President asked.

'This is Latin America. The word freedom doesn't mean the same thing here. They called Fidel a ponce in the *Diario de la Marina* the other day, and it's still in business.'

'They also threw forty US citizens out of the country only last week,' the President said.

'Including a New England mafia boss called Di Stefano. Owned all the big hotels and most of the night spots. The famous Spina ran the world trade in narcotics from this city. Sure the Cubans threw them out.'

'Are the Communists going to take over?'

'No,' said Petcher. 'Fourteen men run this outfit, of which two

33

are commies. Fidel hates them. They stabbed him in the back.'

'How about the airline business? They still let you run it the way you want?'

'So far,' Petcher said. 'The only capitalists who burned their asses here were in sugar. And they deserved it. I think they made a great mistake in closing the embassy down.'

'I'm glad to hear you say that, Steve,' the President said.

The next day passed in enjoyable activity confirming the President's existing opinions on the situation, and strengthening his determination to resist the pressure to which he was constantly being subjected. Shepherded by Petcher, the party visited the city's evil old madhouse, now in the course of conversion to something like a country club. They looked in at the open prison at Campo Florida where the counter-revolutionaries were kept. Petcher chatted with several of them and translated what they had to say. They seemed to spend their time playing soft ball. The visitors tasted their bean stew and found it good.

After that they took a turn in the old town where the President's nostalgic memories were thickest. In the Prado the girls were promenading by the hundred, to place on display the tiny waists and the mighty haunches that were a speciality of Cuba. The barflies streamed in and out of Sloppy Joe's, as ever. Typical orchestras played *guajiro* music to packed audiences in the cafés.

Wealth from the sugar boom of the nineties had struck, like light prehurricane winds, in a gusty and haphazard way, sparing the grey colonial buildings of the Cathedral district, but freakish in its impact in the Virtues and Souls area near the city's centre. Here rich upstarts had torn the fronts from their plain houses, rebuilding them with balconies carved with sea-monsters from Castaneda's Bestiary – wave-riding gryphons being the favourite.

There was money to burn. Italian specialists from Milan paved the streets with terrazzo, following the voluptuous and intricate designs of the mosaic pavements of third-century Piazza Armerina. Upon these the President trod with respect.

These narrow streets were ingeniously shaded by trellises over which vines had been trained, and innumberable small, yellow birds were dodging through their foliage. 'Canaries, did you say?' The President assumed Petcher to be joking.

'Batista's idea,' Petcher told him. 'He always did the first thing that came into his head. Someone told him the birds here couldn't sing, so he let a couple thousand canaries loose on the town.'

A fruit-crushing machine on the street corner fountained colour and incense into the air and the two men stopped to refresh themselves, just as a man clip-clopped past on a long-tailed, delicately-stepping horse. His eyes were bulging and imperious, and white, curling moustaches covered his cheeks. A peon shuffled after him dressed in an imitation of an old fashioned servant's shift cut from fine material, with a cord hanging from his neck to symbolize the bondage of the past.

Petcher told the President that this arrogant-looking horseman was the brother of the richest man in Cuba.

'Not the famous Julio Bravo? He still around?'

'He sure is,' Petcher said.

'Well, that certainly surprises me ... And do they still beat the old curfew drum on the Vedado?'

'Punctually at 7 p.m.'

'I was hoping it would all be as it was,' the President said.

'It's all here,' Petcher assured him. 'Just the same as ever.'

Everything the President saw he liked. Although in theory the Cubans had no idea as to the true identity of their visitor, his party was under discreet vigilance by plain clothes Cuban G2 agents, who knew that they could expect to spend a year or two on the Island of Pines should any mischance befall their distinguished guest – whoever he might be.

Later, back at the opulent villa on the Malecón, the President and Petcher had demolished the best part of a bottle of Carta D'Oro. Springfield had gone to bed with an attack of the migraine and the secret-service men were in the next room, playing stud poker.

The President, who suffered from fatigue these days, and was taking injections for his anaemia, felt re-infused with energy, and better than he had done for many months. The two men lit up cigars supplied by one of Petcher's friends who owned a small tobacco property down in Pinar Del Rio.

'Nice cigar,' the President said.

'Good, huh? They roll them by hand.'

'Taste even better when you've had to stay away from them for a while.'

'So many things do,' Petcher said. He laughed, able almost to relax at last. Petcher did not particularly care for rum, but it stripped away the inhibitions faster than any other drink he knew. Studying the room's curvature in the amber lens of his glass he no longer felt a barrier between him and the President.

'The stars still shine as brightly as ever at El Paradiso?' the President asked.

'And a moon,' Petcher said. 'They put in a moon since you were last here.'

'I'd like to have gone round there again,' the President said. 'For old times' sake. But Howard wouldn't hear of it. Remember the last time?'

'I'm not likely to forget it,' Petcher said. 'That was Eddie's party. He knew some nice girls, huh?'

'That was a tremendous party. And what's the news of Eddie?'

'Didn't you hear? He was drowned in a twister we had last year. There was a warning on, but he went out just the same. He couldn't stay away from the fish. That was last September, round the Cayo Coco area. Vanished off the face of the earth. He'd been a bit depressed. It could have been a death wish.'

'The worst of the job I'm in,' the President said, 'is the loss of contact with old friends. So old Eddie's dead. Imagine that. We had great times together. Remember the day we all went out on sábalo fishing down at El Morón?'

'That's where the twister hit him. El Morón, right next to Cayo Coco.' Both men shook their heads over this vanished scrap of a shared past.

'That poet – Carlos López? Is he still around?'

'I ran into him only last week. He's a member of the magic circle now. He gets invited to read his poetry to the big chief.'

'He was a nice guy too.'

36

'If you paint or write poetry, you're in these days,' Petcher said. 'You can live off the high hog and Fidel picks up the tab.'

'I see no objection to that,' the President said. 'Artists are the life blood of any young nation.'

There was a long pause. 'What was the name of that girl?' the President asked.

'Which one? I seem to remember we took three or four of them along.'

'The one who started life as a laundress.'

'That was Paquita Rosario.'

'She was a very sweet girl,' the President said.

'With a remarkable history,' Petcher said. 'From two dollars a day ironing shirts to supper parties at the Palace. But completely untouched by it all. Unspoiled. Beautiful, charming and natural in every way. What the Cubans call *una noble mestiza*.'

'I liked her.'

'And she liked you. That was a girl who could have had anything she wanted. Last year she was supposed to have been seen around with Fidel, but she still lives in a one-room flat and walks to work.'

'Beautiful as ever, I suppose.'

'More beautiful if anything.'

'What makes a good woman, Steve?'

'That's a very big question, Mr President. One I'm afraid I'm unable to answer.'

'Don't let them tell you that anything ever makes up for it, Steve.'

'Makes up for what?'

'The loss of the simple things of life.'

'I'm in no doubt about that,' Petcher said. 'That's what I live for, and that's why I'm here.'

The President sighed. 'Well, what's done is done, I guess. Water under the bridge.' He thrust out an arm suddenly in a gesture of defence as if to drive back the wolves of melancholy that watch and wait in the shadows of successful lives. 'The question right now is, what do we do with the evening? I'm out on parole, Steve, and I've only one night left. Do we go out?'

'You want to take Springfield and the gorillas along?'

'No,' the President said. 'Not this time. I want this to be more like one of those parties we used to have.'

'I see,' Petcher said. So here it came at last, he thought. The Achilles heel of old. 'I gather Springfield takes his duties seriously,' he said. 'How do you propose to get rid of him?'

'On second thoughts, do we have to go out? Maybe we could have a party here?'

'Nothing to stop us. I could call Carlos if you liked. One or two friends who'd keep their mouths shut.'

'That's a pretty nice idea. So long as we don't go out we don't have to worry with Springfield. He's smart enough to know when to keep out of the way.'

'Maybe I could even locate Paquita,' Petcher said. 'If you want me to. I could try one or two numbers and see if she happens to be free.'

When Petcher left the President he drove a short distance to the villa on Thirty-Fourth street where, by arrangement, members of the government could be informally contacted. Never had the situation, he believed, been more delicate. One wrong move and Cuba would be lost forever. As Petcher argued with the expatriates, 'So far we've lost nothing. The only people who've suffered at all are the big boys in sugar. We don't owe anything to them. Leave well alone.'

Julio Vargas of the Foreign Commission saw him, a moderate, pro-American, the only rebel who had been too young to grow a successful beard in the Sierra.

'How was the house?' Vargas asked.

'Perfect. And thanks for the champagne.'

'Anything else I can do for you?'

'We're having a party tonight. Any hope of getting hold of Paquita Rosario?'

'Difficult,' Vargas said. 'You know who she's with these days?'

'Rumours have reached my ear,' Petcher said.

'Why Paquita?' Vargas asked. 'There are plenty more.'

'This is one of those irrational things,' Petcher said. 'He made a play for her last time he was here, and she wouldn't come across.'

'We can but try,' Vargas said.

'Do your best, Julio. It could be important for us all.'

'You know they are preparing to attack us?'

'Everybody knows that. This guy is all against it. He hates the idea. This is something he inherited from the last administration. It's the Agency baby, and they're gunning for him.'

'Why did he come here?'

'He wanted to convince himself how things were before taking a stand.'

'And has he done that?'

'Paquita could tip the balance.'

Astonishment showed in Vargas' unlined face. 'Such a small thing could make such a difference?'

'It all helps. Paquita is a very clever girl.'

'Well, I will speak to her,' Vargas said. 'That is all I can say.'

Next morning when Springfield came down he noticed a faint odour of perfume in the room where they'd all been sitting the night before. The first person he saw was Teller, whose look invited questions which Springfield ignored.

'The President's having breakfast,' Teller said. 'He wants to see you.'

Springfield nodded. A trained detective, he noticed – although a woman had almost finished tidying up the room – the tell-tale traces of disorder that remained. Someone had moved the furniture round. There were glasses on a tray waiting to be taken away. He spotted a hair-grip on the tiled floor, and bent down to pick it up, and put it in his pocket. Springfield had a pretty good idea of what had gone on the night before while he had been sleeping off his migraine.

He found the President seated at a table out on the verandah, backed by the delicate peach of the Havana morning. He was scooping out a half-grapefruit, and there was a special briskness about him, a readiness to wrinkle his eyes in a quick smile, that confirmed the theory he had already formed.

'How's the head today?' the President asked.

'Fine, Mr President. All I needed was a good night's sleep.'

'That turned out to be quite a party. You were wise to get away when you did. How about some coffee?'

The President rang the bell, and a negro servant was at the door with the tray almost before he'd taken his finger off the bell-push.

'On second thoughts it was a pity you didn't feel able to stay. Petcher knows some wonderful people. I wish you could have talked with Carlos López, the poet. They're going to give him the Ministry of Culture. In this country poets rate higher than hand-shaking politicians.'

'Maybe it will be the same with us one of these days, Mr President. I gather the trip's been a success.'

'It's opened my eyes, Howard. I was on the point of doing something stupid. I've been pressured out of my mind over this Cuba thing. What do you *really* suppose is troubling these people's minds so much?'

'They're worried about their investments. They were picking up a profit of 900% on sugar, and it comes hard to see that cut to 100%. Nobody likes having to kiss easy money goodbye. That's human nature.'

'But,' said the President, 'they forget that I don't work for the multinationals. My employers are the American people. This exercise was set up a year before I took office, and now the guys I look to to help me conduct the affairs of the nation say it's too late to stop it.'

Tell him what he wants to hear, was Springfield's maxim. 'You don't believe that, do you, Mr President?'

'No, Howard. It's an absurdity, but it puts me in one hell of a predicament. Right now I have ten enemies for every friend. If I break this up I can forget about a second term.'

'How about pretending to go along with them? Tell them, okay boys, go right ahead, but play it so that they get no backing. Keep them starved of funds. While you're about it, why not take out a couple of the Agency heads and give them jobs as ambassadors, some place like Kano? I don't see the need to get into a fight. Pursue a policy of attrition. Wear them down.'

'That is the answer, Howard. Wear them down. But there's a full-time job here for someone. A lot of planning comes into this. Is this something I could persuade you to take on?'

40

'I'm a private citizen. I'd be up against the establishment.'

'Howard, I've just decided to look around for a new DI. He'd be in a position to do anything, short of changing the constitution. How does that sound to you?'

Springfield flushed with pleasure. He swallowd. 'Mr President, you have a higher opinion of me that I have of myself.'

'Give me a straight answer. Can you do it?'

'Yes,' Springfield said. 'I can do it.'

That same morning Petcher was back in Julio Vargas' office. 'I'm seeing him off in an hour's time,' he said. 'Thought I'd stop by and put your mind at rest. My feeling is that it's going to be all right.'

'Another six hundred mercenaries arrived in the Miami camp yesterday,' Vargas said.

'It doesn't matter,' Petcher said.

'Two thousand more are training in Guatemala.'

'Let them train.'

'You are complacent,' Vargas said.

'Only one thing matters, whether or not the President is behind this,' Petcher told him.

'And you insist that he is not.'

'Not now. No.'

'They will attack us all the same?'

'It's highly likely,' Petcher said. 'But without air cover.'

'Are you sure of this?'

'That is my opinion. I'm not given to over-optimism.'

Vargas seemed puzzled. 'I still find it difficult to understand why a capitalist should work so hard for us.'

'I'm a capitalist, but I'm a realist, too. I have a big stake in this country. You ought to thank Paquita. I'll bet he never knew a woman like that. He was heading in the right direction, but she tipped the scale. Do you people have any decoration for women?'

'Not even for men,' Vargas said. 'In the new Cuba we have ceased to crave for personal commendation.' He smiled, and the smile aged him. The only revolutionary he had ever met with a sense of humour, Petcher thought.

41

'So virtue is its own reward,' Petcher said. 'Does that go for us foreign capitalists too?'

The smile returned, with even deeper lines than before. 'We value our friends,' Vargas said. 'A sense of virtue and our own soft currency are all very well for internal transactions. I should like to make a hard currency gesture of appreciation. What have you in mind?'

'I heard an alarming rumour the other day that there's been talk of taking my company over.'

'You would receive compensation.'

'In five percent bonds,' Petcher said. 'I might as well take the virtue.'

'If it's to be taken over, Steve, there's nothing I can do. On the other hand, if no decision's been taken I may be able to help. Rely on me.'

'It's all I could possibly ask,' Petcher said. 'All I could ask.'

LA PLUME DE MON AMI

by

Rose Tremain

Rose Tremain has published three novels and a collection of short stories. She also writes regularly for radio and television and in twelve years has had sixteen plays performed. She was one of twenty young writers chosen to represent the Best of Young British Novelists in 1983. In the same year she became a Fellow of the Royal Society of Literature. In 1984 she was the winner of the Dylan Thomas Short Story Award, and her new novel The Swimming Pool Season *is to be published by Hamish Hamilton shortly.*

Rose Tremain lives in Norwich.

On an April Thursday, Maundy Thursday in Gerald's Letts Diary, Gerald strolled in his city suit through the lunchtime crowds in Covent Garden and saw, through the window of an expensive shop, Robin buying knitwear. Until this moment – Robin, moving towards a full-length mirror with a beige and burgundy cardigan held tenderly against his shoulders, glances up, and his round blue eyes that haven't faded with time behold, through the artful display of home-knitted jerseys on wooden poles, Gerald looking in – Gerald and Robin hadn't met for twenty years. If they sometimes thought about each other, or had a dream in which the other appeared, or sent, on impulse, a Christmas card, they also knew that their friendship belonged too delicately to the past to survive the present or the future. They doubted they would ever meet again.

Gerald, at thirty-eight, was a tall, powerfully fashioned man, with a fleeting, blazing smile of touching emptiness. Robin, at forty-two, was neat-waisted, springy, very hesitantly balding, small. As they sighted each other, as if through an ancient, long-discarded pair of binoculars, both knew unerringly what the other would see: their separate mortality. Both felt, on the same instant, a sweet sadness. Gerald smiled and walked into the shop. Robin, still holding to his chest the burgundy cardigan, moved neatly towards him and silently embraced him.

Because it was lunchtime and because, as Gerald neared forty, he had become an innocently gourmandising man, he prolonged this meeting with Robin by the space of a meal, during which they discussed – very gently, so as not to lay on this fugitive encounter a feeling of heaviness – the past. That night, they went to their separate homes on different sides of London and began to remember it.

Gerald liked to remember things chronologically: cause and effect; beginning, middle and end. So he started by remembering the play – the Crowbourne school production of *Antony and*

Cleopatra, in which he'd played an acclaimed Antony and in which, at the last minute, because of the appendectomy of a dark-browed boy called Nigel Peverscombe, Robin had played a petulant Cleopatra. Hand in hand with his memories of his Crowbourne Antony went Gerald's memories of Palomina, his first woman.

Robin preferred to remember more selectively, starting with days, or even individual moments when he'd been happy or at least carefree, and only then proceeding, holding fast to the rim of his duvet in his dark and reassuring room, to those other times when he'd begun to see himself as a clown, a fool, a player in a tragedy even. He managed, however, a rueful smile. His life since that time hadn't been disagreeable. Certainly not tragic. Next term, he was taking over as Housemaster at Shelley, Crowbourne's premier house.

Gerald remembers staring, smiling as he bows, beyond the hot flood of the stage lights on their scaffolding, at the dark space above the heads of the audience, and feeling the future touch him lightly and beckon him out. School is over. He is eighteen and a man. Palomina is out there, applauding. Ahead is the summer. No child's beach holiday with his mother and father and his two baby sisters, but a journey this year, a man's adventure, two months of travel before the start of the Oxford term. He wants to applaud with the audience. Applaud his good fortune, his youthfulness, his potency. He wants to shout. 'Bravo!' cheer the Upper Sixth, sitting at the back. Gerald and Robin move forwards, separating themselves from the rest of the cast. The clapping and stamping is thunderous. Gerald shivers with ecstasy and hope. He smiles his captivating smile. 'We did it,' Robin whispers. And Gerald's wellspring of optimism is turned to admiration and affection for Robin, the young teacher, his Oxford already in the past, producer of the play and, finally, its bravest star. '*You* did it, Robin,' he corrects.

He remembers nothing about the school after that night. Not the farewells, nor the packings of trunks, not even the last singing of the school song. It fell away from him and he cast it aside. It was strange for him to imagine, as he sat on the deck of the channel steamer with

Robin and watched the English coast become thin and insubstantial that Robin would be returning to Crowbourne in September. Why live through Oxford and get to know the proper world and then go back? I will never do this, he promises himself, I will never go back to Crowbourne except as the father of future Crowbournians. Robin will teach them and remember me. In his repetitious life it will be me, not my sons, who will count.

It's chilly on the boat, windy and grey. Near Dieppe, it gets rough and Gerald and Robin sit huddled up in their coats. Robin produces a hip flask of brandy. The silver mouth of the flask has a warm and bitter taste. They don't talk much.

At Dieppe, their legs unsteady after the long boat crossing, they lug their suitcases to the Paris train. This was before the days of backpacks and weightless, shiny bags. For two months, they carried those heavy cases around, re-labelling them for each new stage of the journey. They were scraped and scratched and dented and buffeted and sat on. Arriving back at Victoria, they seemed like the sad trophies of a battle. Gerald can't remember what became of his suitcase, but he remembers the look and feel of it in his cheap Paris room, opening it and laying out on the shiny coverlet a clean shirt and the kind of striped jacket that used to be called 'casual'. Men's clothes. He'd become a man. Now Robin would show him France. All the places he'd learned about he would see and touch, wearing his casual clothes. With Robin he walks out into the Paris night. Robin leads them unerringly to a noisy, whitely lit brasserie and advises Gerald, 'Have *pied de porc*. They know how to cook it here.' When the meal arrives, Gerald stares at the trotter on his plate and thinks, good, from now on I shall seek out the unfamiliar. That night, he has a dream he's snuffling for truffles.

Of course, says Robin to himself, as if in answer to a question, I remember Paris! We were in the *sixième*. The hotel proprietor wore an eyepatch. I had room No. 10. We didn't go into each other's rooms, but stood only on the thresholds. Paris was the threshold of the journey. Gerald wore clean, smart clothes that got dirtier as the summer went on. He seemed large in that French city. I was a better size for Paris. He was golden and greedy and loud. I disliked him, suddenly. He tried to make me get up early to take him to the Louvre, but I didn't want his enthusiasm for the pictures, I wanted

47

to go on my own and spend some time with the Cézannes. I felt in need of foliage and quiet. I said, 'Go on your own, Gerald. I've seen the Louvre.' I walked to the Luxembourg Gardens where, every time I've been there I seem to see a nun, and started writing my diary. I'd arranged to meet Gerald there and he came running at me, waving like a lunatic. I blushed for him. 'Leave me here,' I wanted to tell him, 'go on on your own.' But he sat down and began to chivvy me about – of all people – Rubens. 'I can't stand Rubens,' I told him. So he shut up and sighed and began to kick dusty pebbles like a boy. Yes, I disliked him then. Some nuns passed and he smiled at them. I started to write down 'N' in my diary for every nun I saw. I decided they were bad omens.

Another thing I didn't like about Gerald then was his piety. It was a false piety, born out of his successes at Crowbourne and his romantic love of the girl, Palomina. He displayed it, though, in all the grand churches, Notre Dame, the Sainte Chapelle, the Sacré Coeur. Of these three, only the Sainte Chapelle is quiet and the other two mill with tourists in ugly clothes, exhibiting their own brand of false piety by lighting candles for people far away. Watching them, I try to imagine the names of the people getting the candles. Over the years, the names have changed. Now, they're mainly Japanese: Kyoko, Nukki, Yami, Go. Then, twenty years ago, they were American: Candice, Wilbur, Nancy-Anne, Buck. They disgusted me. Gerald's lighting of candles disgusted me. I was, then as now, a very unsentimental man. I saw several N's in the three churches that day. N's look as if they're always whispering to Jesus and I can't abide these private conversations. They could be talking to God about me.

Of our three nights in Paris, I prefer to remember the third. We are asked – a prearranged date – to dine with Monsieur and Madame de Bladis, friends of Gerald's parents. Gerald refers to these people as 'The Bladders'. Brushing our cuffs, shining our shoes with paper hankies, we take the Métro to Neuilly, where the Bladders have a *maison particulière*. 'She's rather fun,' Gerald tells me, 'she has a sense of humour.' And the thought flits into me like a bat: do riches alter the jokes you make, the things you laugh at? I feel poor on the stuffy Métro. For the first time since leaving England, I'm at peace with Gerald's size and air of wealth. I decide, on the morrow, to grow a beard. My first beard. I don't tell Gerald my decision. I'll let him notice it himself.

The de Bladis house is emphatically grand. Porcelain black-amoors hold on their turbaned heads a marble table in the hall. Madame de Bladis is chiffoned, pearled and rouged and sweeps down her cascading staircase like a dancer. She leads us to the roof, where there is a canopied garden, complete with a tiny fountain, the noise of which creates in my own bladder a perpetual yet not unexciting desire to piss. 'Gerald, Gerald,' she says in her soft French voice, 'you are getting so beautiful. Why don't we have a daughter to offer you?!' Gerald is quieter here, awed by the roof garden, very beautiful indeed. And it's to me, in his shyness of these people, that Gerald turns – for encouragement, for the right word in his hesitant A-Level French, for confirmation of an idea or an opinion. I become the teacher again and the old intimacy we had for the weeks of the *Cleopatra* rehearsals and then lost as we arrived in France, returns. As Gerald's friend, I am made welcome. We are served *anguillettes* – a kind of minuscule eel I've never eaten before or since – as a first course. All along the roof, as the sky deepens, pink lanterns are lit. Above and between these, tilting back my happy head, I see the stars. 'Your friend is smiling,' says Madame de Bladis, 'I like this.'

Gerald remembers a feeling of admiration, of envy almost for Monsieur de Bladis. A bank to run, a sumptuous house to own, a pretty wife with a plump, high-sitting bosom to be deliciously unfaithful to – these earthly rewards could be worth striving for. I will, he decides, watching the plash-plash of the fountain, watching the gloved hands of the servant who brings a hot chocolate soufflé, try to make a success of things. Oxford and the Law. The route is straight. I'm on my marks. Yet there's a little time, such as now, sitting on a roof in Neuilly on a warm night, to be *savoured* before the race begins. Even Robin is allowing himself to savour this night. He's stopped feeling cross. He's started to enjoy himself. And tomorrow we go south, as far as the Loire.

'Ah,' says Robin, 'ah, yes, yes,' as we see, admirable and stately above the town, the Château de Blois. And I know that this little lisp of pleasure he lets sigh conceals his abundant knowledge of French and Italian architectural caprice, that he will guide me through the complexities of the building in the same delighted way as he guided me through Shakespeare's verse. He's twenty-two. How has all this knowledge been crammed into him? I feel as empty of history as a willow bat. As Robin prances round the dark well of the François Ier staircase, he murmurs, 'Brabante, you see. Used by Il Boccadoro. Note the balustrade. Shallow relief ornamentation. Very Brabante.' And I want to mock him. 'Very Brabante, Robin? Really?' But I don't. I let him bound on, gazelle-like in his light-treading reverence for stone, and I am invaded with my longing for Palomina. I want her there and then on the staircase. Her pubic hair is lightly brown. I want to tangle my life in her little brown briar bush. I lean on the balustrade and look down into the sunshine. A couple below me seem small and I'm dizzy with my Palomina-lust. 'Gerald!' Robin calls sternly, 'come on!'

The *pension* Robin has found near the station is poor. Outside my window is a vegetable garden where an old man works till dusk, hoeing and coughing and lighting thin cigarettes. His cough wakes me in the morning. The place has a cold, green painted dining room where, for dinner, we're served a watery consommé followed by some lukewarm chicken. We don't dare ask for vegetables, though in the garden I've seen peas and beans and marrows, but a dish of these arrives long after we've eaten the chicken. '*Je m'excuse,*' says a thin, vacant-eyed waitress as she plonks the dish down. We eat the beans obediently and talk about money. We should economise on rooms, says Robin. All right, I say.

I've begun to worry about how, in all the weeks to come, I'll ever get my underpants washed. At school, you put out all your dirty clothes on your bed on a Friday morning and made a list of them and they were returned to you, washed and ironed, the following week. Who washed and ironed them exactly, or where, I'm not able to say. I've never washed any clothes myself ever in my life, though I've heard there's something called Tide you're supposed to use. Can one buy Tide in France, or is it called something else? '*Marée*', for instance? I sense, by the set of Robin's nostrils as he plans our next day's visit to Chambord, that he's become too unearthly for these kind of questions. But I rather love and admire his enthusiasm for buildings and feel pleased I asked him to come with me. I notice, in the cold light of the green dining room, that he's unshaven for the second day running. Is he, I wonder, going to model himself on more intrepid travellers than us? Scott, for instance? Or Alfred Russell Wallace? But I don't ask him this. We go to bed rather early, me to write to Palomina, he to write his diary.

Extract from Robin's Diary. July 31st 1964.
Ch. of Blois v. calming. Size has a tranq. effect on me. Renaiss. arch. seems so sure of itself, so sophisticatedly playful, nothing *mean* in it. Not hard to imag. my life in a turret.

G's arms and face are getting quite brown from sitting about. I think there's a kind of impatience in him to get south. I shall rein him back – he my horse, me his chevalier!

This room is mournful.

Saw two NN at the Ch.

Chambord tomorrow, hooray.

Extract from Gerald's letter to Palomina. July 31st 1964.
My darling Palomina,

One week now since I saw you. I miss you, my darling. Do you miss me? I miss you so much. Please write Poste Restante to Avignon or Nice.

I saw a fine Renaissance staircase today. I missed you on it. Do you miss me on staircases?

At Chambord, Robin remembers, he was still in his carefree time. After Blois and now here, he's becoming a Francois Ier admirer. At Chambord, the great king had a river, the Cosson, diverted to his castle's feet. Robin lies on the sunny grass, eating bread and a carton of brawn salad, and imagines all the everlasting things he would like to re-route towards his master's cottage at Crowbourne: the Spanish steps, Michelangelo's David, Cézanne's jungles, Dylan Thomas's house-high hay, the golden vestments of Saladin. He's aware, with his face tipped up to the blue sky, of the Loire valley as a kind of cradle where he and the grand houses can quietly affirm their remoteness from the modern, the discordant, the utilitarian and the plebeian. Tiny orchids, wild as weeds, grown near his head. *Bliss.* Order and beauty and grace. *Blissful.* He doesn't move. Gerald gets up and struts around, taking photographs. Robin thinks of the frail King Charles IX who would hunt in this park for ten hours at a stretch and blow his hunting horn till his throat bled. Gerald is daring like this with his limbs. In the high-jump, he'd hurl his big body at the bar. 'Run, Gerald!' Robin wants to call to him. He loves to see him run. But he's gone off somewhere with his camera and Robin is alone.

He's gone off, in fact, to try to buy a stamp for his letter to Palomina. He thinks the little kiosk where they sell postcards and slides might also sell him a stamp, or rather several stamps, because he plans to write to Palomina a lot. He's heavy with his Palomina-lust and writing to her assuages it. *'Ah non, Monsieur,'* snaps the kiosk woman, *'nous ne sommes pas un bureau de poste.'*

'Pardonne...' says Gerald, *'pardonnez-moi.'*

'Allez!' says the woman with a sniff. It's as if he'd asked for a French letter. He blushes.

Robin remembers the Avignon train. It's the Boulogne night train, but there are no sleepers, nor even any seats. It's crammed with Parisians going south, sitting wearily shoulder to shoulder, like in wartime. He and Gerald stand at a corridor window and as the darkness comes, they begin to sense the air getting warmer. They're lulled by the thought of a lavender sunrise in Provence. They lie down in the corridor with their heads on their suitcases and doze and all the shoulder-to-shoulder people lean and nod and pull down their blinds and a general tiredness overcomes the train.

The train stops several times, but no one seems to get on or off. Robin sits up and stares at the names of stations: Vienne, Valence, Montélimar... Gerald seems to be sleeping soundly, enfolding his suitcase like a lover, his long legs in creased trousers heavy and still on the dirty floor. Robin takes an old cardigan he used to wear at Oxford out of his own case and covers Gerald's shoulders with this.

At six o'clock at Avignon-Fontcouverte, where the air is chilly and white with a dense mist, they stumble out, shivering, and follow the upright Parisians to a clean, new-seeming station restaurant serving croissants in their hundreds and large cups of coffee.

Now, tasting this good, hot coffee, they feel the traveller's awareness of deprivation and blessing, warmth after cold, shelter after storm. They don't talk, but each is privately happy. And they're south at last. Along the station platform, a hazy yellow sun disperses the mist and starts to glimmer on the plane trees. Gerald's hair is tousled, giving him a shaggy, unruly look that Robin finds disturbing. On his cheek is a pink blotch, where it's lain pressed against the suitcase lid.

Gerald remembers how they walked through suburbs where buildings were sparse then, past plumbers' yards and garages and a vast, empty hippodrome to the centre of the city, lugging the heavy cases. Buses passed them, taking people to work. Gerald suggested they should get on one of the buses, but Robin said no, he wanted air. So they walked till the city streets started to narrow round them and the Pope's Palace was there above them, then sat down at a pavement café and saw from the milling crowds and fluttering banners and flags that Avignon was in the middle of a festival. 'There'll be a problem with rooms,' Robin said, and in the hot sun Gerald felt tired and sleepy. Then he remembered that at the central post office there might be a letter from Palomina, and wanted to run to the letter and press the envelope against his nose, breathing in the translucent airmail sentences of his woman.

'I've got to go to the post office,' he said, getting up. 'I'll be back in half an hour.' And he darted away, leaving Robin sitting on his own with the luggage.

The room is shadowy, remembers Robin, in a kind of well of buildings which shoulder off the light. There's a double bed with a hard bolster and no pillows. The bedcoverings feel heavy and chill.

They're lucky to find the room. All the cheap places have *complet* signs up. This is the last vacant room in the last hotel...

On either side of the bed, back to back they lie in the early evening and try to sleep. Robin is acutely aware of Gerald's breathing. On a rusty washbasin near the bed stands an orange

53

packet of Tide Gerald has bought. In the absence of any letter from Palomina with which to pass a secret hour before dinner, he's washed out all his underpants. They're hung on a rail at the side of the basin and drip steadily onto the lino floor. He's naked in the bed except for a short sleeved T-shirt, and as well as his breathing Robin is aware of his firm, round buttocks very near to his own, and feels, for the first time since the night of *Cleopatra*, a fatal stab of desire. He buries his face in the bolster and forces himself to remember the dark, Italianate features of the girl Gerald loves, Palomina, four years older than him, staying *au pair* with Gerald's family, helping with the baby sisters. She's a plump girl, not beautiful, but wide-eyed and wayward-seeming, with a mane of brown frizzy hair. The antithesis of blond, handsome Gerald. Yet pious like him, probably, with an exaggerated, lying Catholic piety. Confessing after he fucks her.

The room's above a café in the tiny, hemmed-in square. At the window, Robin can hear swallows and the sound of tables being laid for dinner.

Extract from Gerald's letter to Palomina. August 8th 1964.
My dearest Palomina,

I've written to you almost every day. When we got here (to Avignon) I went straight to the PTT and God I was so miserable when there was no letter from you. It was so beastly, and I began to ask myself jealous questions: have you found another boy? Please reassure me, my darling, that you still love me. I feel like dying. This dying feeling is so horrible I think I must break my promise and visit you when you get to your parents' house on the 23rd. Please say I can. I'm in torment without your breasts.

Extract from Robin's Diary. August 8th 1964.
Prog. into Avig. is through draperies announcing a music and theatre festival. So no rooms of course. Boulevards choc-a-bloc with German youth. Thighs etc.

Tourists are teeming coarsefish. G. and I try to behave like surface feeders, Mayfly gourmets. This will be diffic. here. We're sharing a room, for reasons of econ. mainly. G. is washing his knickers in Tide.

54

Had a dream last night in the train corridor Aunt M. was dead. Hope she isn't. She's the only intell. woman my family produced.

Avig. teeming with NNs.

Lost count after 9. Bad sign.

NB. P. des Papes looks monolithic, just right for the Church, but wrong for me. Adieu la renaissance.

Gerald remembers waiting in Avignon for the letter that never came. Day after day, he goes to the central post office and says his name, Gerald Willoughby. *Je crois que vous avez une lettre pour moi, Gerald Willoughby.*

'*Non,*' they say, '*non, rien pour vous.*'

He dreads it then: *rien pour vous.* You have nothing, Gerald, *are* nothing without the embrace of Palomina.

The city is hot, choked, dusty. They follow the tourists in a line up the ramparts of the Pope's Palace. The wind brings gusts of litter. One night, they sit on planks to hear the voice of Gérard Philippe reciting Victor Hugo at a Son et Lumière performance, and the vast walls of the Palace are lit with strange violet light, behind which the sky seems violet and the bats like black musical notes, bodiless, flying to nowhere. They return penniless and sorrowful to their room. Robin's wallet has been stolen. They spend the next day telephoning Lloyds Bank and Thomas Cook and Robin's mother in Swindon and wait, with the letter that doesn't come, for money to be sent to them.

They walk out to the famous bridge, the Pont St Bénézet, and the Rhône is slow, majestic and green as the Amazon. Gerald remembers the blue of the Loire and feels the change in river colour to be one among very many confusions: Palomina's silence, the mood of sadness that seems to have settled on Robin, the feeling of heaviness this city imparts. For the first time since leaving England, he's lonely.

Robin spends hours at the Musée Calvet. He tries to perceive where, in the Daumier drawings, amid the torrent of lines, the artist has changed his mind. Unconsciously, he's seeking out the rage in the pictures, yet hoping to be calmed by them. He sits down very frequently on the hard *banquettes* and the image of Gerald's turned back in the bed comes unasked-for into his mind. And he looks round and sees Gerald some way off, staring at the paintings, but not *entering* them, as Robin does, just vacantly gazing, unmoved, untouched.

On the eighth day in Avignon replacement traveller's cheques arrive and Gerald re-packs his underpants which have dried stiff and powdery, not quite like they were in the days of the school laundry. 'I expect there's a knack to washing, is there?' he asks, as he examines the French writing on the Tide packet. Robin merely shrugs and touches his new beard, in which there seem to be little clusters of grey. It's only since the night of Son et Lumière that he's stopped answering all of Gerald's questions. Very often, the boy looks hurt.

The absence of an airmail letter from Palomina is hurting. All Gerald can think of now is getting to the central post office in Nice. He can *see* the letter in its little metal compartment. He can *see* Palomina's bunched-up continental writing. Yet the thought that Palomina has stopped loving him is giving him pains in his bowel. 'I feel strange,' he tells Robin, as they climb onto a hot, mid-afternoon train and sit down opposite two nuns, 'I feel weak.'

He leans his head against the burning glass of the train window and closes his eyes. The train's crowded with young people, German, Dutch, American. The seats opposite the nuns were the only two available. '*Milano?*' asks a big Italian with hairy thighs, as he pushes past with his rucksack. '*Non,*' says Robin.

The Italian looks distractedly up and down the train. A tin mug, strung onto a canvas loop of his haversack, almost bangs the wimple of the outer nun, who lowers her pale face and folds her arms. '*Questo treno. A Milano, non?*' the Italian asks the nuns. '*Nice!*' they whisper, in unison. '*Ah fucki shiti!*' he says, seizing a hank of springy hair, and pushes himself towards the door, arms held high, like a wader. Robin smiles, liking the horror on the faces of the Sisters. 'God!' says an American girl, 'wait till I tell Myrna I touched Gérard Philippe. She'll die!'

The train starts to move. Cool air comes in above Gerald's blond

56

head. Gerald remembers, on this train, the feeling of becoming very ill. He remembers falling in and out of a deep and sickly sleep and dreaming of the sea. He remembers the nuns looking up at him under their pale brows. He remembers Robin soaking his handkerchief with Evian water and giving this to him and, when it touches his head, feeling cold to his marrow. 'I'm sorry, Robin, so sorry . . .' he keeps repeating. And he walks past all the hot Dutch and German bodies to a foul-smelling toilet and shits his soul out into the stained pan. There's no paper in the lavatory. With shaky hands, Gerald pulls his wallet from the shorts that lie round his feet and wipes himself with two dry cleaners' tickets saying 2prs gr flannels and 1 blue blzr. His school clothes. Swilled away somewhere between Brignoles and Vidauban.

Over Nice, where they arrive towards six o'clock, rolls a gigantic thunderstorm. Outside the crowded station, the rain begins to teem and Gerald's enfeebled brain wants to cry for England and familiarity and shelter. He's forgotten the letter waiting for him at the central post office. He's incapable of Palomina-lust. He can barely walk. Sweat is running off him like the rain off the station roof. 'Stay here,' says Robin, sitting Gerald on a bench with the luggage. 'I'll go and find us a room.'

And he watches hopelessly as Robin darts out into the forecourt, where people mill and shout and wait for taxis and buses. NICE COTE D'AZUR says a white and blue sign, and Gerald remembers that they are, at last, by the sea. Yet the bench towards which his head soon falls and rests smells of city soot. He puts a limp arm round the suitcases and longs for Robin to return.

It's dark by the time a Citroën taxi takes them into the *vieille ville*. The storm has moved inland and is hurtling far off, over the mountains. The sea's calm in the big bay, silvery in its glut of reflected light. 'What a show,' Gerald mumbles, 'Nice is.'

Their room is an attic. Robin remembers the pigeon's noisy existence on an iron window bar and the depths of quiet falling away below them into a courtyard. For most of his life, at least two or three times a year, in a dream, he's returned to this room with its view of gutters and chimney pots and balconies and washing. The hotel is called the Jean Bart. There's one lavatory every other floor. In the room below them an eighty-year-old Finnish woman

57

struggles with the stairs. She tells Robin she's well known in her country for her translations of D.H. Lawrence. Robin feels light and happy among the roofs. Twice a day, he carries bouillon and bread up all the flights of dark steps to Gerald's bed. He and a pert maid tidy the room around their golden invalid, who is humble in his sufferings, cut down to size. For three days, Palomina isn't mentioned. At night, Robin and Gerald lie side by side in the dark and talk of going on into Italy. Robin writes a postcard to his mother in Swindon saying: Arr. Nice. Old Town v. congenial. Trust yr hip not playing up in hot weather. Blessings, Robin. Gerald sleeps. Robin unwinds the sellotape from the Tide packet and washes, with gentle attention, his patient's underwear and his own. He dries the clothes at the window where the male pigeons wear their showy tailfeathers like long kilts.

Gerald remembers his resurrection on the fourth day. He's standing in the PTT. The building has a vaulted roof like a church. It's cool and dark. An Irish girl is weeping and being comforted by a friend she addresses as Dilly. 'Oh Jesus, Dilly,' she sobs, 'oh Dilly, Dilly...' And a pale PTT employee snaps, *'Monsieur Willuffby?'* and slides a glass grille open and pushes towards Gerald an airmail letter.

That night, as Robin and Gerald sit on a pavement in the *vieux port* and eat red mullet and a brilliant sunset the colour of the mullet tails descends on the cloudless evening, Robin takes out his postcard to his mother and adds, in angry schoolmaster's red biro, PS. Weather here lousy. Gerald looks helplessly from Robin's card to the sky and sighs. It's intolerable, Robin, he wants to say.

The house of Palomina's parents in the hills behind Ajaccio is remembered entirely differently by Gerald and Robin, the smell of the *maquis* and of the eucalyptus trees being the one sweet, sad memory common to both. Robin remembers the unpleasant feeling of grit under his bare feet on the tiled floors. Gerald remembers gliding on these same floors like a silky ghost to Palomina's bedroom door. Robin remembers the terror of finding himself, for the first time in his life, astride a horse. Gerald, on a bay mare, remembers the joy of it, and the blissful sight, not far in front of him, of Palomina's bikini-clad buttocks going up and down on her Mexican saddle. Robin remembers the feeling, in these hard hills, in the shadow of the granite mountains, of becoming soft, boneless, vulnerable, too easily crushed and bruised, the feeling of helpless flesh. Gerald remembers arranging his big body next to Palomina's in the sunshine and letting his eyes wander in the topmost pinnacles of rock, and thinking, I could climb those. With my bare hands and wearing only my football boots, I could master the Monte d'Oro.

The storms have gone north. Over all of Corsica shimmers the breathless heat that seems, in Robin's brain, to suspend time, to make every day long and blinding and purposeless, a month of empty sabbaths, everyone and everything monotonously sighing and humming and burning.

The house sits on a small hill, itself contained in a wider valley hemmed in by the mountains. Below the hill is a stream, torrential in winter, now slow but cold and clear and full of minnows. Each evening, Robin comes down here and lowers his hectic head into the water and opens his eyes and sees in the green river his own foolish lovesick feet planted on the sand. He wishes it was autumn. In the crisp beginning of the new school year, there was purpose and dignity. In his diary, which he can hardly bear to write during this futile time, he makes plans to abandon Gerald and go on into Italy on his own. His writing in the diary is so bad, the language so truncated, he has trouble, some years later, deciphering what he wrote.

Extracts from Robin's Diary. August 24th – August 30th 1964.
Miserab. arriv. G. so puffed up to see P. I cld wring his neck.

No car avail. So we're stuck in this idiotic 'ranch'. G. thinks he's Yul Brynner. Or worse.

G. gets me on a f. horse. Failure.
    Lg to see some sights, even if it's only Napoleon's House.
    Boredom.

P's mother, Jeanne, is an enig prd shallow persec woman. You sense

59

no one loves her. We lnch in Ajacc. Then she show us the fam. tomb. Hideous. 4NN.

Alone today. G., P., and J. went riding. Allwd car. Saw N's house. Dispp. One gd portrait by Gros. Also Chap. Imp. Welcome brush with Renaiss. order. Coming out into the sun again, wanted to die.

Mst get to Italy. Flor. Sienna. La bella Toscana. Je souffre. Je souffre. Dream again Aunt M. died. Buried her behind some frescoes.

For Gerald, this valley contains like a casket the precious possessions which are Palomina's ruby nipples, her amber arms. His body is a slow avalanche of desire, engulfing, obliterating. Palomina. Paradise. His blood enquires about nothing but the act of love on Palomina's single bed at dawn, before her mother is awake, before Robin comes sighing out of his dreams, before the sun has fallen across the shiny rumps of the horses in their dusty stables. He remembers a thin line of white six o'clock light coming under the shutters. Day. Everything in this coming day glitters with hope: the smile under the lipstick on the lips of Palomina's mother; the sun on his knuckles as he eats his breakfast melon; the silver of the shivery eucalyptus; the fatal, alluring, far-off blue of the horizon. *I'm in paradise.* He wishes that he was keeping a diary like Robin's, so that he could record each new ecstasy.

He's sharing a room with Robin. In the room are twin beds, covered with white Portuguese lace, a painted chest of drawers, an oak wardrobe, a blue and yellow china lamp and a dusty bit of rattan serving as a mat. This modest arrangement of furniture now contains the bountiful happiness of Gerald and the silent misery of Robin. As a kind of poultice on his wound, Robin remembers the room at the Jean Bart and the carrying of broth and Gerald's sweet gratitude. 'I'd have died if it wasn't for you, Robin,' he said. Now, in Corsica, with these two dark, thick-browed women and Gerald's fair hair going pale as honey, Robin feels he's dying. Not precisely of love, but of his own foolishness. He can live without Gerald. What he can't seem to manage is to live with him and yet without him.

60

'I know,' he says one night to Gerald, 'you'd probably like to stay on here. But there's a ferry back to Nice tomorrow and I think I'll get on it and then press on to Italy like we planned.'

'On your own?'

'Yes.'

'Don't you like it here? You don't like Palomina, do you?'

'I just want to get to Italy.'

'Don't you love the mountains? You love the river, don't you?'

'They're all right.'

'You mean it's churches and paintings and things you miss? But you saw Napoleon's House, didn't you. You liked that.'

'I want to leave, Gerald.'

'But we agreed, Robin, we'd have this holiday together.'

'I know.'

'So you can't just desert me. And, listen, Palomina's father's arriving tomorrow. We'll get taken to more things. He's a big wheel. The Tomasini family are big wheels here.'

I should, said Robin to himself, twenty years later, have left the next day. Why didn't I leave? Why did I do what Gerald wanted?

Obediently, he puts on a clean shirt and trims his startling beard for the return of André Tomasini. This man, who has made a lot of money by Corsican standards, arrives in an ancient Chevrolet and is accompanied by four slender-hipped young men, wearing medallions. These man are embraced by Palomina like brothers. Tomasini is a small, cruel-faced man, whose authority seems to reside in his thin-tipped Roman nose. He greets Gerald and Robin unsmilingly ('oh, I see, my daughter invited you, did she?'), covers Palomina's face with intimate kisses and ignores his wife until she informs him that lunch is ready, when he bangs her bottom like a dinner gong.

They sit down to the meal. Tomasini begins a lengthy, superstitious grace, invoking the name of *'notre ancêtre illustre, Letitzia Ramolini, mère de l'Empereur'*. What this had to do with the eating of *saucisson* and trout remains, to this day, a mystery to Gerald, part of all that he suddenly couldn't understand. Now, the house where he's lived in ecstasy is invaded with conversation and gesture and innuendo and private knowledge from which he's deliberately excluded. Outside, the light is as fierce, the crickets as

61

noisy, the horses as elegantly restless as on all previous days, yet Gerald knows – in Tomasini's patriarchal behaviour, in the reverently lowered eyes of Palomina, in the withdrawal of Jeanne's friendly conversation – that his status is altered. No matter if Palomina works *au pair* in his family, here it's only the Corsicans who count. The strangers are inferior. Gerald looks helplessly at Robin, who is eating his tout primly, in utter silence. He refuses to catch Gerald's eye. His lowered and impassive face is, the boy supposes, still dreaming hopelessly of Florentine marble. Fleetingly, he envies Robin his detachment.

'Who,' says Tomasini, as the meal ends, 'is coming riding with me this evening? Palomina?'

'Yes, Papa.'

There are four horses. Two of the young men are invited. Gerald thinks of Palomina's bouncing bottom and her mane of brown hair and stares with dismay at his mess of trout bones. Palomina and the young men have started to giggle at some private joke. Then the afternoon unfolds: Tomasini takes his wife to bed; Palomina and the young men and Gerald go down to the river. While the others play like children and splash about, Gerald sits on his towel and feels too large, his skin too pale, his hopes too serious. Robin goes and lies down on the Portuguese lace. He can hear, on the other side of the wall, Tomasini's brief and ritualised exertions. With a kind of weariness, he tugs out his diary and writes: NNN. Negative. Null. Nothing.

The following morning, Gerald wakes as usual at dawn. In this valley, the importance of each unfolding day seems to fatten with the sunrise. He stands with his eyes narrowed to the crack in the shutters and is filled with his own longing. The house is silent. Towards midnight, the young men drove away in the Chevrolet. Robin sleeps. Gerald's tall, brown body is twenty-six paces from Palomina's bed. He wants, in the touch of Palomina's stubby hand, to be forgiven his jealousy and restored to favour. He feels old – at the very centre of his life. The boy who played Antony is far off, left behind in his silly paper armour. Antony the man is here, clenching and unclenching his man's fist. He pulls on his shorts, glances at Robin's face made gentle and sad by sleep, and goes out into the dark passage. The tiled floor is icy under his feet. He's afraid. He thought love was easy, just as Latin verse and cricket and the worship of God were easy. Until yesterday, he thought this.

He's at Palomina's door. He opens it as slowly, as silently as he can. On the other mornings, her room has been dark, darkness his ally, shaping the room softly round him as he slipped under the thin sheet. Today, light startles him. He stares, his eyes wide. Palomina sits on her bed eating a nectarine and smiles at him. Juice from the fruit wets her chin. Not far from the bed, sitting in a wicker chair, wearing a towelling robe, is André Tomasini. Gerald draws in a breath, begins to back out of the room.

'Come in, come in, Gerald!' Tomasini calls kindly.

He hesitates, his hand on the door. Palomina sucks her nectarine. 'Come in and sit down,' says Tomasini. Gerald moves into the room and looks blankly at the tableau of father and daughter. Palomina looks at him wistfully, but her eyes are hard. 'Sit down,' says Tomasini again. He perches on a hard chair, where some of Palomina's clothes are strewn, smelling of sun oil and her ripe body.

'Now,' says Tomasini, 'don't look so alarmed, Gerald. We're not barbarians here, you know, we're not *banditi* like you English always suppose, but we like to get everything right for our families, you understand?'

'How do you mean, "right"?' says Gerald.

Palomina licks the nectarine stone. Tomasini lights a cigarette.

'My daughter is twenty-two,' says Tomasini. 'Do you think I want her to spend her life *au pair* in England?'

'No...'

'No. This is for learning a language, no more. She is twenty-two and she must have a future.'

'Of course she must...'

'Boys of eighteen do not marry.'

'I could –'

'No, no. Don't be silly. Boys of eighteen do not marry. Now, I think you have had some hospitality in this house from my wife, no?'

'Yes. Yes, we have...'

'Good. So you will tell your parents we made you welcome?'

'Yes...'

'Good. But this is enough. You understand?'

Gerald gapes. Palomina turns her head to the window. 'I think you understand,' says Tomasini, 'I think you're a clever boy, Gerald. I think you're going to do well at Oxford.'

'Sir, I –'

'And a boy who's going to do well at Oxford can understand what is being asked.'

'You want me to leave.'

'Of course. And your friend. You take the ferry today.'

Finding no words in him, Gerald merely nods. Palomina. Paradise. Over. She won't save him. He stares in silence at her as she puts down the nectarine stone and licks her fingers, one by one.

During the lunch in Covent Garden, Gerald said, lighting one of the cigarettes he was trying so hard to give up, 'I suppose our happiest time was after Corsica, in Italy.'

Robin, who didn't smoke, passed Gerald the ashtray. 'I've always,' he said, 'loved Italy. I always will, I expect.' And he smiled across the table at his friend, to whom it was pointless to say, no, Italy was worse than anything. All you thought about was that stupid Palomina. Standing in front of the David, even right there, I could still see it in you, your silly longing. It marred everything we did.

'I go to Nice sometimes,' Robin said, taking a toothpick out of a white china jar. 'Once I went to look at the Jean Bart.'

'The what?'

'The Jean Bart. Our hotel.'

'Was that what it was called?'

'Yes. It's still there. Our room's still there. The room where you were ill, remember?'

'Oh that was an awful time, wasn't it! Poor you. You were so kind to me. I remember you used to have these dreams about an aunt or someone you thought had died.'

'Aunt Mabel. Yes. She had died. She died the day we arrived in Ajaccio.'

'Oh, I'm sorry, Robin.'

64

'Yes. She was lovely. She's buried in Tintagel.'

'Tintagel?' said Gerald, raising an arm to summon a waiter. 'Can't say I've ever been there. Time to get the bill, do you think?'

THE EAR

by

Colin Thubron

People call Leningrad 'the Venice of the North', but it has none of the benign warmth of the Italian city. Its canals seem incidental to it. Along their grassy crescents the palaces and terraced mansions stand serenely ungiving in pastel yellow, blue or tangerine – chromatic rectangles of the purest classical, broken only by an occasional moulding or pediment. They withhold themselves even from the water. Their reflections are clouded and indistinct in its grey. You cannot tell what they are thinking.

Perhaps it is merely November, with its mists and threat of ice along the Neva, that sends this chill through me. Yet there is something impersonal and ambivalent even in Leningrad's beauty, which strikes me as eerie. All its spaces are huge. Yesterday, walking where the river bifurcates among built-up islands before pouring into the Gulf of Finland, we even felt this hugeness to be threatening. Joanna's hand slipped automatically into mine. Beyond Suvorov Square and across the Field of Mars we walked almost alone. To our right the barracks of the old Pavlovsky regiment stretched for literally hundreds of yards in a buff façade diversified by countless columns. Yet the houses and palaces seem eyeless. There is no feeling that you are being watched, you are too insignificant. Even the Russians appear not quite to belong here. They trudge the streets with the anonymity of visiting peasants. But, paradoxically, the city could not be anyone's but theirs. They share its vastness, its impersonality, sometimes even its look of not really being inhabited at all – but simply there, like a force of nature.

But of course, as Joanna says, Leningrad is beautiful. Simply its beauty is not the gypsy kind I love (like hers). It is blond and cool. Its gardens are magnificent. Its bridges are balustraded in elaborate wrought iron. Not a single bullying skyscraper overhangs its centre. We wandered down smaller streets over a ruffled slipstream of cobbles, cut by tram-rails. The air held a hard brilliance, healthier than our English damp. It was our first holiday together – three fleeting days – and we clung on to one another for love as well as warmth.

We also had our first argument.

The hotel had already upset her. (She is highly strung, and frightened by what she calls my impulsiveness.) The concierge on our landing had agitated her by what Joanna thought a purposeful scrutiny, and the anonymous men who inhabited the foyer conformed to her jittery cliché of KGB agents (and to mine too). So when, last night, I said, 'You'll come with me, won't you?', I wasn't surprised by her response.

'I can't, I couldn't.' She had been staring out of the window but now turned round with her fingertips touched to her lips, like a scared child. She turned up the volume on her transistor radio, to drown our voices to anyone listening. 'You shouldn't go either.'

I said: 'It's not dangerous. Nobody can do anything to us. There's no law against visiting people here.'

She came close to lower her voice, but looked at me scathingly, as if I were purposely, conveniently, thinking her stupid (and perhaps I was). She said: 'They're dissidents.'

'But I'll know if anyone follows me.' I thought this was true, but wasn't sure.

'They'll be watched themselves,' she said. 'And bugged too. You know damn well they will.'

We sat on the bed with the transistor between us. It played marching songs from an all-male choir. Our voices drowned in it. I knew we were in for an argument, and I felt tense and cold because I didn't know where arguments with Joanna would lead, or what we might end by saying to one another. At least for the moment, it seemed, we were arguing about my safety. But we sounded like children.

'Well I'm not going,' she said.

'Well I am.'

And I knew that I was. For some reason I had to, although I had no idea what religious dissidents might be like. They were simply relatives of Russian *émigré* friends in England. ('We're frightened for them,' they'd said, 'they've stopped answering letters. We haven't heard anything for two years.')

I touched Joanna's shoulder. 'How can we go back to England

and say we were too scared? We promised.'

'We can't help them.'

'How do you know? Just to hear from somebody outside may help them. These people are isolated, Joanna. Can't you imagine how isolated?' I heard my tone growing moral, but couldn't stop it. 'If they're prepared to risk themselves by propagating what they believe, at least we should have the guts to go and see them. Nobody's going to touch *us*.'

She was looking at me with disquieting appraisal. This look was usually touched with a smile; but not now. She said: 'You've never liked evangelism in religion.'

'It's not religion. It's people in trouble.'

'How do you know they're in trouble?' She turned the transistor higher. 'The way you insist on this makes me feel it's you that's in trouble.'

'What do you mean?'

'You know what I mean. You're still your father's child – the son of a priest, trying to maintain that Daddy is right and God exists.' She turned her back. 'Well, count me out. You know what I feel about your father – and God. You'd be better shot of both.'

Our words all came in a monotone under the radio's noise, so I could not tell how loud they would normally have been, how angry we were. It was like arguing underwater. Her turned back seemed to be asking for comfort, but I couldn't give it. 'How the hell can a pair of Russian dissidents affect my ideas about God?'

She turned to confront me. Her expression, under her peppery tumble of hair, was an odd mixture of fear and derision. 'You're just romanticising them. You're using them. Their courage seems to prove the existence of something, that's all. And it's something you want to believe in.' She laid her hand on mine, but accusingly. 'But martyrs don't prove a damn thing. There've been diehards in every religion. They're not heroes. They're just martyred to their own conditioning.'

I said incongruously: 'For God's sake, Joanna, I'm not expecting a revelation.' I stared down at her hand on mine; it looked suddenly fragile. 'Of course I admire these people.'

'Well I don't. Let them keep their convictions to themselves. Nobody stops them worshipping. It's just their spreading of ideas

71

that the authorities don't like, and I can sympathise. Why do they have to ram their certainties down other people's throats? I call that arrogance.'

'And if they kept their certainties to themselves, you'd call it selfish.'

She allowed herself a smile. 'It would be less of a bore.'

I said: 'You're frightened.'

'Yes. I'm frightened for you. You're such a fool sometimes.' She gave my hand the faintest, conciliatory squeeze, then stood up. 'But I know you won't change your mind, so you'd better go now and get it over with.'

I stood up beside her, feeling sheepish. When I kissed her she was trembling. I said: 'I won't be late.'

'Please don't.'

Outside, the snow was falling in a faint dust out of the dark. Only where the street-lamps shone could I see its thin descent across the light, and underfoot the prints of recent passers-by showed black and clear. I lingered melodramatically in a doorway in case anybody had followed me from the hotel, but nobody passed. The streets were almost empty. It was eight o'clock, but it seemed much later. I started to walk.

As I trudged outwards from the city's centre, the concentric arcs of the canals grew longer and quieter. Slowly the houses overhanging them lost their classical refinement and degenerated into flaking stucco terraces and down-at-heel warehouses. The larger streets were lined by nineteenth-century apartment blocks, sombrely handsome but going to seed. Their courtyards were stacked with firewood or rubbish, and their entrances gave onto balustraded stairways twisting into darkness with a gloomy grandeur.

It was in one of these that Anatoly and Ekaterina Zhitkov lived. By the time I reached it the snow was falling softly, heavily, out of a stifled sky. My footsteps made no sound. After entering the block I loitered in a corner of the stairs to see if anyone came. But the place seemed deserted. Its marble steps were cracked and chipped. I listened. For a while I heard nothing in the silence, then only the drip of leaking water somewhere, falling onto polished stone. I climbed to the third floor in semi-darkness. The doors I passed were padded in leather, and set with a makeshift variety of door-mats: discarded vests, old towels.

The Zhitkovs' door looked the same as all the others. A street-lamp shone faintly onto the landing through the stair-window. But for a moment, although nobody was in sight, I hesitated, and peered down into the stairwell. I felt suddenly guilty. After all, what could I bring them? Simply greetings from relatives comfortable in the West. None of us belonged in their world, or ever could. Our sufferings, such as they were, had nothing to do with God or belief or anything truly outside ourselves. Even my appearance – my Western suit and digital watch – seemed an offence. I had no right even to cross their doorstep.

Momentarily, as I pressed the bell, I remembered Joanna's accusation that I was using them. But I don't think this is so. God is not an urgent presence or absence to me now. He merely remains unravelled, in suspension. I think it is only here, in the Soviet Union, ironically, that I have come to feel Him important again. Belief has meaning here, danger.

The door jerked open. 'Da?'

'Anatoly Zhitkov?'

'Da.'

He was small and dark, with sharp, mobile features. It was not a face I had expected. His grey-streaked hair was combed back meticulously from a wide forehead. His cheeks appeared grey too, but his thin body was plumped out with pullovers under a carefully-pressed jacket. He looked difficult, too sensitised.

'I'm English,' I said. 'I've come from the Barinovs...'

For a moment his expression clouded. I thought he might close the door. Then he said: 'Aha, Vasily and Tanya ... aha ... Come in.'

I followed him into a gaunt sitting room. Its walls and ceilings were high and showed traces of moulding, but were void of any other decoration. Thin cracks spread like spiders' webs over half their surface. The floor was carpetless, and the furniture was of utilitarian squatness. A bare light bulb dangling into the room's centre shed a bleakness over everything beneath: a black-varnished desk, three chairs, a few books, two icons propped on a chest of drawers. In one of the chairs Ekaterina was sitting, but levered herself up when I entered.

'He's come from England, Katya,' said Anatoly. 'He has news of Vasily and Tanya.'

Ekaterina was fair and heavy-bodied, with a vague, unfocused expression. All her movements were vague and ponderous too, and she was dressed without her husband's neatness, in shapeless trousers and jacket. She took my hand absent-mindedly, while her eyes wandered over my face like two pale moths. 'Tanya . . . yes . . . how are they?'

'They're well,' I said. 'They've written to you.' I did not know what more to say. Their letters might have been intercepted. And of course we were bugged. I glanced foolishly round the walls, as if the microphones might have left some tell-tale mark.

Anatoly said: 'Yes, they've written.' His English sounded fluent, but his tone was non-committal. He seemed to be saying: 'Of course they've written, but of course we've heard nothing.'

I said: 'They were anxious to know how you were.'

'We've been all right,' Anatoly said. 'But busy . . . you know.'

I didn't really know. Dissidents in the Soviet Union were deprived of employment, but the concept 'dissident' was nebulous. I realised I knew almost nothing about the Zhitkovs, except that they had recruited members to a small, fervent circle of Orthodox believers, and had worked for a Helsinki Human Rights monitoring group that had been forcibly disbanded. They now looked deeply uncomfortable. Anatoly sat on the edge of his chair, crossing and recrossing his thin legs. His words were always accompanied by a flurry of nervous gestures, and he kept knocking his cigarette ash onto the floor with a nicotine-stained finger.

Ekaterina retired inside herself. On the few occasions she spoke she always ended by turning to her husband, as if for judgment. I had the quixotic impression that her face was really a wall, through whose chink the eyes peeped only sometimes; at others they were dead or not there.

'How has your work been then?' I asked. I meant Christian work. I think I needed some hope to take back to the Barinovs, who were devoted believers. That's all. I wasn't seeking to buttress my own faith (if that is what it is) by tasting theirs, whatever Joanna says. I'm sure I wasn't.

'Work.' Anatoly pulled at his cigarette with a slightly bitter expression. 'Better now, better. I'm working as a librarian at the Petrovsky Institute. It's not well paid, but it's adequate.'

His gaze kept shifting between his wife, myself and the ceiling. It was impossible to know what he was thinking. His presence – all our presences – had shrivelled before the microphones, the nameless listener. Sometimes I fancied I could hear this listener breathing, so tangible was he. He turned the place into a courtroom: all private life a courtroom. We spoke to him, not to one another.

I felt my breathing quicken. I was already growing angry with the hidden ear. I looked round for a radio or record-player whose music might drown out our words, but could see neither. I said softly: 'And your other work?' I crossed myself (self-consciously) so that they could be sure what I meant.

'Ah,' Anatoly said, 'Christian work.' He glanced at Ekaterina who went on gazing at the floor. Then he raised his voice, as if addressing the ear: 'I think Lenin was right when he said we should leave all that behind us. The Church here has no future, you know.' The tap of his finger on his cigarette was more like trembling. 'There are only three seminaries left for priests in the whole country, and even those are turning out many men who are barely literate. It's government policy to guide the better-educated seminarists into other paths. Priests are a waste of manpower. The country so much needs manpower.'

The bones of his face seemed to have tightened. I noticed again how grey he appeared. I tried to understand what he was really saying. What news did he want me to take back to the Barinovs and to England? I interpreted: the government is destroying the priesthood by refusing it to any but the illiterate.

Anatoly was not looking at me. Suddenly I realised that I had grown bitterly angry: angry with the invisible ear that had reduced this fine man and woman to playing out a farce of pretence even in their own home, masking their faith with the fatuous formulas of a later religion (because that is what Marxism is to me).

Anatoly said dully: 'Will you have a drink? Or eat?' Then he got up and moved into the kitchen with Ekaterina. I thought: perhaps

75

there are no microphones in the kitchen. But when I tried to follow them, they waved me back: 'You're our guest.'

I sat down in the gaunt room again, momentarily alone. Except for the ear. Joanna says I get angry too easily, and perhaps I do. But when I thought of the System massed behind that listener – the lifeless orthodoxy so narrow and self-sure (or perhaps so unsure) that it had to crush out everything that was not its own – I fell into a bitter, undirected fury.

I strode belligerently up and down the room. At one end hung the black rectangle of a curtainless window, at the other the open door of their bedroom. The bed looked too big: huge and low, so that the blankets lay loose on it. That room too, I imagined, was bugged. So even their lovemaking was violated.

I threw myself back into my chair – the Zhitkovs were still in the kitchen – and suddenly found myself addressing the ear. The fury in my voice was muted, the words coming in a rushed whisper. I said – and it became more and more like a statement of faith: 'I just want you to know that it's not you who are sitting in judgment. No, it's you who are being judged. History will show you as so small-minded that posterity will laugh at you. Whatever these Zhitkovs think (I had to protect them) your shabby little doctrine won't last. Nothing like that lasts. You haven't abolished God at all, you've just tried to replace Him with yourselves. But make no mistake, you can't blot out life for ever. Not for ever. You think you're on the side of order, trying to control anarchy. But you're not. You're just on the side of dullness, trying to suppress the thoughts that are everybody's right. So why don't you just go home?'

I heard a faint shuffling, and for one grotesque moment I thought that an answer was about to emanate from the wall in front of me. But it was only the footsteps of Anatoly and Ekaterina. Before they came in I added something which surprised myself a little. I said to the wall in a measured, distinct voice: 'There *is* a God.'

They returned with a bottle of three-star Armenian brandy, which they poured gingerly into little mugs. Anatoly smiled. 'These are our little luxuries.'

Then they sat in their chairs again, close together. I thought how vulnerable they both looked sitting there, concealing even their courage. Nobody who has not been to this country, I thought, could realise how profoundly isolated the dissidents were, surrounded by the deep, hot patriotism of their people, and branded as traitors. I wanted to applaud the fragile-seeming pair, but the ear forbade it. I even wanted to hug them, but they mightn't have understood.

I said: 'I wish I had brought you something from England.'

'Never mind,' said Anatoly. 'Things are better here now.'

Ekaterina echoed: 'Yes, better now.'

Anatoly said: 'We used not to be able to afford such drink. But my wife's brother found her some work in a summer camp of the Komsomol. That's quite well paid.'

'Komsomol?'

'The Communist Party youth organisation.'

'Oh.'

Ekaterina smiled her sleepy smile. Then for a moment her eyes awoke in their chinks and she murmured: 'You'll tell Vasily and Tanya that we're all right, won't you? We just haven't much time for writing...'

'I'll tell them.'

'Things have changed a lot since the time they left.' She poured out more brandy. 'They'd hardly recognise it here.'

I was feeling uneasy now. My anger had dissipated. Anatoly went on smoking cigarette after cigarette, his gaze flickering back and forth over the floor. I wanted to smoke myself, but he did not offer his packet. His cigarettes seemed a personal part of him, like his clothes or a prescribed medicine.

My voice suddenly sounded thin, anxious. 'Is there anything I can do for you after I get back? Any messages? Or can I send you anything?'

Anatoly smoothed his fingertips over his sleek hair and smiled. 'Well, there may be. What do you think, Katya?'

But she only looked back at him.

'Perhaps you could send us a cassette.' He leaned forward, and I in turn leaned towards him. 'Do you know the music of Victor Silvester? We always liked that.'

I bit my lip. I was afraid my laughter might degenerate into something else. 'You have a cassette-player?'

'Yes, yes.' Ekaterina picked it out of her jacket pocket and laid it proudly on the floor between us. 'It's Estonian. Very good.'

77

I could sense some tension, desperation even, in my own words and gestures as I said: 'Let's turn it on.' I pointed a circling finger at the walls around us, staring first at Anatoly, then at her. At last we had the means to drown out the ear: the simple means familiar to dissidents over years of persecution. At last we could talk. 'Let's play it.'

But as I said this I felt an odd, despairing premonition, as if I had known everything all along. Perhaps it was even a relief to know, like an ache lifting because its cause was located. So when Anatoly looked blank and said, 'The cassette on? Why?', I was not even surprised, but only felt a dark, tired current spreading through my whole body, immobilising it. When I looked at them now, they seemed broken. I, too. I even wondered how I was going to get back to my hotel and Joanna, I felt so weakened.

I mumbled: 'Victor Silvester. Yes. I'm sure I can find you something.'

For the first time, Ekaterina glowed. 'Could you get us "Dancing in the Moonlight"?'

'I expect so, yes.'

We fell into silence. They stared at the floor near one another's feet. She seemed to have lapsed almost into sleep, her arms folded over her stomach, while he still glanced up occasionally, his eyes shifting and black against his white skin. He looked wretched. I stared numbly round the room, at the furniture, the few books whose titles I could not read, the bare bulb, the innocent walls. My gaze halted only at the icons, and remained fixed on them, as on a last hope. They stood on the chest of drawers – a saint I did not recognise, and a dark-skinned *Eleousa*, the Virgin of Tenderness. She was austerely beautiful, her head inclined to the preternaturally adult Child in her arms, her expression one of presaging sadness.

I stood up and touched the icon's rim. 'It's fine.'

Anatoly took it and turned it over in his long, nervous hands. 'I sometimes wonder if it's not a fake,' he said. 'They do these things so cleverly nowadays. Down in the Caucasus they'd fake up your grandmother for ten roubles.' He laughed, and put the icon back. 'But I think it's genuine.' He squinted at it. 'There's a nice economy there. And a subtle use of colour.'

I said weakly: 'I find it moving.'

Anatoly's fists came together at his chest, as if holding himself firm. 'As art, yes. But those things are all gone here now. They aren't a part of us any more.'

'No,' I said. I glanced at Ekaterina, but she was wearing her vague, inchoate look. 'I think I have to be going.'

They did not demur. We shuffled into the passage and she helped me on with my overcoat. Anatoly opened the door. I stepped outside and shook her hand. She said: 'Remember us to the Barinovs, won't you?' For a moment I felt she wanted to say something more. She frowned and hesitated, suddenly awkward in the doorway, holding onto the tips of my fingers as if unwilling, at last, to release me.

'Yes, I'll tell them.'

She dropped my hand, moved slowly behind her husband, and vanished inside.

Anatoly's gaze was fixed somewhere on my chest. 'Yes, we're sorry not to have written.'

'They were worried about you.' I took his hand and gently pulled him onto the landing. I said: 'I wasn't sure if your flat was bugged or not. You must have thought me strange.'

'Bugged?' He looked at me, then his lips tightened and he said abruptly: 'No, we're not bugged. Not any more. That's all over.'

'I see.'

He repeated: 'That's all over.'

I started down the dark stairway. For a while his face remained above me, looking whiter in the filtered light of the street-lamp. Then it disappeared. I pushed out of the apartment block and into the snow. It was falling in huge, unearthly flakes now, obliterating all but the nearest street-lights. I walked back through it, ankle deep. Already it covered the rooftops, and was descending into the canals in a pale holocaust. Along the road a few cars were nosing homeward, their lights dimmed and small, like disembodied eyes. Sound itself seemed to have been banished from the earth, along with the secret ears that listened to it. I shivered and covered my mouth with my scarf. No, nobody was listening. Nobody else had been present in the room at all. There had merely been the three of us: my uncertainty, and their brokenness. That was all. Even my statement of faith had been delivered to a blank wall.

I looked up at the suffocated sky, and hoped I could find my way back.

IONIAN WHITE AND GOLD

by

Anne Spillard

*Born in Leeds and now living in Cumbria, Anne Spillard
began writing four years ago. She has had short stories
published in* Loving Couples, New Stories 7 *and several
magazines. She has broadcast for BBC radio, and at present
she is writing a novel.*

Limpid. Limpid. Sylvia kept saying this to herself, where she sat under the twisted shade of an olive tree that gave little shelter from the hot blue afternoon. Sometimes she looked into the green sea, thinking limpid. Sometimes she picked tar from between her toes with a white pebble. The beach was spattered with dollops of black oil. Yet the sea was limpid, clear down to its steep-sided bed, where the white pebbles became turquoise, though the dollops remained black.

Humph came up for the third time. He ran his hands through his hair, adjusting his mask, and looked around, orienting himself, as though he had just been born, thought Sylvia.

He saw her. 'Hi!' he called.

'Hi,' said Sylvia.

'Come here,' demanded Humph, without much hope.

'Too oily.' Sylvia began picking at her heel.

A few yards from Humph a long iridescent fish hovered, not looking at him; apparently not aware of his presence. The fish seemed to be looking at her. From the shore even its eyes looked as green as limes, and it caught Sylvia's attention.

'What's that?' she nodded in its direction, and Humph disappeared sneakily back into the womb, with hardly a ripple.

Into the limpid womb he went. She saw him as though she was looking into a telescope. He flipped his feet gently, moving towards the fish, which hovered, as if waiting for his attentions.

'Be careful! It may sting,' she called.

Her voice ran over the surface of the water, which was so still that she was able to watch Humph as a god might watch creatures in an alien world.

Humph looked so much bigger than the green fish. Yet, as she watched him moving towards it, Sylvia shivered. He couldn't hear her; couldn't see her either. In the limpid water she was as far away as the moon.

The sound of goat-bells came faintly from the plateau high above her, while Humph's black shadow swayed among pearly goldfish.

'Come on!' he called, breaking out of the water like a sea-cow.

Above her too was the bleak black Crag of the Ravens, where the birds called and swooped on random air currents.

But no people. Only Humph, waiting, half-smiling at her.

She stood up, undressing quickly in the impetuous way that people use when they make up their minds suddenly and want to act before they change them.

Naked, she picked her way over the pebbles and the oil patches. Humph trod water, watching her.

Above them, the bells came nearer, the silhouette of the first goat ambling over the skyline, where Odysseus came when he landed secretly to evade Penelope's suitors.

For moments the ravens swooped and hovered in silence, as Slyvia walked slowly down into the shelving Ionian Sea.

Behind her, on the shoreline, there were sudden uneasy ripples, as if the water had been pushed unwillingly from underneath, then settled back to its calm. But the small waves had made her pause, and, rather than lose her balance, she leaned forward, her feet left the pebbles, and she was afloat.

'Good girl,' said Humph, as though she had done something clever.

Sylvia, conscious of the silence round the deep basin of the bay, had tried not to disturb it. But Humph had no such inhibitions. He flapped and splashed towards her, head half-submerged, holding his hands out. He touched her. He began to run his hands over her.

They were totally visible from Arethusa's Spring, near which the goatherd crouched, watching them. He saw every detail of her white back and whiter buttocks. Her legs trailed behind her, kicking desultorily, two blue-shadowed white ribbons. And round her shoulders her hair floated in a gold cloud, so long that it modestly allowed no more than glimpses of Humph's caressing fingers as they slid over her.

When she turned to swim back to the beach, the goatherd was standing under the olive tree, leaning against its trunk. His jeans were bleached and stained. But the kerchief round his neck was clean and very white and – without consciously being aware of this –

it reassured Sylvia, whose first thought was for the passport and travellers' cheques that she had left in her handbag tucked in the roots of the tree, near to her discarded clothes, that lay, obscene almost, she thought now, by his feet. Panties, wide cotton skirt, faded turquoise vest, thrown in what had seemed an innocent carelessness, but now seemed immodest in someone else's country.

About to lift herself out of the water, she relaxed her elbows, pushing herself back into deeper (such limpid) water. From the olive tree, the goatherd watched, never taking his eyes from her. A pair of binoculars hung round his neck.

Humph had slipped back under the water, and Sylvia turned, swimming towards him with her most splashy crawl to conceal her nakedness. Humph, seeing that she was coming back, swum underneath her. His hands cupped her breasts, which hung down like two white amphorae into the water.

She wrenched free. 'Stop! Stop!' and he began to chase her, at his ease at last. It was a game.

When he saw the goatherd, he was half-angry, half-amused. 'So what?' he said. But the goatherd had encroached on his territory – was now standing on the hem of Sylvia's wide green skirt, so it was not so easy to laugh it off.

'What shall I do?' Sylvia was frightened now. The goatherd was big and bronzed, with black curly hair and fierce yellow eyes. His arms were folded across his chest, and the binoculars, resting on their strap against his forearms, moved slightly up and down as he breathed. There was no expression on his face.

Humph got out of the water, not removing his mask or flippers, a prehistoric toad, picking his clumsy path over the stones. '*Arrivederci*,' he said, and in the sea Sylvia, hearing, shuddered at his crassness. Yet to Humph, the fact that he had used a foreign language at all, irrespective of it being the wrong language and the wrong word, was a measure of his meeting the goatherd more than half-way.

The goatherd made no reply as Humph picked up the clothes, pulling the skirt with a jerk from under his foot.

'Excuse me,' said Humph sarcastically.

He took the clothes back to the sea and stood a few paces in the water, holding them out to Sylvia, who, as soon as she could get her

85

balance, stood in deep water, putting them on over her head. The green skirt billowed over her, then settled like a deflated parachute on the sea. Awkwardly, holding Humph's hand for balance in the now-wet clothes, she began to walk ashore, the clinging skirt making her progress difficult and teetering.

As she came nearer the tree, Humph, now angry, stepped up to the goatherd. 'Go away!' he shouted.

For a moment it seemed as though the goatherd was going to ignore him. Then, shrugging his shoulders, he moved away towards the sea. He didn't look back, walking straight into the water till he plunged forward and began to swim in strong crawl away from the shore. Presently he rounded the jutting rocks that defined the end of the bay, and disappeared from sight. As if to clinch his disappearance, the water repeated its earlier convulsion, bursting about a metre further up the beach than usual.

Hung from a branch of the tree, the binoculars swayed on their strap, a pair of sightless black eyes.

'Fancy leaving those,' said Humph. He unhooked them, and inspected them carefully. A piece of zinc oxide tape had been stuck round the strap.

'Dr M. Bracken,' he read out. He looked out to the empty sea. 'That didn't look like Dr M. Bracken.'

'Of course it wasn't. He found them somewhere.' Sylvia found herself suprised that she didn't suspect the goatherd of stealing them.

'That's right.' Humph hung them back on the tree. 'That explains why he wasn't bothered about leaving them behind. Easy come, easy go.'

They turned to leave.

'He lives in Bristol,' said Sylvia. 'Moved there from Oxford.'

'Who?'

They had turned their backs to the sea now. The blank eyes swung to and fro gently, looking towards the sea.

'Dr Bracken. He's in aeronautics. Accepted a post with less prestige because his wife likes sailing, and they wanted to be near the sea.'

'You know him?' asked Humph, surprised.

But Sylvia skipped ahead of him up the path, her skirt pulling sharply on the dry thorns and twigs of the brush-wood.

'Of course I don't, silly. Never heard of him in my life. Anyway it couldn't be right, could it?'

Humph was never quite sure how to take Sylvia, and was put out by falling for her story.

'Why couldn't it?' he defended himself.

'Because,' said Sylvia, 'Dr M. Bracken is a woman.'

She laughed and ran ahead nimbly as he lunged for her, half-amused, half-exasperated.

'Dr Marghanita Bracken,' she called. 'You must have heard of her.'

So, laughing, half-affectionate, they climbed the path and came to Arethusa's Spring, which was marked by a yellow sign that had fallen on its side. They scrambled up the crumbling scree and peered under the low branches of ilex and elder. A cleft hollowed back into the rock, its lips stained with the mud-coloured lichen that grows in shadow. After the glare outside, the cleft looked bottomless, as though it might split down into the centre of the earth. Then, at the base of the chasm, they saw stones looking bare and dry.

'There's no water,' said Humph. 'Must be a drought.'

They peered down, thwarted.

'Arethusa,' said Humph, who had waited for this moment, 'was a beautiful wood-nymph. Alpheus fell in love with her, and she ran away to an island to get away from him. Artemis turned her into a spring, to disguise her. But Alpheus found out where she was, and he turned himself into a river and flowed over from Peloponnesus across the Ionian Sea to the island, and found her.'

'That's not fair,' said Sylvia. 'It's not fair to turn her into a miserable spring that hasn't even got any water in it just because she didn't fancy him. And it didn't work anyway, because he found her.'

A small pebble rattled down from the rocks above the mouth of the chasm. Straightaway the stones at the bottom began to shake and twist.

'It's full of water!' They leant over, amazed at its depths and utter clarity. For a moment they looked in silence. The ruffles on the water settled, and the spring was still again.

'Limpid,' said Sylvia.

But Humph was looking at the stone facing above the spring. He was wondering where the pebble had come from, how it had been dislodged, and whether any more were likely to fall on them as they knelt above the water.

Hanging on a piece of string from a branch of the ilex tree was the bottom half of a plastic bottle.

'It's to drink from.' Sylvia unwound the string and they weighted the cup with a small stone and let it down into the water. The cup tipped on its side, and with difficulty they managed to persuade a trickle of water to just cover the bottom of it. They drew it up carefully, and when it reached the top of the well, they grasped it with almost reverential pleasure.

'What shall we do with it?' asked Humph. 'We can't drink it. Not from that cup.'

'Anoint me with it,' Sylvia demanded. She leant her head back, closing her eyes, waiting.

Humph wasn't sure what she wanted him to do. He dipped one finger in the cup, then drew it across her forehead.

Sylvia shivered. The sun fell on her hair, almost white against the dark green leaves. Her skirt fell round her in a circle of soft green cloth, and her white shoulders and throat and –

'Ohh!' She leapt up, shaking her hair in disgust. 'Pig!'

For Humph the moment had been too magical. Embarrassing, melodramatic. He had tipped the rest of the water over Sylvia's head.

When he had made his peace with her, she said, 'Now it's your turn,' and she knelt over the spring again, letting the bottle down into the water.

As she did so, a shower of gravel and small stones began to bounce down the rocks towrds the spring. Humph pulled her backwards, and they rolled under the ilex tree. The stones bounced on past them, down to the grassy platform below.

'Come on.' Humph had had enough excitement for one day. Seizing her hand he half-pulled her away from the spring.

But before she went, Sylvia turned and carefully wound the cup's string back onto the tree.

'There was someone up there,' said Humph. 'Someone was watching us all the time.

They both thought of the goatherd.

'Well,' said Sylvia, 'at least we know he didn't have his binoculars.'

They climbed the path to Eumaeus' Cave.

'Myrtle, arbutus and oleander,' Sylvia intoned, and the fragrant shrubs caught at their legs and tangled in their hair. They stood at the narrow entrance to the cave, surprised at the green light which shone from its depths.

'Eumaeus was a creep,' said Sylvia. 'Odysseus did his own thing, adventured around, lived it up with goddesses and all that. Then he came home and went on this macho trip of expecting everyone to give him a hero's welcome, wiping out poor old Penelope's suitors, and generally creating havoc. Her heart must have sunk to her knees when she heard he'd come back.'

But Humph had heard it all before, and wasn't listening. He had entered the cave, and now stood inside, looking upwards.

'Hey!' he laughed. 'That's why it looks bright. There's no roof.'

They stood together on the sheep-pelleted floor of the pit that had once been a cave. Above, myrtle, arbutus and oleander trailed branches over the fallen-in edges. And above everything, the sky showed, still clear and blue.

From the town came the deep cry of a ship's siren that meant the ferry had returned from Patras.

'Seven o'clock!' They began to go down the path, surprised at the lateness of the hour and the brightness of the evening.

They ate supper on the verandah, while Aliki watered her geraniums that lined the steps to the house in feta cans. Then she dragged the hose past them, apologising with a gesture half-surly, half-defiant. She flung its end into the tank above the shower-room and walked back past them into her own tiny living-quarters.

'Demetri's been drinking,' said Sylvia. Aliki's husband usually filled the tanks, and the huge terracotta ali-baba urns that were the guests' water-supply and stood in the shade at the back of the house, where the tree-covered hill rose steeply to the next level of the road.

Sitting under the vine, they looked down at the lights of Vathay, the horseshoe harbour. The ferry towered above the quayside houses, resting in monstrous blue benevolence for the night.

Or so they thought, till, unexpectedly, its siren boomed again. Sylvia stood up, agitated. The ferry began to nose round.

89

'It's going! What'll we do?' They had planned to go back to the mainland the next morning.

Now the ferry began to leave the harbour, swinging round the lepers' island where the small chapel gleamed pink in afterglow.

But the German students at the next table reassured them.

'It goes to Corfu this evening. It'll be back very late tonight, ready to go to Patras tomorrow morning.'

So that was all right. But in the harbour was an unfamiliar empty space, where the water swilled blackly. As the *Ionnis* left, the island seemed too isolated, too independent, and for a moment Sylvia felt afraid, watching its lights as it disappeared round the point.

Water began to pour over the top of the tank, running along the verandah, so that they had to move their feet.

Aliki came back, looking straight at them, in silence reproaching them for not turning off the water, for just sitting there.

'Let's go for a last stroll around,' said Humph, and Sylvia said cautiously, because she had had enough walking for one day, all right, but only the town, not miles from anywhere, which he promised.

Nevertheless, she slipped her torch into her handbag before they set off.

Coming to the lower end of the town, they saw in the darkness the outlines of the ruined walls of cottages looming along tall weeds and bedraggled vines. They stopped to look, imagining the night, thirty years ago, when the whole island had shuddered violently, and most of Vathay had been destroyed in the earthquake. Difficult to believe that this neat-painted town had been rebuilt from ruins like these.

Where had the owners of these cottages gone? Had they been killed in the earthquake?

'No,' said Sylvia. 'In areas where earthquakes occur, people simply leave when there is a disaster like this. They lose heart. The site can stay derelict for hundreds of years. Sometimes for good, like at Olympia.'

They came to the iron gates of the cemetery. Sylvia tried them, and even though it was now dark, they opened at her touch. They went in.

The torch flickered over plastic flowers and paper satin bows and wreaths. Round the walls, they peered at photographs and talismans. The messages they were unable to decipher, though they transliterated a few names.

'There's an English one here,' said Humph, and Sylvia brought the torch nearer. And nearer.

'In loving Memory of Dr Michael Bracken, born 1930, died 1982. Drowned at Sea in the Pursuit of Knowledge.'

In their minds the binoculars swung on the olive tree, and the frayed, faded name leapt vividly as a sharp colour in front of them.

'Dr Marghanita Bracken,' said Sylvia, but she did not laugh, and each looked into the face of the other for some sort of comfort in the dusk-filled cemetery.

The figure of the goatherd seemed to loom around them among the masonry, the dead flowers, and the tawdry decorations.

They both turned as a black shadow moved, lifting itself from a stone seat, and footsteps crunched on the chippings.

'Hello,' said a woman's voice. 'You're English, aren't you?'

She had been sitting very still, very close to them.

'That's Michael Bracken,' she said, nodding her head to where they had been looking.

Sylvia said, 'We were wondering who he was, why he's buried here.'

'He was doing rather controversial stuff,' said the woman. 'Carrying on where Wilhelm Dorpfeld left off. There was a squall, and his yacht sank.' Her tone was terse, not encouraging. She jingled the keys in her hand.

'I'm afraid I've got to lock up now. I've borrowed the keys and I promised to get them back to the janitor tonight. I don't want to disturb him too late.'

Lying in one corner of Dr Bracken's niche was a fresh bunch of wild cyclamen.

They picked their way back across the cemetery. The woman followed them, sure-footed though she had no light.

At the gate she said goodnight. Her manner was brusque yet polite. She made it clear she did not wish to talk to them any more, and when she had locked the gates she turned in the opposite direction and began to walk uphill. Presently she disappeared in shadows, and they stood listening till her footsteps faded.

'Wilhelm Dorpfeld,' said Sylvia. 'Wasn't he the one who tried to

91

prove that Odysseus came from Lefkas?'

'That's right. It wouldn't go down very well in Ithaki, I shouldn't think. The Odyssey's part of their life here. They're steeped in it.'

They had both noticed the crisp freshness of the little bunch of wild cyclamen.

'She put them there,' said Sylvia. 'She'd come to see his grave.'

'Perhaps she was his wife,' said Humph.

The woman had been thirty-ish, with strong handsome features and thick black hair.

'Perhaps she was his mistress,' said Sylvia.

They walked back to Aliki's, Sylvia unnerved by the coincidence of their experience, and Humph assuring her that it was not *so* unlikely.

'He was English, so of course his name would stand out in a cemetery of Greek names,' he reasoned. But he had had the same eery sensation as Sylvia when he first saw the name engraved on the plaque.

They packed most of their belongings ready to leave in the morning, and sat on the bed drinking the remains of the *ouzo* from paper cups.

They washed outside, in the narrow yard between the house and the hillside, scooping water from the cool deep jar to fill the plastic washbowl. On the road far above them, light filtered down through the trees from the street-lamps.

In bed, they lay with the shutters pinned back, looking down at the harbour lights, and the black outline of the hills beyond.

They slept.

Into her sleep thudded the distant sound of engines. Sylvia turned, half-waking. The vibration came nearer, her body seemed to be pulsing with it.

Awake now, she saw that the moon was up, throwing the pattern of the lace curtains across the crucifix on the opposite wall. Other, brighter, lights moved across the room, and the seemed to hear a single footstep on the verandah outside.

Sitting up, she looked out of the window. The *Ionnis* was manoeuvring into her place along the harbourside. Her ramp was down and people moved silently on her decks.

Sylvia sighed with satisfaction.

Something moved near the window. Moving gently to the sill, so as not to disturb Humph, she peered round the curtain. No one was there. Moonlight threw cold green light onto the verandah. There was the table, with its floral cloth, and the empty chairs. Young green grapes hung from the vine. Towels and swimming-gear hung from the balustrade.

Treading softly on the cold linoleum, Sylvia left the room, and crossed the kitchen, opening the door that gave onto the backyard and the toilet.

For a few instants she stood looking up into the shadows of the trees. There was sudden silence as the *Ionnis* switched off her generators. Shafts of moonlight fell on the stone flags of the yard.

And onto Sylvia herself, where she stood, hair falling across her face, her white cambric nightshift outlining her body above slender legs. She moved, and the shadows of trees fell gracefully across her. A wood nymph, she moved to the ali-baba jar, lifting the tin lid, and putting her hand into the cool dark fluid.

Shimmering in the water was the still green fish, looking at her with pinpoints of green fire.

Sylvia gasped, pulling her hand back so violently that the lid of the jar crashed down onto the stones.

Someone moved high above her in the wood. She heard the stealthy footsteps, the sharp crack of a twig, the rustling of branches. Someone up there was watching her.

She opened her mouth to call, 'Humph! Humph,' and even as she did so, she knew that he would be useless; that it wasn't Humph she needed, but someone who would understand what she could not even conceive of.

Someone was coming down towards her, and she couldn't call out, couldn't move. Green fire flickered round the inside of the ali-baba jar. The ground seemed to sway under her feet. She was standing still, yet she felt herself to be falling, to be falling...

Above her, the trees rippled, then lifted. Earth and stones fell over the retaining wall, at first in a trickle, then heavily, bouncing against the house wall. The hill was moving towards her, myrtle, arbutus and oleander, it rose in a great wave, above which there was the crash of street lights, and a deep rumble as if a train was passing over her head.

Then the hill split. There was a wave of earth, and on it, balanced as if he was riding the surf, the goatherd was scudding down towards her, his hands outstretched.

With a crash a rock splintered the ali-baba jar; water spilled round her feet. Earth began to engulf her, pinning her against the wall of the house.

A wild shout burst open with the door to the house. Aliki stood there, seeing everything: the landslide, the jar, Sylvia.

But Aliki saw something else too. She stood in front of Sylvia and shouted up the bank, and her voice raised above the terrible noise, was raucous and hostile.

It wasn't a dream. In the moonlight Sylvia opened her eyes to find herself lying in wet mud. They had pulled her clear, and Humph was wrapping a blanket round her. There were uniformed policemen; there were firemen, arc lights. There were officers who had rushed up from the *Ionnis*, their white uniforms stained with red mud as they scrabbled with their hands, moving the stones and earth to free her.

They carried her down to the ferry. But before she went, Aliki bent over her, as if to wash her face.

Neither could speak the other's language.

'Aliki, Aliki,' Sylvia moaned. For only Aliki had seen. Aliki knew everything.

But Aliki bent over her, and her face was still and severe. Putting her finger surreptitiously on Sylvia's lips, she murmured, 'Oxi.' No.

Humph came with her, and the luggage. He was shaking, shocked by the nearness of disaster.

'A tremor,' he said. 'We were all lucky. It's just blocked their yard. It could have engulfed the house, and all of us. As it is, no one's hurt. Except you, poor old love.'

'The fish. The goatherd.' Sylvia tried to tell him.

'Shock,' said Humph. 'You've had a terrible shock. Just try not to think about it.'

He came with her to the women's showers; they moved freely

94

round the ship, empty till the passengers boarded later. She sat weakly in the footbath, unable to stand, and the water cascaded over her, running the earth away, leaving her cleaner, yet not feeling any cleaner, no fresher. Still she seemed to feel the earth pressing round her.

She moved her feet suddenly, impatient with the wetness. He dried her tenderly, and she dressed.

'I want to go on deck,' she said.

They went out into the cool air, where rosy dawn glowed above the black skyline.

At Aliki's house on the hillside, she could see activity. Behind the house was the fresh red scar of the landslide.

'Why are the fire-engines there? Is someone trapped?' She saw the moonlit goatherd, balancing, floating almost, as he had come with the hill, towards her.

Humph put his arm round her. 'No one's trapped. There's nothing to worry about. There's a stream there, that's all.'

'A stream? You mean water?'

Humph hugged her, laughing. 'Yes, water. They even found a fish in it. Why are you looking so horrified? It'll be all right, you know. Apparently it's a spring that used to come out further down, but now the land's shifted, it's begun to run into Aliki's house. They're diverting it. No problem. Of course they'll have to do a bigger job on it later.'

Sounds of engines and pumping and voices came to them from Aliki's house. They saw Demetri come round to the vegetable plot below the verandah. He lifted his hand and shouted something.

Moments later they saw water flowing through the gate, then down the steps. Aliki ran from the kitchen. A row of red blotches, her geraniums, grew jerkily along the stone coping, as she lifted the *feta* tins to safety, while water swilled round her flip-flops.

'It's coming here.' Sylvia, as if hypnotised, was watching the water make its way down the steps into the street below.

'It'll flow down into the harbour, of course.' Her concern surprised him, and he decided she was still in shock.

The water reached the street, and seemed to hesitate, spreading uncertainly in both directions along the gutter. Then it rose to the level of the kerbstones and started to cross the street that ran along

95

by the side of the docked ferry. A small crowd of people hung around, watching its progress.

Sylvia began to cry. 'Keep it away,' she sobbed, 'keep it away,' and Humph, at a loss, comforted her.

'It *is* away. It's just running down into the sea. That's what water does, you know. Finds its own level.' He tried to distract her. 'Come and have some coffee.'

But she shrugged him off.

The water had risen to the level of the dockside, and the first fingers of liquid felt along the bottom of the railings, then slipped down the wall into the green water alongside the ferry. Presently it was curving over in a steady waterfall.

Almost on time, the ferry drew away from the quay.

'Did you pay?' Sylvia suddenly thought of Aliki.

'No,' said Humph. 'But we'll see she gets it. I'll give it to the purser, he lives in Vathay. Don't *worry*. Everything's all right now.'

They had left Vathay behind. Ahead of them the hills of Cephalonia drew nearer. They were passing the south-east side of Ithaki.

'There you are. There's the Crag of the Ravens.' Humph tried to get her interest. 'There's the Spring of Arethusa.'

Their eyes travelled down to the shore, where the olive tree was a small dark mark against the white beach.

'What's that?' Sylvia was pointing halfway up the path from the bay. The sun had risen, lighting the scrub, and the ribbed greys and blacks of the crag.

Something glinted on the hillside.

'I don't know what that is,' said Humph.

But an Australian, leaning on the rail near to them, turned and smiled helpfully.

'That's the sun shining on field-glasses.'

And seeing their blank faces, he grinned. 'That's how it is,' he said. 'We're watching them, and they're watching us.'

I NEVER EAT CRABMEAT NOW

by

Lisa St Aubin de Terán

Looking back, I don't know what is worse to live with; I suppose I just try and forget what I can. There are some things that never go away though, like the smell worming its way back into everything and clinging to the inside of my brain; and then the Daily still missing Fred and asking after him. Then pushchairs, and fish shops just make me feel sick. Last week I saw a budgerigar in a cage picking at a cuttle-fish bone, and that triggered everything off again; now I can't sleep for thinking about Amadeo. What was it? I feel I'll never really sleep well again until I know, but I realise that I might not sleep at all if I really knew the truth.

Why did you go to Diélette, a place you'd never even heard of before, a place nobody seems to have heard of? What was the allure of that desolate stretch of Normandy with nothing but sand and stone and discontent wedged into its disproportionate harbour? 'Why go anywhere?' you had said, and shrugged, and I knew that your restlessness was impenetrable then, at least by me. I contemplated trying to hold you back, detain you by some devious means, but I believed your indifference to be incurable. Wherever you went you would look out to sea, scanning the horizon for someone or something you missed. You lived in a state of orchestrated lack; when there was no sea you would invent it. It was just another layer of your dream, like me, to be peeled away and discarded at will; and then drawn back in from time to time to wrap around you. You were locked in fantasy, turning the weeds of our back garden into waves. Our house was like a mad-house again. You read my thoughts and said: 'The only incurable thing about me is my need for movement.'

I wasn't impressed, since you refused to take me, or rather let me go in any capacity. I tried to understand this need of yours for solitude, but when I saw that you intended to travel with your customary circus, I was so annoyed that I didn't even haggle over the terms of my defeat.

You moved with a troupe of girls ranging from late adolescence through the various stages of precocious delinquency and charm, compromising only with the androgenous Amadeo in his pram with his angelic curls and frills. It struck a genuine chord of consolation, the only one, to be released from Amadeo's distressing eating habits for a month. Apart from that, he was the only one who ever really accepted me. He managed with his smile to make me an honorary girl like him. Unlike the others – our twins, eight years old and congenitally impossible. I used to worry that they might be autistic, but they were just savages. Then there was their nanny, the luscious but otherwise singularly useless Candy, and her 'little sister,' Rachel. I don't know what possessed you to take Rachel. Ever since she had installed herself, uninvited, in the spare bedroom the year before she had done nothing but vent her nymphomania on the neighbourhood and breed resentment.

You took them all with you, though, that potentially lethal human zoo, as though in your inner lonliness you found security in clutter. You even drugged the cat and put it in the picnic basket, and smuggled Fred the tortoise across the Channel in a hollow compartment of the pram. And Fred was my tortoise, too – but then Amadeo was my son.

I went as far as Waterloo and saw you off. The station was insufferable, inundated with people and luggage, and most of the luggage seemed to be yours. You billeted your party around the cafeteria and then sat down to your toast. It was dry and hard and you became obsessed by it. Whatever I said, you came back to that toast. 'I actually can't chew it. What is it made of? What is one supposed to do with it?' Amadeo, temporarily released, had spread raspberry jam on his, and was intent on wiping it off across the table tops and people's knees. You were too involved, however, in the nature of the bread to notice, and the girls paid no attention. Only the new-spread fellow-breakfasters retreated one by one, protesting and ignored by you.

Nobody could staunch your urge to travel, but in the more practical aspects of your life, even you had to give way occasionally. Getting your three-foot-six-inch pram through the three-foot door of the train to Portsmouth was one such example. Amadeo got a foretaste of the seasickness to come, rammed and battered against

100

the ungiving hinges of the door, while you charged at the inadequate space time and again. I don't know if it was fascination or despair that stopped me from intervening. If the guard hadn't come and taken you through the double doors of his wagon, I suppose I would have done something, if only for poor Fred.

After you'd left, I began to hate Diélette. It just seemed wrong from the start: it wasn't on the maps, people didn't go there. You said you were going for just that, to hide away in a fishing village in a land of warm bread. How do you hide with four extravagant females in your wake, and an overgrown baby? And that stale station toast only came up during your departure; we always ate fresh bread from the *pâtisserie* at South End Green. It wasn't what I felt that seemed to matter then or now, so much as what happened to you and the others.

I've pieced together what I can, from you, from the twins and from my own trip out after your phone call. So I know that you sailed to Cherbourg and arrived somehow and disembarked out of the bowels of an impersonal ferry and then ferried your troupe by taxi to the Hôtel de France there. You stayed for one night only, anxious to move on to Diélette, that unknown place of your perverse dream. Amadeo always had to sleep alone: the slightest instrusion would wake him, and once his usual almost narcoleptic sleep had been disturbed, he would cry and moan all night. In the absence of a cot, Rachel made him a mattress of pillows inside a capacious wardrobe, and then locked him in. When the maid unlocked the door on an apparently empty room and was met by a piercing cry from the coffin-like wardrobe in question, she dropped her breakfast tray and ran.

'What kind of mother would do such a thing?' the taxi driver who was taking me to Diélette asked after he had regaled me with the details of this apparently iniquitous neglect. I didn't attempt to explain that Amadeo liked contained spaces and the dark. The driver remembered you clearly and needed no prompting to unravel a list of further aberrations. He referred to you as 'the Lady with the strange eyes', and he told me, in his clear coastal French, how he had enjoyed sitting beside you for the half-hour of the ride. He explained that he had been feeling nervous the day he drove you, and the thought of going to Diélette had filled him with dread, but that your presence had somehow calmed him down. I remember I warmed to the man for understanding these things. He seemed nervous, though, again with me.

'The baby carriage scratched all the paint off my car,' he said. 'I didn't want to charge her for it, but... even if she'd been the blessed Virgin herself... a man has to live.'

He shrugged, and we drove on in silence for some minutes, well away now from the prim shuttered rows of houses and the outlying estates of modern flats. That was when I started to feel sick. On either side of the road, mixed hedges straggled into small, well tended fields interrupted by the occasional *hameau* of grey stone houses. It was unnaturally hot, and every time I paused to think about it, it seemed to be getting hotter.

As we passed through Virandeville the taxi swerved to avoid a group of conscripts who looked as though their feet had melted into the tarmac. The driver whistled angrily through his teeth. 'Some people like trouble.'

I nodded.

'They look for it,' he said.

Again, I agreed politely.

'That lady of yours, she is like that,' he smiled with a mixture of horror and admiration.

We drove on, faster now, as though to prove that he too could be reckless when he chose.

'And why go to Diélette?'

I found myself repeating your own words. 'Why go anywhere?'

'Yes, yes... but Diélette, ever since they put the nuclear plant there five years ago, it is not the same place, not what it seems; there's something bad there now, you can feel it in the air. It isn't safe, especially not for her – not for those girls either.'

He paused, and I sat back uneasily.

'They're riff-raff, not even French,' he said, jerking left to bypass Les Pieux, 'they're Arabs.' He paused again.

'If it weren't for the crabs, God knows what there would be found floating in the sea.'

102

'Crabs?' I repeated, holding back a wave of nausea as the taxi charged yet another hill in third gear.

'That's what they used to fish for.'

'Used to?'

'There's hardly anyone left now, of the old lot, and those that are are fishing for trouble.'

The driver was impressed into momentary silence, then the spectre of the sea came into view from over a hill, and he shuddered, and his voice seemed to break loose again, insinuating its way into my innermost thoughts like the frothing rope of spume dragging at the sand.

Outside Cherbourg, when we passed our first ribbon of grey stone cottages – the *boulangerie*, bar and that straggling row of identical dwellings – it struck me that they were spaced almost as though they were afraid to huddle together, like defeated soldiers limping backwards to some familiar ground. At first that air of semi-regimented despair had seemed quaint, but as we passed one hamlet after another, all as grey and as unforgiving as the last, I grew tired of them. Until that half-hour ride to Diélette, I didn't know I could grow tired of a colour so quickly, and yet the greyness showed me: the walls were grey, and the road, and the sides of rocks that occasionally overhung the road, and the gulls and houses, and the sky, for all its heat, still shimmered grey, and even the skin of the peasants peering out from behind grubby curtains was grey. Only the greens, the oaks and sycamores and the turning green of the ripening corn contrasted with the dour twilight shades. By Les Pieux, though, the drone of my driver's voice had so effectively blended with the forced roar of his engine and my own fears as to make me believe that the green itself was a tremendous growth of mould.

When the sea came into view I felt a kind of dizziness grip the back of my head. It was hard to breathe in the heat. The tide was low and I felt, looking at the sweep of dunes and rock that joined the sea to dry land that it was pulling and grasping at all it could, at me on the hill, at the taxi, at the haze of sand, sucking it out into its

103

mysterious depths and giving nothing back. The driver matched my mood with one of sombre reserve: where before he had talked out of a wish to communicate, he spoke now out of a reluctant need to annihilate silence. This time round, though, I refused to listen. I had the sea to torment me now, so I blocked out his ramblings about the evils of the nuclear plant and the alleged bandits that ran it. Instead, I dreamt that I had buried my head somewhere in those coves of bleached sand, and the sea was dragging out my entrails.

It was only meant to be four more miles to Diélette, and the taxi was doing a steady fifty, and yet that last lap from the crest of the hill to you was the slowest. I could drown the monologue beside me, but I could not ignore the heat or the strange atmosphere. It was like stepping off an aeroplane into the tropics. My ankles were beginning to swell, and they got worse as we crawled towards our destination. The air conditioning appeared to have broken down. I opened the window on my side, but the driver shook his sweating face sadly.

'That'll only make it worse.'

By the time we entered the village itself, I realised that your description of the house was a useless guide to finding it. I was there because of your strange call; you had spent most of the time saying my name, and then repeating over and over again, 'Are you there?' The line was crackling, and somewhere, an irate operator was cutting in. I heard you say, 'Come', and something about Amadeo and his pram; and then you had said, as an afterthought, I suppose, 'The house is grey.'

The taxi driver tried to leave me at the crossroads, but I refused to get out there. I knew he must know where to go to find you in that exposed warren. We climbed the hill to Flamanville and away from the stark sign pointing to the nuclear plant and the beach. For once, he was driving slowly. The last lap of the route had smelt like a fishing village with its sour barnacled odour of stale shellfish and damp nets. I had noticed little piles of dead crabs and their remains outside one or two of the houses. We stalled outside a row of three tall cottages standing on their own. The driver seemed unwilling

104

either to stop or get out of the car. He pointed to the middle door and asked for two hundred francs. I opened my door and remained half-in and half-out. I paid him and straightened my crumpled clothes.

'*Quel molosse!*' he whispered, letting the banknotes fall to the taxi floor, then he drove off up the hill with the car door swinging free. I looked in the direction of his last horrified stare, and saw an enormous slavering hound straining at a rusty chain in the next doorway. I flattened myself instinctively against the wall and watched while an elderly man, wearing the traditional *bleu*, stumbled out after the dog. It appeared to be a hybrid race somewhere between an alsatian and a bear, a brown shaggy matted beast with huge teeth and yellow eyes. The man dragged it back in with great difficulty, and I nodded to him, but he was so drunk I couldn't tell whether he could see me or not. He gave the impression of not having managed to focus on anyone for years.

There were flies everywhere. Outside your door there was a heap of long-dead crabs looking more deliberately gathered or discarded than elsewhere. As I knocked on the door, a wizened face appeared at the window of your other neighbour. This time, when I nodded, I was met by a glacial stare before the ancient face disappeared, letting the cobbled net curtain slip back into place. Although most of your windows were broken, your door was locked; and the house seemed deserted. I thanked God that I wasn't travelling with the kind of luggage you always trailed behind you, picked up my holdall and made my way back down to the village and the beach – where else would you be at lunch time in this heat? It was a relief to be away from the taxi, there had been something sinister about his manner. I went into a little bar and drank a cognac. The locals were engrossed in a game of cards, so they scarcely looked when I went in, and although the barmaid was sour to me, she had a sour face and lines around her mouth that came from more than just ignoring me that day. I asked about you, and she shrugged; when I asked again, she smiled knowingly. I was not deterred though, I had travelled across the Channel often enough to know the low opinion that all Frenchmen have of my French. Then I went out and down the coast road for a hundred yards or so. There was the lighthouse standing out on its stone rampart, the abandoned harbour, and the massive nuclear plant on one side, barely visible beyond a beach. And then on the other side there was a stretch of sand and rocks curving round for mile upon mile lined by low cliffs and fields. It was a magnificent view, and I felt that you would be out that way. After twenty minutes of trekking over the hot sand, it was a mystery to me how you could have gone further with the pram and the circus and the picnic that you would inevitably have brought. But by then I was too hot to bother, and I sat down to rest. I think I sat and stared at the bare cuttle-fish bones and the circling gulls and at the sea itself, and then I buried my face in my bag and fell asleep.

I woke up, hours later, feeling dizzy from the sun. I scanned the littered shore for you, but the beach was deserted. That was when I started feeling really angry. I resented your indifference, and your alternate clinging and rejection. Disappearing then into the fifth dimension just seemed to me to be another example of your perversity. I vented my wrath on the stray bladderwracks, bursting the drying sacks of brine. Where I had thought to find you lying waiting, there were only the torn pincers of crabs, and little piles of dismembered limbs quilted in flies' wings. I walked back past the bar and on across the sands in the opposite direction, and I was unconsciously gathering bits of crab and consciously thinking bad things about you when I saw the pram.

It was standing on its own, as lifeless in its way as the lighthouse, but I didn't see that at first. It had what appeared to be a new dark sunshade, and between me and it, the twins were digging in the sand. As I approachd them, they looked up once, but made no sign of recognition. They were burnt the colour of baltic pine, and their hair looked almost irrevocably tangled; they seemed so intent on shovelling their sand that I thought they were purposely ignoring me. Even when I stood right beside them, they kept shovelling, manically, heaping up the slipping sand into a long mound.

'Aren't you going to say hello?' I asked.

'We're burying crabs.'

'Where's mummy?'

'She's back at the house, she doesn't come out any more.'

There was a strange smell of old crab meat, of beach debris, of shells and fish and rotting flesh in the sun, and then an undertow of something else. It mixed in with the heat and made me feel physically sick. Halfway to the pram, the twins stopped again, shaking out their frilly swimming things and then squaring themselves to dig once more. They marked out a rectangle some three feet by one.

'Still burying crabs?'

'Yup.'

'Why?'

'They've eaten Rachel,' one of them told me, then the other one interrupted, 'Well, she fell in the sea, actually.'

'... and then they ate her!'

They had stopped digging now, and were poised to fight, with their eight-year-old fists trembling to be right.

'When did Rachel fall in the sea?' I asked patiently. They both paused and a sudden wave of boredom registered on their identical faces.

'Oh, ages ago.'

It was their boredom that made me fear for Amadeo, since they too, like you, were irritated by certain aspects of reality.

I couldn't get to the pram without my handkerchief as a gag. I cursed the place that had nothing but bad feelings and dead crabs, and I was angry for once with the twins for using the pram as a sea hearse. When I looked in, I was too shocked to even be sick. I pushed it blindly through the haze of hovering flies, struggling to force its wheels through the dry sand. The twins were calling now but their voices were as unintelligible as the gulls to me. Then one of them was tugging at my shirt.

'Don't go that way, daddy, that's the Centrale, it's bad, that's where the smell comes from.'

I tried to push on, but they blocked the way of the pram, staring down sadly at Amadeo's prostrate body. His hair was bleached almost white, and his face was parched and peeling, his lips cracked and caked with dry blood where he had been mouthing, and the frills of his lace shirt looked more like layers of a soiled dressing. He lay completely dull and listless, incarcerated by the abominable smell.

'How long has he been in there?'

107

'Oh, ages.'

'Jesus!'

They seemed annoyed suddenly as though by my stupidity.

'He can't hold up his head. He can't do that since we went to the Centrale. He's got the sickness, and so has mummy. Mummy's hiding at the house. She says she has to stay in the dark, and Amadeo has to stay in the sun.'

'Why?'

'Because of the smell, of course. But you mustn't take him near the Centrale, or she'll be furious.'

Amadeo whimpered when I touched him, so I didn't dare lift him out. Instead, I pushed the pram back up the slope. The villagers were there, staring. I noticed that the ones who had tolerated me at the bar were now out on the street, frowning and muttering too. Someone spat as the twins passed, and the gobbet fell a few inches away from their sandalled feet.

'Why do they hate us like this?'

The twins didn't seem to mind.

'I suppose because of the smell; they hate most things.'

'Like what?'

'Like the Centrale, and Rachel, and the others.'

Even with Rachel in the sea, only four were accounted for, that left one more of your circus to account for.

'Where is Candy?' I asked, hopefully, I don't know why.

'She's gone.'

'Where?'

'Just gone.'

I didn't ask any more questions after that, I didn't want to be told any more answers. The twins wanted things, they wanted gobstoppers from the slot machine outside the shop, and they wanted new spades to bury more crabs and they wanted horsemeat for the cat; but I didn't dare go into that shop, it was all I could do to walk past the villagers, shoving that foul stench up the hill and watching them exchange their looks as we passed. The twins walked ahead of me, apparently unconcerned by the fuss. As we neared the crossroads I felt myself leaning more and more heavily on the pram as my knees weakened from the excessive heat and the smother of Amadeo. A fat slow-eyed boy was leaning against a wall, he looked about sixteen and very sweaty. As the twins passed him, he lunged forward, trying to touch the nearest on her flat sunburnt chest. As he reached out, he leered at me with an unpleasant complicity. I didn't see what happened next, but the soldier pulled his hand back bleeding from a deep gash.

'*Putains*,' he said and turned back to the wall, clutching his wound.

The twins were proud of themselves, and they showed me the sharpened cuttle-fish bones they were holding in their hands.

'They're not going to touch us.'

'Not after what they did to Rachel.'

'What did they do to Rachel?' I asked, despite myself, breaking my earlier vow of silence.

'Well they're not going to do it to us,' they said firmly and then continued up the hill, swinging their worn spades.

I never liked Rachel, you know, and I didn't want to know what they had done, had they pushed her into the sea or had she fallen, or had she jumped because of something else they did to her, or were the twins lying, they did after all, lie a lot. I didn't care somehow, not for Rachel or the others really. I had to care about Amadeo, and keeping the flies off him, and getting him back, and somehow making the twins be eight again, and most of all I had to find you.

When we reached the house the drunkard was sitting out by the road fondling his dog.

'That's Pierre,' one of the twins whispered, then: 'Hello, Pierre.'

He stared at her, looking somewhere halfway between her and her double, looking confused, probably seeing four girls instead of two. He turned his head away without replying.

'He never talks,' they explained.

The door was still locked when I tried it, but the twins had gone on past the house, beckoning me round after them. I pushed on up a dirt track, feeling that at any moment the pram would run back over me. Once in the back garden, there was a tiny flight of stairs to negotiate, then a footbridge, and then a door.

'What about 'Deo?'

'Oh we always leave him here, you can't get it down the steps, it'd tip.'

There was a view out over rooftops and the bay, curving slowly round to the tip of Normandy. I tried to lift poor 'Deo out again then, but he was stuck to the mattress, and the smell when I moved it was more than I could bear, and I gagged.

'You do go on about it,' one of the twins moaned. 'We've been living with it for weeks.'

There were, it seemed incongruously, a briar rose and a sweet pea growing out of the nettles that lined the steps.

Why were you hiding in the closet? Who were you hiding from? You'd always had such an array of camp followers, why had they suddenly gone? You just wept, you wouldn't tell me anything, and now – you still won't tell me. Amadeo was my son, I want to know how he died. I could have sworn I felt him whimper in the pram, but now I know that it was just the flies. When I came to bury him, he was rigid and had been for God knows how long. Was that all you called me for, to bury the baby? What would you have done if I hadn't come? And I wonder, what strange thing has settled over that village that lets a dead child wander up and down stinking the place out and no one intervenes? Were they all child molesters, as the twins imply? Or was there radiation sickness, as you seem to think? I wish I knew what you did think, and sometimes, if you think at all. Life is all toast to you, how do they make it? why do we eat it? what is it there for?

It's just you and me now, and the *pâtisserie* at South End Green, and the croissants on Sundays. At night sometimes I just lie awake and wonder, who did what to the baby?

I would have taken him to the police, but there was no one to take him to. And then there was something about your crying that frightened me. What would you say to the police? And what about Rachel? And could the twins be trusted not to say something outrageous, not to lie . . . ? By the next morning, I felt that smell was in my hair, behind my eyes, everywhere. I suppose that was why I buried him. It seemed the least I could do really. I put him in the sand, one night's digging deep. I expect he's still there.

When I go down to Kent now to visit the twins at school, I have to force myself not to ask them about 'Deo, and I find myself looking at them in a funny way, wondering if they could have done such a thing. If it wasn't them, was it you? Who did it? And why in Diélette? The ferry back was a nightmare: I got so seasick I thought I'd turn inside out over the rail, thinking about Amadeo in the sand, and Fred, poor Fred rotted down to a puddle under his shell inside the pram. By the time I got to him I'd had enough, I couldn't even bring myself to tip him out, so he's still rotting there, rusting into the garden with its beautiful view – there didn't seem any point in lugging the pram back empty.

So some nights I can't sleep, and some nights you can't either. Meanwhile, we've got your wretched toast to discuss; and now the wonder is wearing off, finally, after all these years, I don't know what to do with you; but I've had a vasectomy – just in case; and I never touch crabmeat now, of any kind, not even in a sandwich. And every summer, when the swelter sets in, I get an urge to go back to Diélette.

111

UMBRIAN AFTERNOON

by

Michel Déon

Novelist, travel writer, and member of the Académie Française, Michel Déon is regarded in France as one of that country's best living writers. His work has been widely translated, and Graham Greene called Where Are You Dying Tonight?, published by Hamish Hamilton in 1983, 'a fascinating and complex novel about the relation between fact and fiction'.

'Umbrian Afternon' is extracted from his latest novel Je vous écris d'Italie. The translation is the editor's.

Who can describe the pleasure felt by a young man still full of enthusiasm and hope, a young man in pursuit of a memory, retracing his footsteps along a road in Italy at the end of the nineteen forties? Though to say 'retracing his footsteps' is a slight misnomer: better to say retracing his tyre-tracks. He was driving a pre-war Fiat, the model that got itself nicknamed the Topolino on account of its resemblance to a mouse, a clattering but sturdy car that garage mechanics would bend over lovingly each time it overheated or hiccupped or shook itself free of a vital part, each time the brakes failed or it refused to start. And the road he was following was one he had covered before, in June 1944 on board a jeep at the driver's side, as a second lieutenant in the infantry. In 1949 he felt he ought to be able to recognise every detail of the countryside, but perhaps in five years one's memory could forget or confuse it all, and one's sensation of 'déjà vu' become so fleeting that one could begin to doubt every part of it? Vaguely disappointed, he asked himself if this unfaithful memory of his wasn't playing a trick on him, knowing full well what the reality had been. Instead of remembering, it had decided to imagine something else.

Several times he had had to stop to check his route on the map. No, he was heading in the right direction and, save for one detour caused by a bridge being rebuilt that had sent him half a dozen miles out of his way, he was following the same road as he had in 1944. It was simply that the countryside whose image he had preserved had been, it seemed to him, less harsh and less severe, more richly coloured than the scene he was driving through now. From time to time there were signs to reassure him. Over there, for example, that big fortified farm on the hill: it was there that his platoon had stopped for the night, so that his men could bivouac by the side of a torrent. The farmer and his family had barricaded themselves in the main building. The men had broken down the door with their rifle butts to make sure that there were no Germans hidden in the

115

cellars, and had come upon the Monticellis – he suddenly remembered their name – seated at their long kitchen table with bread and plates of soup in front of them: they sat there, the grandparents, the mother, the children, all dressed in black, struck dumb, their eyes glued to their food, refusing to meet the soldiers' stares, awaiting their fate. Germans, resistance fighters, Allied soldiers: they no longer knew who was the enemy. At the farm the platoon had enjoyed a brief moment of peace in its race to the north, in pursuit of the grenadiers who were mining the roads and dynamiting bridges. After bathing in the stream, the men had stolen a sheep, roasted it on a makeshift spit beneath the olive trees and sung part of the night away.

He had followed this road alone with his thirty men as it wound deeper into Umbria, detached from the main company to carry out mopping-up operations in the Varela sector. On his flanks, advancing in parallel, were three platoons hard on the heels of the straggling Wehrmacht troops. For four days, in the wake of the massed battles on the Rome road, he had had the intoxicating sensation of waging his own personal war in unknown territory where the enemy vanished at the first blow. It was after this escapade that he had rejoined his company commander, Captain de Cléry, and the great and exciting difficulties had begun. Yet – those four days had been unforgettable.

Now he regretted all the more sharply his inability to remember what had happened in sufficient detail. Perhaps the difference stemmed from the fact that, for that particular part of the Italian campaign, the weather had been glorious. The light lay on the Umbrian Appennines and the poppies mixed with the thin green corn cultivated on plots hard-won from the stony ground. Today the sky was grey and the hay was rotting where it stood on the small ricks which the pesants still turned, without conviction, to dry it. They watched the Topolino go by with a certain curiosity, but without waving or acknowledging it: to a far greater extent than in 1944 he had the impression that he was advancing through hostile country. What did it matter! The young man was happy as his car bounced and creaked along the broken, potholed road, and negotiated without mishap the bridges hastily rebuilt by the Allies' engineer corps. Despite her vitality Italy had not yet managed to rid

116

herself of the war's aftermath – or, to be more accurate, she had rid herself of her more visible scars, putting off indefinitely the reconstruction of the poorer, less picturesque parts... In Umbria the roads were still as they had been after the pounding they had received from the motorised divisions. Here and there villages offered the spectacle of gutted town halls, dwellings torn apart, mutilated trees. The driver of the Topolino came upon a German artillery piece trapped in a ditch, its yawning breech overgrown with grass, and a lorry with its black cross being used as a chicken coop in a farmyard. He wondered whether he hadn't simply thought of all these conflagrations as torches to light the victors' path, whether he hadn't heard the bombardments and volleys of machine-gun fire as the drum rolls of a triumphal parade. The more joyful war is as one races towards victory, the sadder is the silence that descends on the ruins left behind. *Post bellum anima tristis est.*

Since his return to Italy Jacques Sauvage had amused himself by giving his name as Giacomo Selvaggio – an act which had been the cause of a slight delay in Rome when, at his hotel, he had filled out the police registration form in his new name. The detectives who had come to arrest him for false declaration of identity took a great deal of persuading that all he had done, in an access of enthusiasm, was to Italianise his French name, just as another Frenchman, Arrigo Beyle, had done so long before him. But Jacques was not easily cast down, even when he was thrown into a stinking cell and left there for six hours while all the linings and seams of his cothes were unpicked to make sure that he wasn't smuggling foreign currency, and greasy fingers leafed through his notebook and his Italian dictionary and grammar. These local difficulties were the price he paid for a glorious initiation. Nothing worthwhile can be acquired with ease once a war is over, once one no longer carries a badge of rank on one's tunic. That's part of the game. Equally, Jacques' impetuous spirit excused everything because, well, that was Italy; and so he was rescued from the most deflating disappointments.

★

117

The road wound down into a gorge with a torrent of clear green water at the bottom. This stretch of the route was the most recognisable. In 1944 the young lieutenant had had to study it carefully for likely danger points before he could advance with his small convoy of jeep, armoured car and two lorries. Two miles further on the gorge had opened out to reveal, a hundred yards lower down, the mouth of a broad and deep valley. After the wild and stony Umbria they had so far traversed, the valley had seemed like an oasis with its neatly laid-out fields, its olive groves and its rustling orchards.

Jacques pulled up at the exact spot where, five years earlier, he had raised his arm to halt his convoy. The soldiers had stood up in the GMC transports to find out what was going on. Artillery fire boomed out and, from east and west, two tanks from a support company trailing clouds of dust converged on a smoke-blackened hamlet. The scene had looked exactly like those naive *images d'Epinal* depicting the battles of the Napoleonic wars, save for the fact that here the enemy was invisible, entrenched in its hamlet at the junction of three roads, and that the infantry was closing up fast behind the tanks – tiny ants far down in the valley. In the distance stood the fortified town of Varela with its beige ramparts shining in the sun.

Jacques extracted himself from the Topolino with difficulty. Over any long distance he was slightly too tall for a car of its size: he had to fold himself up, then, once outside, unfold himself again, his knees and back aching and stiff. The valley stretched out in front of him. From the lightening sky a harsh light fell on the oasis and the ruins of the hamlet whose position had been so heavily contested. A tractor crept along, raising a smudge of pink dust on the same road by which Captain de Cléry's supporting tanks had approached without cover to conduct their flushing-out operation. The first, its tracks damaged, had stopped, and the second, firing blind, must have reached the ammunition dump. For several minutes the mountains ringing the valley had resounded with the echoes of the explosions while a mushroom of black smoke streaked with red and yellow flames billowed upwards. By radio 2nd Lt Sauvage had received the order to deploy his forces in the direction of the hamlet to complete the outflanking manoeuvre. One armoured car with its

118

black cross had made good its escape to the north, but men in field-grey uniforms, worn out and choking, had streamed from the furnace with their hands up. They had been swiftly piled into a covered lorry, and the operation had continued towards Varela, led by de Cléry standing erect in the front of his jeep, hanging on to the windshield with one hand and with his fieldglasses in the other. Petrified, the town showed no sign of life.

Even today, it still looked aloof and forbidding, proudly encased in its high walls. The sight of it conjured up exactly one of those middle-distance views from a portrait by Piero della Francesca, in which a meditative profile dominates a landscape of colours softened by a haze of heat. Jacques could clearly make out the olive trees, the rows of vines, the fields of yellowing maize, the ribbons of the irrigation canals and, in the far distance, a mountain chain whose ridge-line dissolved into the blue-grey of the sky. The valley of Varela was a painter's canvas; but what moved Jacques even more was the re-discovery almost down to the last detail of the image he had cherished during his long absence. He had thought about this valley for so long, about the sight of Varela ringed by its high walls, that he had often wondered whether this town wasn't a mirage he had dreamed up, along with the onward march of the column of infantry down the road leading to the fortifications which held Beatrice prisoner.

Jacques got back into his Topolino. The car was a true sardine tin. Cooped up inside its cage, it was impossible to see more than a hundred yards ahead and a few inches of the verge on either side. He missed the jeep driven by his faithful Mehdi – a soap-box on wheels in which one rode exposed in all weathers. Half a mile further on lay the hamlet, or at least what remained of it. Everything had caught fire: trees, roof, doors, windows. There was nothing left but sections of charred wall and some rustling hulks of cars. From the hamlet the road led straight to the north, spanning irrigation canals and passing by a *casa cantoniera* of which there was nothing to be seen bar the pediment with the inscription 'Varela, 1½ miles', and an arrow. A tank had fired two shells and blown it to pieces, for no reason apart from the pleasure of seeing it vanish. Was this the bridge? No, it was too exposed. At the next crest in the road, Jacques stopped and got out. Muddy water ran between the banks

119

of reeds. In the culvert there was room for a man. The wounded *Feldwebel* had hidden there. He had thrown his grenade almost blind and it had exploded in mid-air. The jeeps had already passed by, but in one of the GMC transports two soldiers and Sergeant Lévy had been injured. A soldier had jumped to the ground and emptied a full clip into the German. Why a whole clip when a single shot would have sufficed? But it was always the same: when the infantry had a man at their mercy, they would turn him into a sieve with a terrifying rage. Minutes afterwards, the column had arrived at the gates of Varela, exposed and without cover, in one of those bold strokes of which Cléry was so fond.

Jacques stopped his Topolino at the foot of the mounted statue of Francesco di Varela. The *condottiere* stood guard over the entrance to his walled city, and one could not present oneself at the gate without coming face to face with his furious stare, as furious as Colleoni's. Standing on his stirrups, brandishing his sword, he forced back all intruders. The statue carried his name, two dates – 1510-1560 – and the name of the scupltor: Alberto del Cimino. The pose was so strikingly true and real that it seemed as if the slightest thing would bring it to life. Francesco di Varela was bursting with vitality, and his face, twisted by a rictus, expressed such a concentration of violence that it would have terrified any visitor – had it not been for the sadly derisive trick that time and the wood pigeons had played in plastering it with an ignominious layer of excrement. Up until the arrival of the Allies, the mayor had entrusted one of his employees with the task of cleaning the statue daily. The new administration clearly felt no such duty towards the *condottiere*. Perched on the edge of his sword, on the raised visor of his helmet and between the ears of his horse, the pigeons relieved themselves with an ineffable satisfaction; and it had taken barely five years for the mounted personage to be covered in glutinous white matter from head to foot, so that now it looked more like the snowy peak of a hill than anything else. It was only the helmet's visor that had protected the face from these depredations – and the terrible gaze which Beatrice's ancestor brought to bear on his valley.

Cléry, in 1944, had jumped down from his jeep and walked all the way round the pedestal. The statue had impressed him so much that, forgetting the surrounding dangers – the possibility of an ambush by rearguard elements who might have taken refuge in the fortified town – he had taken photograph after photograph of this work of Cimino's which had gone so unappreciated by art lovers for so long. At the time Cléry cherished the ambition of financing an encyclopaedia of such neglected masterpieces, forgotten flowerings of Italian genius, a reaction, he claimed, against the decadent aesthetics of Berenson. This project, like many of Cléry's other grandiose ideas, had sunk beneath the weight of new ambitions. But had it been left to the captain commanding the 2nd company of Algerian infantry to direct the Italian campaign, there is no doubt that the route of the Allied armies would have been very different, passing more often through small market towns still with their Romanesque churches and their frescoes dating back to the *trecento* than via the shrines which were the landmarks of every aesthetically minded tourist.

At the foot of the statue of the *condottiere*, Jacques was struck by an intense emotion. He recalled the sight of his friend taking photographs from all angles, before the disbelieving eyes of his soldiers. How Cléry would have relished the opportunity to point out, once again, the triumph of carelessness and of pigeon-shit over art! Jacques in his turn took some photographs, just as a covered cart drawn by a donkey was passing through the studded gate: the first sign of life the town had imparted since his arrival. Apart from this wrinkled, indifferent old man driving his donkey with a dry clacking of his tongue, Varela, enclosed in its ramparts, gave the impression of having been shut in behind such thick walls of silence that one might have thought it had had a spell cast on it to sleep for evermore. Taking the wheel again, Jacques passed through the gateway. At last some faces appeared: women on stools in their doorways, bent over their lace-work cushions; mummified ancestors glued to their chairs, the backs of their heads pressed to the wall, once-bright blue eyes faded by the years; children playing in the gutter; craftsmen in aprons at the doors of their workshops.

The town had been conceived on an odd plan. It had been built on an eminence in the middle of the plain, but at the centre of this eminence was a small crater, and the streets and alleys now converged in a gentle slope down to the *piazza del condottiere*. This meant that, from the outside, there was not a single roof to be seen. There was neither campanile nor steeple (the church was Romanesque) and the palazzo's terrace went no higher than the level of the fortifications. Subsiding at its centre beneath the weight of its most solemn monuments, the town shrank back behind the shelter of the crenellated walls and the six guard-towers that surmounted them.

A small boy of about twelve suddenly materialised at the bonnet of the Topolino, offering the newcomer his services as a guide to the Albergo del Condottiere. But Jacques was not going to the hotel; he was looking for the house of the Varela family and fully expecting, at that moment, soon to be utterly lost in the network of dark, narrow streets.

'La Contessina Beatrice!' the boy cried joyfully, opening the right-hand door and setting himself down uninvited on the free seat to guide the Frenchman through the labyrinth and bring him out on the *piazza del condottiere*, facing the palazzo.

Little by little Jacques reconstructed the layout of the town to himself. It had always seemed difficult to keep one's bearings there. One-way streets, a road closed because there was a house in danger of collapsing – he would have been hopelessly lost, without the assistance of the small boy shouting in his ear in the way people have when they are worried that a foreigner doesn't understand the language. '*A destra, a sinistra, tutto diritto.*' Eventually they arrived at the *piazza del condottiere*, a sight all the more beautiful for having to be earned by the traveller's resolve and enthusiasm. Why was it not better known? Cléry had stated categorically that it was one of the finest in the world, certainly the equal of the *campo di Siena* with its elegant arcades, the tall central fountain with its bronze statue flying over a pyramid-like construction of decorated basins, the pure and uncluttered façade of the church, and the austere-looking palace, saved by its Renaissance flourishes and – its one ornament – the balcony faced with porphyry gryphons from which the counts of Varela had once addressed their subjects. His re-discovery of the square, the exaltation that he felt at this uniquely lovely scene unchanged over centuries, the abrupt plunge back into a past of his own that was hardly five years old, filled Jacques with such irrepressible joy that he grabbed the child by the shoulders and clasped him tightly to his chest.

'It's very nice, isn't it?' said the boy.

'Very, very nice.'

'The Contessina's house is over there, under the arcade.'

'Thank you. I recognise it.'

But eager as he was to see Beatrice again, the open doorway of the church and its dark shadow drew him irresistibly. In 1944 the two jeeps and the GMC transport carrying the wounded had pulled up on the square, and a makeshift sick bay had been swiftly set up in the transept to nurse the two soldiers wounded with Sergeant Lévy, four horribly burned German survivors and an old shepherd whom they had picked up at the roadside with a bullet in his stomach, still surrounded by his flock.

The moment he was through the doorway, Jacques caught again the smell of the incense which had so effectively masked the smells of the orderlies' disinfectants and the men's leaking wounds. All the time they were there a choirboy had walked up and down the nave with his censer, and it felt to Jacques as if he could still hear the crunch of the boy's cleated shoes on the flags and the creak of the chain as it swung the burner back and forth. From time to time the boy had stopped behind a pillar to spy on the wounded and cross himself whenever they moaned or rocked in their delirium.

The church's interior was as austere as ever. The empty recesses had not been filled with coloured plaster statues; the rough benches worn smooth and shiny had not been replaced by new chairs; and the altar was still the same impressive table of granite covered with an embroidered cloth. Thus had Francesco di Varela ordained it four centuries earlier: there was to be no competition in this house of God with the grandiloquent luxury of the Medici, or the Ferrare, and certainly not of the popes whom the *condottiere* considered to be hardly better than a crowd of heretics sacrificing to pagan rites. In his church prayers would be offered in all humility and, thanks to the rose windows in both transepts, in a seraphic light which traced its dazzling carpet of flowers – shapes of blue, yellow, pink and green – on the floor. It was next to the pillar at the corner of one of

123

the transepts that Sergeant Lévy, a student from Algiers, had died from a wound that had not been thought serious at the time but which had turned out to be caused by a grenade splinter lodged in his liver. Still lucid as he lay with his head on a cushion staring up at the window filtering its long, flexible tapers of sunlight, Lévy had asked Jacques to reach into his haversack and get out his copy of Proust. The book was incomplete, covered in notes and grease stains. Would he read him the page on the stained-glass windows of Combray, which 'were never so brilliant as on days when the sun scarcely shone . . . this dazzling and gilded carpet of forget-me-nots in glass'? At the sound of Jacques' voice, whose naturally deep tones were amplified by the vaulted roof, the other injured men had ceased their moans and calls for water, bathed and soothed by the words, illuminated by the burst of rainbow colours from the rose windows. Proust was applied like a balm to a student already touched by death's shadow, to soldiers from the Algerian infantry, to Feldwebels from Pomerania, to an Umbrian shepherd. Thus the semblance of a speech may be more powerful than the speech itself.

The feeling of quite suddenly finding himself, thanks to the peace and quiet of a church, back in a past life which had not so long ago been thrust aside, dislodged by so many events, so many new phases in his life and even in his way of thinking, this feeling was so complete that Jacques stood where he was without moving, his feet in the shimmering pool of light, for an instant of time which seemed to keep on expanding, and which would have lasted long minutes had the church's spell not been suddenly broken by a new and silent presence which he could clearly sense behind him, as if Sergeant Lévy had stepped out of the kingdom of shadows and come to thank him for his visit and beg him to read aloud once again the passage on the stained-glass windows of Combray.

'So,' said Beatrice, 'you feel it's not the same? You think we should have kept the beds and the kitchen table the doctor did his cutting on – that we should have kept the confessional as a dispensary cupboard? It's all over, my friend. We've disinfected, cleaned up, swept, put all the benches back, rubbed off all the graffiti. The priest hopes you'll forgive him. It's his house, after all.'

Leaning against a pillar, she smiled at his surprise. Straightaway he noticed the white strands in the young woman's hair and was touched. On pretty features lacking all animation and interest the years will often pass without leaving a trace, only imprinting themselves suddenly, very late in the day, to reveal a pitiful faded reminder of what they once were; in other faces the stigmata of age can only enhance features illuminated by a passionate life of the spirit. Beatrice's beauty, full-grown, came to Jacques as a revelation. Was it possible that five years earlier he had not had the maturity to be struck by it, and had been content to judge the young woman on appearances: a proud mouth, a soft complexion, a difficult aquiline nose which she carried with dignity, eyes of an oriental blackness which darkened her whole face. At the time she had belonged to another world, to a set of aesthetic values which left him at a loss and which, in his inexperience of life, he desperately feared he did not know how to appreciate. If, after the armistice, Cléry – who had not set eyes on Beatrice for more than five minutes – had not told him in very forcible terms one evening that he had allowed himself to pass by the most startlingly beautiful apparition of their entire Italian campaign, Jacques would not have returned to Varela in 1949. As it was he had returned, armed only with the perhaps wild hope of rewriting an already closed page of the past.

'You've missed the point as you always do,' Cléry had said. 'The minute you can find the time, go back and see Beatrice. You went around Varela with your eyes closed. All your skinny, nail-biting girlfriends won't teach you a thing. There was life, and you walked straight past it. So she's six or seven years older than you. What difference does it make? Let me tell you: if you can get to know her, she'll teach you everything you need to know. You'll have a memory that will last you for the rest of your life. I promise you, if I weren't a married man with three children, I would have gone straight back to Varela when the war was over. But look at me. I'm not out to turn the world on its head. In any case, she's six inches taller than I am, and that's too much. She is a mystery who could devour a man. I've got too many plans to let myself be distracted. I'm delegating my intuition to you. You can consider it an order if you like.'

One had to go back to the newcomers' extraordinary entry into a shuttered and untrusting Valera: to the laying-out of the wounded in the church; to the infantry patrols that covered the town with a fine-tooth comb to ensure there was not a single German left concealed there; to the five corpses discovered in an alley with their throats cut – all known fascists; and to the captain's instant proclamation, printed an hour after his arrival on the press next to the town hall:

CURFEW

Patrols will shoot on sight any person who is found on the streets of the town between the hours of 9 p.m. and 6 a.m.

The responsibility for any such summary execution rests on the shoulders of the local authorities.

Signed: the Resident Commander and provisional King of Varela,

Cléry I.

Postscript: In the absence of Captain de Cléry, 2nd Lieutenant Sauvage will perform the functions of Regent and Resident Commander.

It was a bizarre, not to say farcical ploy, but one which had so astonished the townspeople that the feuding and settling of scores had ceased immediately.

'You cannot get people to respect the rule of law unless you show them that it is inviolable,' the captain had told Jacques. 'The moment I arrived I set myself above them, and all you have to do is maintain that superiority, until they eventually find out that we aren't royalty at all – I mean royalty with absolute power, not some sort of constitutional figureheads. Italy is a country in complete disarray. What it needs is unity, and to restore that unity we shall have to restore the monarchies, or the duchies and principalities at the very least. What we must do is find ourselves a few available kings, and there are princes and dukes by the bucketful; then, later, we can give the question the serious consideration it needs. I might tell you that this is project No.66 on my list, to be dealt with the minute we sign the peace treaty, before all the would-be Metterniches have a chance to build a Europe of phoney statesmen

– giants with feet of clay. Dismiss . . . no, at ease . . . have a glass of this rather choice local wine – a demijohn I requisitioned from the mayor – before I hand over the command of Varela and disappear to the north, where all those glorious challenges are waiting – the storming of Berchtesgaden, fixed bayonets . . .'

Beatrice was still leaning one shoulder against the pillar of the church, a smile on her lips, looking at Jacques, who faltered beneath the onrush of his memories and the shock of this vision come to meet him at the end of his journey. He recognised her without being certain that she was the same, much as he was no longer certain of being himself. In reality it was she who had changed less in the intervening five years, despite the white strands in her thick black hair. Jacques had stripped off the uniform which had once made him look like a young warrior, a victorious but casual young blade, aide to the brilliant Cléry in whose reflected glory the 2nd infantry company had basked. In his beige corduroy trousers and his leather jacket he could no longer rely on anyone apart from himself to help him awaken Beatrice's feelings and carry off a new conquest. At that precise moment he suddenly had the sensation that this conquest, if not impossible, would at the very least be horribly fraught with risk.

'Well, lieutenant,' said the young woman, taking a step towards him as if she were coming to his assistance, 'it's time to come back down to earth.'

'I was remembering.'

'Come on. Your room is ready for you. I've had a desk put under the window, so that while you're working you'll be able to see the palace.'

On the square the Topolino was surrounded by children. Beatrice clapped her hands and they flew off into the side streets. It occurred to Jacques that the desertion of Varela was identical to the day when Cléry had taken the town, marching through streets with closed doors and shuttered windows which rattled from the metallic uproar of the jeeps, the truck full of wounded men and the armoured car. In the silence of his return Jacques recognised the Varelans' instinctive suspicion; all were probably at this moment hidden behind their drawn shutters to catch sight of whoever it was the Contessina had gone to look for in the church. The day was

127

slowly failing and the fronts of the houses cast a serrated shadow as far as the foot of the palace.

'Do you have much luggage?'

'No ... no ... not much ... just the materials that any pen-pusher needs ...'

'Pen-pusher ... what's that?'

Though her French was excellent, the sense of the expression escaped her.

'A pen-pusher is someone who uses dictionaries, books of grammar, pencils and rubbers, card indexes, a typewriter and lots of books out of which he copies things that a little while later he will present as his own work.'

Beatrice laughed, a clear, open sound.

'I should think that if you want to be taken seriously as one of those, you'll have to shrink a little. At the moment you look more like a sprinter than a ... what's the word? A pencil-pusher.'

'Pen-pusher. You know, that really got in the way when it came to exams. When I was nineteen I was French university champion in the 110 metres hurdles ... Do you know what that is?'

'I have no idea, but since you won it, it must be terrific.'

'My tutor said I would have to decide between what he called a career as a clown on the race-track and a serious career as an historian. I didn't have to, in the end, because a war suddenly turned up.'

It was true that Jacques was far from the image of the conventional academic. His six feet two inches posed a problem when he climbed in and out of his Topolino, but this belied an athleticism which had imparted an unmistakeable manner: the easy, open stance, relaxed in spite of his natural timidity, and, occasionally, instances of rather gauche behaviour. It would have been difficult to imagine a nature more different from that of his captain Cléry, who would draw himself up to his full height – what there was of it – and bristle furiously before roundly denouncing whoever it was had had the effrontery to be physically superior to him.

'Folco will help you with your bags,' she said.

Folco? Ah yes, Folco had been there in 1944. The French had called him 'the Contessina's killer', despite the fact there was really nothing of the assassin about him at all. But the way he looked after Beatrice; the way he dogged her footsteps in the street; the way he even followed her into the church where, while she helped the auxiliary medic to change dressings, he knelt with a floor-cloth to wash the flagstones wherever the object of his respect chose to place her feet; his way of always being there to open the door before she had raised her hand, of anticipating her orders, of watching every movement of her face for the next service he could render her: all these things made one think not exactly of a killer, but of a guardian angel – or guardian devil, since there was nothing in the slightest bit angelic about him.

When Folco appeared in the doorway of the house, Jacques recognised him immediately, although in the short time that had elapsed the face of the factotum had become if anything more shrivelled. Now the baleful look could hardly be made out between the wrinkles and the shaggy grey eyebrows, and the huge mouth – a split from one ear to the other – was without lips, lost to the last departing teeth. He had a sickly air about him, but Jacques knew him to be possessed of great reserves of nervous energy. Born in a shepherd's hut in the Appennines, he could walk for hours on end with a pack that would floor a normal man. To say that he had appreciated what his 'liberators' had done for him would be an exaggeration. Throughout the occupation he had affected not to see either the soldiers or their officers. And yet, on the final day, when the wounded men had been evacuated by an ambulance up from Rome and the infantry company was about to leave Varela, he had asked Jacques if he could travel some of the way with them as they headed north. Then he had left them twenty miles down the road, deep in the mountains, in a place that was so inhospitable it looked as if no human being could survive there. Jacques remembered his slight silhouette, his pack on his shoulder, moving away down a goat-track towards a deserted hollow. Folco had not once turned round as he disappeared into the distance.

The house of the Varela family faced the palace, whose ground and first floors were occupied by the local administration; the second floor housed the so-called *'museo del condottiere'*, little visited but kept up by Beatrice as the honorary curator – 'the cleaning woman', as she said, laughing; and the third floor, low-ceilinged, lightened by square, regular windows, held the archives and what had once been the servants' quarters beneath the flat roof. The house itself rose for three storeys above the arcade and, without possessing the nobility of the palace where over two centuries, from 1550 to 1755, generations of Varelas had commanded both town and valley, it was nevertheless a house with a definite patrician pride, as its balconies of pale sandstone testified, and its crazed and rough façade of pleasing smoky yellow.

'I thought you would like to have the same room as last time,' said Beatrice. 'In any case, the choice isn't endless. I don't keep up the whole house. There are some rooms I haven't been in for ten years.'

Ahead of them, a suitcase under each arm, Folco climbed the steep steps up to the first floor. Halfway up, the stairwell was suffused with the light from a crudely coloured stained-glass window. It was a watery, drizzling light that chimed in with the smell of the house, a smell of beeswax and stuffiness that assaults the nose in any provincial Italian town where the shutters, closed for fear of the sun's rays, harbour a hothouse atmosphere from spring onwards. Folco opened the double doors to the bedroom. Nothing had changed: the heavy curtains, half-drawn, of red velvet, the yellow immortelles inside their glass globe, the ebony desk banded with copper, the four-poster bed which was so vast a single man might disappear in it altogether, or at least seek hopelessly for another warm body next to his own. He had stolen brief hours there when he could get away, mainly in the afternoon when the silence and closeness of the day plunged Varela into torpor: fitful moments of sleep tense with the worries of overseeing with barely thirty men a town of two thousand inhabitants and a valley so vast it needed a regiment to occupy it properly. Cléry had disappeared to the north with the rest of the company; according to a message delivered by a motorcycle despatch rider, he was meeting with resistance in the Appennines which was blocking his progress. He was left waiting for reinforcements in that part of the front where confusion reigned supreme as the Allied spearhead found itself blunted and harried in the rear by Wehrmacht, commandos.

As had often happened before Jacques, lost in thought, in the images evoked by his return to this room, and believing that Beatrice could read his mind, turned towards her. 'Did the driver of

130

the German armoured car ever turn up here?'

'I knew you'd ask me that, the moment you arrived,' she said. 'What does it matter? That wasn't what you came back for, was it?'

Had she hesitated, betrayed a moment's anxiety? With the curtains half-covering the windows and the room in semi-darkness, he could not say.

'Do you mind if I shed some light on things?' he said, moving over towards the widow.

Beatrice misinterpreted his remark, thinking he was still preoccupied by the armoured car.

'No. It wouldn't be any use. It's all over and done with.'

'I meant the curtains. Is it possible to open the window? I smoke when I'm working, and if there's no draught the room will stink of stale smoke forever.'

'Of course. Open whatever you wish. I'll show you the bathroom. There's only one for the whole house. Tell me your timetable and my younger sister and I will make sure you aren't disturbed.'

'Your sister? Did you say you had a sister?'

'You never met her. She was staying with some relations who live about twenty miles from here.'

'But you never talked about her.'

'The opportunity didn't arise.'

'So,' he said. 'Let's see this bathroom.'

It was an ancient place, full of antediluvian plumbing. The wash-basin, zinc bathtub and lavatory were all boxed in with polished brown wood. Like its counterpart on the stairs, the smoked glass window overlooked the courtyard, and if one wanted to use the mirror, it was impossible without having the electric light on. Beatrice had cleared a shelf for him. On the other two shelves were glasses, toothbrushes, a pot of cream and a bottle of very ordinary eau de cologne. The one sign of luxury in the room lay on the lace runner of the dressing table: a toilet case with brushes and combs in tortoiseshell inlaid with silver, struck in the arms of Varela. In the V formed by two épées were the words 'arela', 'incit'.

'That was the last present from Ugo III to Beatrice before their exile in 1755. Look at the brush handles and the pin box: there's a U and a B entwined. They loved each other.'

The way she said 'They loved each other' made Jacques turn

around and look at her with a sudden sadness of heart, discovering in these words what it was about Beatrice that refused all remedies, her stifling loneliness to which she was already resigned, and a sort of pathetic abandonment. Immediately she seemed to realise what she had given away, lifting her bent head and smiling as if she had just uttered the most natural words in the world, despite having said them in one of those places generally so inappropriate for confidences of that kind – a bathroom where the toilet seat had been left raised.

'I'll leave you,' she said. 'You might like to have a bath. The water isn't very hot, because we still burn wood and it's a very old system. Folco keeps it going. Dinner will be at eight. It's a little early, but on Saturday evenings Folco goes to the cinema. He has no other distractions during the week.'

'So in fact Folco does everything around the house.'

'Absolutely everything.'

She took him back to his room, showed him the cupboard, the drawers, the bookshelves which had been cleared for him to store his own books, the single lamp that he would have to carry from the desk to the bedside table if he wanted to read before going to sleep.

'I hope you'll be comfortable,' she said with a kind of forced gaiety as if, saying it, she could suddenly see just how antiquated, how threadbare, how uncomfortable the room really was, despite its being the best room the house possessed.

'Thank you for everything. I shall make myself so invisible that you'll pass me on the stairs without seeing me, and I'll glide over the floorboards so they won't even creak as I pass.'

'No, no, you mustn't. It's lovely to have you here. Actually I was getting impatient for you to arrive, and I've already brought down a suitcase of old papers that might interest you from the palace. But you aren't going to start work straightaway. Tomorrow is a Sunday, and I thought that since you have a car we'd go to a small farm about eight miles away: the tenants there are friends of mine, and they'll give us lunch. I can't remember where it was that I read it, but if you want to get to know a country and love it, first of all you have to eat everything it has to offer. You'll have kid roasted on a spit and *polenta*. You must try the fruit, our peaches in particular, the best in all Umbria, and I'll bet that Assunta will have baked us an almond

132

cake with almonds from her own trees. And after all that, how on earth can I ask her for the rent of the farm?'

She spread her hands, palms upwards, in a gesture both of impotence and of penury.

'I'm afraid,' Jacques said, 'that we won't all three of us be able to get into my Topolino. But I can always do two trips.'

'Oh, I don't know whether Francesca will be coming, and if she does, it will be on her motorbike. She bought a huge machine from the American army surplus, I can never remember the name, with an enormous number of c.c.'s – 500, 1000, 2000, I don't know – and in any case I have no idea what the c.c.'s are for, but Francesca is very proud of them, and you know she can dismantle her motorbike and put it back together again entirely on her own, without any help. You'll see her on the road one day with her jacket blown up by the wind and her helmet on. She looks like a big insect, something like a scarab beetle that leaves a cloud of dust behind it as it scuttles along. Do you want me to help you?'

'I'll manage, thank you... At twenty-nine, I'm already a practised bachelor. I can even sew on a button and iron a pair of trousers.'

'I'll leave you then. Until later.'

Since he had no desire to empty his yawning suitcases, which only contained the depressing sight of underwear and creased suits, Jacques opened the window wide and leant his elbows on the balcony that overlooked the *piazza del condottiere* in the yellowing light of the sunset. The wide square with its brick-red surface, the heart of Varela, came slowly to life. From their nests squeezed into the cornices of the houses and the palace, the swallows hurled themselves at the fountain, then rocketed back up and skimmed the walls in a dazzling display of aerobatic nerve that traced patterns in the sky, like an aerial ballet conducted by tiny black meteorites with white bellies. Directly below the window, small boys had surrounded the Topolino and were writing 'Clean me' on a rear windscreen quilted with dust. On the first-floor balcony of the town hall a man appeared, lowered the Italian tricolour, folded it with care and placed it beneath his elbows on the parapet to lean and gaze at the activity in the square. Figures moved, tentatively for the moment: groups of men in dark suits listening to the peroration of

133

one of their number; families come for the evening promenade, the wife walking unsteadily in patent leather high heels that pinched; maids in black frocks with starched aprons walking children up and down; the inevitable ice-cream seller in his white jacket, pushing his barrow with seemingly infinite patience as he waited for parents to walk by at least a dozen times before they yielded to their children's pleas and the desire of the mother who swiftly consumed a multi-coloured cone for herself.

What dead weight was it that lay upon Varela, circumscribing life into such narrowness, leaving it in appearance so dispirited, so colourless, so different to the bustle of Naples, of Rome, Milan, Venice? Apart from the groups of men who were probably discussing politics, the walkers ignored each other or acknowledged their neighbours with barely a nod. All had kept their felt hats securely on their heads, the brims turned down as if they were hiding an incipient baldness of which they were dreadfully ashamed. And yet these stiff and formal people walking up and down with deliberate solemnity in their dark, tight-fitting clothes all shared something in common: they loved the *piazza del condottiere* and its compensations for the long day's toil or idleness, and even if they no longer saw it with the appreciative eye that a stranger might have, they shared, deep in their hearts and perhaps even in their blood, an unconscious pride at living in a town that was one of Italy's jewels – however neglected a jewel it might be, however far from the tourist track, or even from the paths of war since the Allies had not bothered to send more than a single platoon of infantry there, and that only for a week before the town was restored to its previous lofty solitude.

On the balcony of the town hall the caretaker picked up his flag and closed the long window behind him. Had he dreamt for a moment that this was his palace, and that he was addressing the crowd thronging the square, as the last count of Varela had done two hundred years before when the town still breathed life? That was it, wasn't it. The town was dead, or as good as dead. It stood as it had always stood, built on this hill with its crater-like concavity, and now it was slipping into the earth and serenely awaiting, with barely a flicker of resentment, that subterranean tremor which would swallow it up.

134

As the first lights came on Jacques was struck by the length of time he had been standing leaning on the balcony and the fact that, already, Varela was exerting a fascination on him which had swept away the cold reception it had given him earlier in the day. He was reassured. He had come to unearth its secrets: the secret of its abrupt decline in the eighteenth century, the secrets of the town's bizarre conduct – and, it had to be said, that of Beatrice herself when he had come to occupy the fortress with his band of men. So vivid had the impression made by Beatrice on the young infantry lieutenant been that in the five intervening years not a day had passed without him thinking about her and the enigma she represented. But Jacques, unlike his commanding officer, was not the type to bull ahead brooking no attempts at resistance. And he might have done nothing at all, preferring to keep a troubling memory at the back of his mind, turning it over and caressing it as time passed until it had worn completely away, had Cléry not one day given him one of his lectures.

'My boy, it is quite fatal,' he said, 'to leave any of these puzzles lying about in the past. They can only poison the present. You run the risk – I'm quite serious – of becoming genuinely ill one day. I met Beatrice for five minutes. It was enough. She's the kind of woman who will give you no peace. Go back, exorcise the memory of her, and then you'll see why every other woman you've met since you left Varela has annoyed you or bored you stiff. Invent an excuse, any excuse will do, and go back there. When your classes are over, just pack up and leave. Tell Beatrice that you've come to write a history of her family. And while you're about it, see if you can clear up that mystery of the armoured car that ran rings around you for a week.'

Reluctantly leaving the balcony, Jacques pulled clothes out of his suitcase until he came across a sponge bag, and made his way to the bathroom. In the warm water of the bath he savoured a moment of bliss. His mind wandered pleasurably as the stresses of the long drive dissolved. Why had no sociologist ever come up with the idea of studying the relationship between people's psychological make-up and the places they bathed in? Tell me the kind of bathroom you keep, and I will tell you who you are. Beatrice and Francesca, perhaps out of poverty, perhaps out of desire for plain living, made

135

do with the minimum. There were no accumulations of creams, perfumes, bath salts or any of the other refinements used freely by women of their age. Apart from the sumptuous toilet case on the dressing table, there was not a trace of vanity anywhere. Beatrice would be thirty-five at the most. When she had mentioned Francesca she had said 'my younger sister'. Francesca might be as young as twenty-five. From the rough flannel on the edge of the bath, the hard hairbrush, the body-building springs hung on a peg, it was easy to see in the motorcycle enthusiast that Beatrice had described a woman who would much rather have been a man. Jacques imagined her, tall like her elder sister, offhand in manner, dressed habitually in her mechanic's overalls. If one were to believe in the notion that names predestine character, Francesca's temperament would have come direct from Francesco, the old *condottiere* with the furious stare. The only difference was that she had replaced the horse with her motorbike. Times changed... though clearly bathrooms did not always change with them. This one in particular was short on ventilation. The mirror over the washbasin was so misted up that when Jacques emerged from the bath he had to rub it with a towel before his reflection could struggle through in a series of spirals: his face with its hollow cheeks and prominent nose, his chin already blue with stubble after a too-early shave that morning before leaving Rome. In honour of Beatrice and Francesca he ran his razor quickly over his face once more before returning to his room.

The dining room was on the ground floor, reached through a small, cosy ante-room where Beatrice was waiting for Jacques, reading a book. As he came in she placed it face down, and he leant forward to try to decipher the name of the author.

'It's Stendhal's *Voyage en Italie*. I was wondering if he ever mentioned Varela. But he doesn't. Nor in his essays. Now and then I think we have never existed as far as strangers are concerned. But I suppose it doesn't really bother me. In many ways it's an ideal situation to be in, like floating in the air or drifting on the sea. Perhaps we really don't exist. We inhabit an idea instead. Didn't you have an odd feeling like that when you arrived here in the valley? A sort of – what would you call it? – disembodiment?'

'No, not at all! I even have evidence to prove that Varela exists. In the Bibliothèque Nationale I came across a manuscript letter by President de Brosses who travelled through Umbria in 1740. He describes to Monsieur de Neuilly how he arrived in the valley in an open post-chaise buffeted by the icy wind off the Appennines. He saw Varela, came into the town, but seems not to have had the goodwill to grant it a second glance. Your ancestor, Bernardo II, wasn't expecting him and couldn't even see him for five minutes. With the result, of course, that the President was furious. It was his considered opinion, he said, that the chicken served in the inn must have come from Rome on foot, that the wine from your vineyards was only fit for sluicing down the tables to wash away the flies, and that the Varelans had lost the power of speech.'

'That seems excessively vengeful for the sake of one unsuccessful audience, but I suppose we can forgive him, since his committing it to paper gives us one of the rare proofs of Varela's existence. I do hope you kept a copy of the letter. I'd like to read it in full. Would you like a drink?'

'No thank you.'

'Let's go in then.'

'What about your sister?'

'Francesca won't be dining with us.'

Folco was waiting for them in the dining room where a hideous, domed green overhead light illuminated the two place settings opposite one another with a cone of harsh light. Almost as soon as he had sat down, Jacques noticed that although their two torsos fell within this cone of light, their faces remained half in darkness. He found himself unnerved by Beatrice's pastel-coloured lips which had become blurred like the shading in a charcoal sketch, and her eyes now so brilliantly black that they seemed to be shining with fresh tears. Around them the chairs and the crockery and cutlery were poor quality, cheap and overdone in style. Well before the war the silver and the dinner service of Faenza porcelain embossed with the family arms had been sold off to various Roman antique dealers and replaced with yellowing bone-handled knives, very ordinary forks and spoons, and some rustic-style earthenware from Vietri.

All that was left were the Bohemian crystal glasses. Few of them matched, so they were unsaleable. That she was in horribly straitened circumstances Beatrice did not try to hide, but now and then a shadow would pass over her features despite her decision to make light of things:

'Since you first came,' she said, 'a lot of things have gone. How can I help it? I'm on my own. The day I get a bill from the tax people, from the men who repaired the roof, from the painter, they seem to appear with their vans. A chest of drawers disappears off to Rome, some chairs, an armchair. It gives me a breathing space.'

Jacques wondered whether the portraits hanging on the walls weren't copies. In the dimly lit room he had only just been able to make out their outline, and he made a mental note to question Beatrice later about the two noblemen and their two elegant companions who were deep in conversation in the shadows. Offended perhaps at having been relegated to minor roles, they gazed out over the heads of the two diners to a point somewhere in the far distance, a place where once the counts of Varela had scarcely had to suffer their subjects' respect at all, so much was it taken for granted. Distracted for a moment, Jacques turned back to Beatrice as she spoke.

'But why are we so forgotten, such orphans of history? This year we had ten visitors to the palace at 6 lire each, and as they were a party of deaf and dumb from the school at Viterbo they paid half-price. *Miseria . . . porca miseria*, Folco says. I sent a letter to Rome, to the ministry. It went unanswered. I went there in person, last year. Nobody knew where Varela was. I think they suspected me of fraud. Why don't we get any visitors apart from parties of deaf and dumb? We must have committed a monstrous sin that we've been ostracised for. Every winter we spend days cut off from the outside world: the passes are blocked by snowdrifts, then the wind turns them into blocks of ice and dynamite is the only way to get rid of them. The power lines come down, the telephone never answers . . .'

'But letters arrive!'

'No one ever writes to us.'

'I do.'

'Of course I'm exaggerating: one or two letters do arrive when the post-van doesn't find it simpler to throw them in the ditch and save itself the detour. Last winter we were cut off for a week. All the mountains around us were covered in snow, but the sky was clear and cloudless and during the day it felt exactly like spring. The fruit trees were confused by it and blossomed too early. We had peaches in May, and apples and grapes in June. That week of solitude was so unreal, so hard to believe, that Don Fabio, the priest, ordered a special service of thanksgiving.'

'There you are. You aren't cursed at all.'

'No, but being forgotten is worse. From a curse you can draw a kind of pride, even a fierce determination to defeat it. When you're forgotten, you can draw nothing from it. You have nothing to hold on to, you flounder in a void; all you can do is make feeble cries for help . . .'

Folco had hurried them through the meal, left the cheese and fruit on the table and disappeared to his Saturday night film starring his favourite actor.

'I don't suggest we go and join him. The film will be scratched to death and the sound inaudible. Since I can't offer you anything else by way of distraction, perhaps you'd like to go for a walk around the town?'

She wrapped her throat and shoulders in a mauve shawl which – Jacques could not help the thought – aged her. As if she guessed what he was thinking, or perhaps because she herself was sensitive to the fact, she sought an excuse:

'Yes, I know it's old-fashioned, but it came from my mother who had probably already had it passed down to her. Imagine one of my relations, long dead, sitting by the window and crocheting this while she watched out for a single passer-by – her sole distraction. After she gets married, an Umbrian woman is condemned to dress in black. There is always someone dying in her own family or her husband's. Even for a distant cousin she has never seen, who has been living in the United States or the Argentine for fifty years, she puts on mourning clothes. Black is a shroud for us. Because they have to wear black, Italian women are weighed down by an incurable dejection that works its way into their souls. Their voices become fretful and plaintive. Mauve is the only colour they are allowed. In any case . . . I have no other shawl!'

The *piazza del condottiere* was deserted and made Jacques

wonder if the feeble signs of life it had shown before dinner hadn't been deliberate decoys, if the people walking sedately up and down hadn't been puppets worked by an invisible puppet-master hidden on the flat roof of the palace. At the four corners of the square stood lamp-holders whose bulbs threw yellowish circles of light in which thick clouds of moths were caught like a swirling storm of snowflakes. Beneath the arcade a single shop-front was lit, that of a café whose pavement tables had been piled on top of each other, ade. Inside there were two men seated at different tables far apart. Motionless, like wax dummies, they sat with their felt hats firmly on their heads. The round table-tops in front of them contained only a coffee cup and a glass dish which had once had ice cream in it. Beatrice drew Jacques to a halt with a hand on his forearm.

'Look at that picture of life in Varela,' she whispered. 'The man on the right, the one who is so pale and emaciated, that's our poet, Gianni Coniglio. He wrote an ode to Francesco di Varela which he got published in Florence under a *nom de plume*. But nobody here would believe he had written it. They thought he was mad, a megalomaniac falsely attributing some great poet's work to himself. After that he shut himself away. Now, every evening after dinner, he comes to the café to eat his ice cream and contemplate the empty square through the window. When we were children we had the same French tutor; she went to him in the mornings and came to us in the afternoons. You will be surprised: when I meet Gianni, we speak French to one another. In five minutes he tells me everything he keeps from everyone else. Then for a month after that he'll pass me in the street without seeing me. All the same I know he is still writing. And guess what he writes.'

'Alexandrine laments?'

'Not a bit of it. Ever since the ode to the *condottiere* he has written nothing but erotic poetry – often erotic to the point of obscenity. He never tells me about his poems, but he sends them to me by post. I often wonder whether he has ever known a woman. Perhaps he was once tempted by one of those creatures who sell themselves on street corners in Rome or Milan. It can't have been anywhere else. Least of all here. Those things are so tightly controlled here that the only females one ever exchanges a few words with are one's mother and sister.'

'There's you as well.'

'Oh, I'm a lost cause. But I can carry my bad reputation cheerfully enough. If, in spite of everything, the people here show me some indulgence it is because I am the Contessina Beatrice and my ancestor Francesco *furioso* still stands guard at the town gates. They are still rather in awe of him.'

Beatrice withdrew her hand from Jacques' forearm. They stood side by side, out of sight of the two men, who were so unmoving that Jacques would have liked some confirmation that they had not simply been placed there as wax models to make believe that Varela had some kind of night life.

'And who publishes his erotic poems?'

'No one.'

'So how do people know about him?'

'The whole of Varela heard tell of his poetry one Sunday in church. Don Fabio was thundering from the pulpit about a corrupter of the town's youth, whom he did not name; nevertheless everyone knew who he meant. Gianni had had the brilliant idea of sending the priest a copy of his poems.'

'What about the other man?'

Jacques caught Beatrice's hesitation, the shiver and the way she stiffened before answering in a voice devoid of expression:

'A painter. Our only artist. It is virtually a miracle that Varela should have given birth to both a poet and a painter. They are regarded as if they were abnormal, degenerate. Belponi they think possesses every vice under the sun, as if in this closed society a person could take up one single vice without being stoned to death by outraged townspeople. He's off-putting enough in appearance, anyway: look at his blue chin and those hands resting on his knees. Do you remember the five Varelans whose bodies your men discovered almost as soon as they arrived? He cut their throats single-handed. He would have cut the throats of others if King Cléry hadn't issued his proclamation. Sometimes I say to myself 'poor Belponi'. He is a victim of the way he looks. People have made him out to be some sort of executioner – just because of his hands. A man who only ever painted nativity scenes, devotional pictures. He did the killings because the others didn't have the nerve; but afterwards his painting changed. All he paints now are things that are so intolerably tragic I cannot see how anyone can want to buy them and live with them. And yet, without him leaving here, without him answering a single enquiry, galleries in Turin and Milan come to him to buy his paintings. Come. Let's walk through a dead town.'

They slipped down dark alleys stinking of refuse and cats. Through the slats of the closed shutters filtered thin rays of light which were extinguished at their passing, and switched back on as they moved away.

'They're watching us,' she said. 'Everyone knows you've come and that you're living in the house with me. They turn out the lights to see you better and so that that you can't see their silhouettes through the blinds. I think it's unlikely that they will have recognised you. Five years might as well be a hundred as far as they are concerned. You aren't in uniform either, and I'd say that you have grown even taller . . .'

The idea that the town locked itself away at night had taken such a hold on Jacques that he was surprised to see the great gate, through which he had arrived with the Topolino that afternoon, standing open. As if they were leaving a prison a cool breeze sprang up, loaded with the valley's spicy scents. He recognised the smell of thyme, faint and so fleeting that no sooner had one breathed it than it faded away, to return in gentle waves to play on the senses.

The *condottiere* had turned his back on them. The only light showing at the entrance to the citadel was too dim to reach him and all they could make out at first were the legs of the horse. Its rump, its head and the *condottiere* himself appeared progressively as their eyes became used to the darkness. His épée raised, he watched over his stronghold, but as the countryside around was silent and no bands of horsemen galloped through the plain to storm the sleeping town, the poor *condottiere* had something of an air of a Don Quixote about him.

'This isn't his rightful place,' said Beatrice as if to apologise for him. 'In the papers that I've given you I found a decree by Ugo I ordering the removal of the statue to outside the town walls. Before, he stood in the square, facing the palace. Ugo I took against him. He liked only things that reminded him of the Renaissance and disliked anything to do with soldiers. Ugo II replaced the *condottiere* with the fountain that you saw. Poor Francesco, deposed in favour of a siren in the style of Giambologna. Not even a genuine one! She wouldn't have stood up to the bad weather, and they had to cast a replica. The original is in the main hall with all the other statues which you will be seeing. I think she must have the most beautiful breasts in the world. Come, I'm cold.'

They made their way back to the *piazza del condottiere* by another collection of narrow streets just as the radio station began to broadcast the latest episode of a soap opera which appeared to be extremely popular with the inhabitants of Varela. From house to house a dialogue punctuated by the noisy laughter of the actors followed the two walkers. This anachronism was unbearable to Jacques. He had arrived in Varela to treat it as a place which was sacrosanct; he was succumbing to Beatrice's charm; he was living in the room from which he had once ruled as regent over the whole valley; he had seen, through a sort of one-way mirror, a poet all but walled up in his solitude, and a painter with blood on his hands; he had walked between high walls of houses in step with a young woman susceptible to the cool night air, whose only protection was a mauve shawl thrown about her; and now, just at the moment when a certain pitch of elation had touched his spirit and lightened his footsteps on the uneven cobblestones, there was a radio soap opera with its thick laughter and piercing voices to send the whole edifice crashing down.

'Don't let it upset you,' said Beatrice. 'It's over at eleven o'clock and then everybody goes to bed. Even Belponi and Gianni Coniglio.'

'What about the *condottiere*?'

'Oh, he spent a great deal of money on a magic potion which would keep him awake all night.'

'Ah. Now you're reading my mind.'

'Yes, I should have warned you . . . A lot of people don't care for it at all.'

'I shall have to watch what I'm thinking in future.'

'Impossible!'

L'AMOUR

by

Clare Boylan

The trouble was that I was an animal lover. I mean to say, that was the source of all our troubles. I was taken from my role of son at the age of eight by the death of my mother. 'Angels lead our sister into paradise,' said the minister. I was left behind on earth with my father and mother's cat which was blind in one eye and had a fungal infection of the fur, but we hadn't the heart to put it down.

My father and I did not know what to do with each other. We had never taken much notice of one another, being perfectly content with the attention of my mother. After her death we abided. At mealtimes we met at table and waited until it became evident that her ghost would not flutter down with meat and pots of mashed potato and then we would rise silently and separately and arm ourselves with jam and cheese and biscuits and things in tins and pots. We did not panic when the food ran out. We had each recognised my mother as the source of nourishment and comfort and accepted that these had died along with her. After a time my father said to himself: 'The boy is growing. I must see to the business of food.'

He made a jelly. It was constructed in layers of different colours. Each shade had to be allowed to set before another layer was applied. It took several days to complete and was displayed on a plate on the draining board. In some way or other it did not live up to our expectations and we left it there until it slid down into a pool of its own rust-coloured water.

'What would you like?' my father said.

'I'd like ... a kitten.'

He bought me two. By the time they were finished leaving puddles under the kitchen table, they were leaving their own kittens in the linen press. I got a donkey from a man in the street by giving him my bicycle. A dog followed me home from school. Boys gave me the things their parents would not allow them to keep – a snake, a pet rat, a poisonous spider. I had a thrush, too, that the cats had knocked about a bit and I had rescued. It grew so tame it would sit on my hand and we would whistle at each other. Other birds and less friendly animals lived in secret places in the garden and I climbed trees to look at robins' eggs and lay on my stomach over a muddy pool to watch the sluggish evolution of frogs. I was very keen on them all, even snails with their outer-space aerials and their pearly trails. Some of them liked me too. In this way, in due course, I learned to do without my mother.

It was different for my father. He could not adapt. Although it was obvious to both of us that no one could ever take the place of mother, he began, quite soon after her death, to look for someone who would stand in her place. I don't think he cared what she was like. The ladies he brought home to tea were of such varying quality that he might have chosen them from a bus queue. One of them had cheeks like raw liver dipped in flour and I had to kiss her. 'This is Miss Dawlish', he introduced (or on other occasions, Miss Reddy or Miss Frostbite or Miss Havanagila, I think); and his eyes would say, 'Be nice to her.' I was nice to them all. I showed them my snake and my poisonous spider. In spite of this they never came back.

'I believe it is because of the boy's animals,' my father confided to an aunt when he thought I was not listening.

'Of course it is,' the aunt said sharply. 'What free agent would wish to take on a zoo as well as another woman's child?'

He never said anything to me. He would no more interfere in my life than I would in his. The stream of ladies ceased and he grew very silent.

One spring, two years after my mother's death, I noticed that he was happy again. He had come back from a business visit to Paris and when he fetched me from my aunt, he was full of energy and jokes, the way he used to be when mother was alive and they were going to a dance. Shortly after this he paid some more brief visits to Paris and then he asked me if I would like to have a holiday there. I said that I would. I was very interested in Paris. My parents had once had a postcard from Paris, from a friend who was on holiday there and on the back she wrote, 'Watching the world go by in gay Paree!' (which is how Paris is pronounced there). I thought at the time that it would be phenomenal to be in a place where one could watch the whole world go by.

When father told me that he had a friend there – a Mademoiselle Duclos – whom he wished me to meet, I took no more notice than I had of the Dawlishes and Frostbites. I was too interested in Paris. A lot of my concentration went on persuading Mrs Crutch, who did our housework, to feed my pet animals and insects. I got over these difficulties, father bought me an astonishing suit of clothes which made me look like a man of twenty, and we were on our way.

I was not able to form an immediate impression of Paris, for we were taken first to our hotel which was a *château* some distance from the city, where we were to stay and to meet Mlle Duclos. It was a smashing place, full of towers like wizards' hats. A long drive hid its curves under trees and in between the splashes of leaves, the starker branches of a deer's horns made patterns on the sky. I had to press myself against the window of the car to make out that the grey bumps, crouched behind swarms of bluebells, were not stones but baby rabbits. We came to the castle entrance. A conference of important-looking little dogs with ears like wigs ranged about the steps, and in the doorway was a princess.

She was the most beautiful lady I have ever seen. A long yellow soft dress, with sleeves like butterflies, reached almost to her ankles. She was tall but delicate-looking and had a cloud of brown hair. I glanced at my father and could see that he too was under the spell of the castle and its princess. He drove the car with his eyes, very bright, fixed on the lady.

'What do you think, Nicholas?'

'Brillo!' I whispered.

'Precisely,' he laughed.

He stopped the car and got out, seeming to forget about me, which I did not mind. He ran up the steps and the little dogs stiffened and shouted angrily.

'Darling!' he called.

The princess turned to him and smiled. She held out her arms and he went into them, humbly, like someone receiving a blessing. After they had kissed he turned and summoned me with an excited wave. I ran out of the car and scrambled up the steps.

'Say hello to Mlle Duclos,' he said.

Nothing had prepared me for this. She bore no more resemblance to the Dawlishes than did the castle to a dog kennel.

With an effort I stuck out my hand. 'How do you do, Mlle Duclos?'

She bent to study me and her hair fell down, framing her face. 'You must call me Marie,' she said. 'I think we are going to be friends.' She kept hold of my hand when she straightened and turned to my father. 'He is exactly like you. What a nice surprise!' she said.

I could see immediately why my father looked at her in such a dazed way. In that moment all I wanted was to have her smile on me, her hand in my hand. We went into lunch and sat at a table, all of us smiling. No one here knows that my mother is dead, I thought. No one knows we are not a proper family.

Father and Marie ordered *escargots* and *langoustes*. 'What would you like, little picture of your papa?' she whispered to me.

'Chips,' I whispered back.

She pushed my hair from my forehead. 'In France, the children are not treated like little animals, fed with the scraps from the plates of adults. Here, you will learn to dine properly, even with a taste of wine. Have you ever eaten *escargots*?'

I shook my head. I could see my father looking at me hopefully.

'Have them to please me,' Marie said.

'All right,' I nodded.

'What a nice boy.' She rubbed my hair. 'I don't think I am going to let you go.'

How happy my father looked then, no longer lonely, reaching out to touch her arm while her hand still rested on my head so that we were all joined together like daisies in a chain. Later I wished we could have all died in that moment so that none of us would ever know loneliness again, or fear.

The *escargots* came, little curls of something in a dish with holes. I ate one and decided that if I thought about something else I could probably finish them. I had got about halfway around the holes when Marie leaned towards me and said, in that confidential way that made one dizzy, 'What do you think?'

I smiled and shrugged, my mouth full of buttery rubber.

'*Escargots!* Do you know what they are?'

I saw that my father looked alarmed when she said this and his anxiety transmitted to me. 'What are they?' I demanded.

'Ha! Ha!' Her giggle was now like a girl's. An older girl's. 'They are snails, my pet.'

I spat it out. The snail. I felt she had perpetrated a terrible trick, not only on me but on my father.

'Nicholas!' My father was horrified but I would not look at either of them. My father kept on chewing until he had eaten all of the snails on his dish.

I might have forgotten the incident. Marie looked as upset and bewildered as I did. Then the waiter came carrying three poor creatures that were trying to escape.

'*Voila/!* Our lobsters!' said Marie in excitement.

'They're alive!' I was horrified.

'Not for long!' Her delicate, teasing laugh rang out as their slow pincers struggled with the air.

I ran out of the restaurant and stayed there, kicking a bed of flowers to pieces until father came to look for me. 'Dirty foreigners! Filthy foreign savages!' I aimed at the heads of quivering daffodils.

'Marie said I should come.' Father looked miserable. 'She thought she ought to leave us alone. She will join us again later.'

I said nothing.

'Don't you like her?'

I shook my head.

'I thought you seemed happy. I was so pleased,' he said.

'She's a sneak,' I shouted. 'She made me eat a snail.'

'No, no! It is the custom of the country. The animals do not suffer. You must learn to adapt.'

He looked as lost as I did. Neither of us was adaptable. I wondered if, like me, he was remembering my mother's meals, shepherd's pies and rice puddings, food that had long lost its connection with any living source. I thought of her apron and her body beneath it, a fathomless cushion, where one could lie when one was confused, and love came out but she never looked for anything as demanding, in return, as friendship.

In the afternoon father showed me Paris. He told me about the buildings, places of art and war and opera, dulling the sunny streets with clouds of history. I preferred the cafés and markets, the little batto boats on the river. 'What do you think, Nicholas?' father said. It was a city of the dead; statues of dead generals by dead sculptors. It reminded me of the place where I had stood in the most inestimable fear with, overhead, the foreign storm of adult weeping and down below, in the ground and powerless to take control, my mother. I said none of this to my father. Instead, I said, 'I'd like to go to the place where you can watch the world go by.'

He brought me to a wide, pretty street with trees and heavy traffic and we sat at a tin table outside a café. We ate ice-creams. A lot of people passed, some who hurried and some who seemed to regard the boulevard as a drawing room in their own home, but although I looked and looked, there was no change of scenery, no yellow hills of Montana nor snow-capped Swiss mountains. 'It's only a street,' I said indignantly. 'You cannot watch the world from here.' Father seemed not to hear. 'Nicholas!' He leaned forward suddenly, his face as serious as if I was another adult. 'You must make an effort with Marie. In due course I know you will come to love her as I do.'

I was confused by this word, 'love'. 'She's not my mother,' I said.

'She will be a sister – a friend.'

'I have my animals.'

For a moment he was silent. 'I haven't told her,' he said.

We were both desperate. 'Don't let her hurt them,' I said.

'She will accept them but first you must accept her.'

The anxiety in his voice made me nervous. 'What if she does not accept them? What if she had a boy and he had a lot of animals, father? Would you accept them?'

'I would accept anything that was a part of Marie. I know it is not fair to speak to you like this, Nicholas, but I cannot lose her. I would be lost without her. I know she liked you but if she thought you did not like her she would not wish to intrude. She is a woman of sensibility.'

I thought of her laughing at the lobsters.

'Promise me, Nicholas' – my father spoke urgently – 'that you will be friendly and behave.'

I felt sorry for him. I was going to say yes, I would behave, but he did not wait for my answer. He saw Marie approaching then and he stood and waved to her. He looked like a blind man, blinded by her bright smile and I thought that he was lost with her or without her.

In another moment my resolve became unecessary for her hand was on my head and her kiss on my cheek and a rush of complicit whispers in my ear and I laughed with happiness.

We were all holding hands again when we moved off. We went to see the Cathedral of Notre Dame, huge and black inside with a big window of many colours 'like a firework in the night,' Marie said, leaning down, close to my ear.

Later, father and Marie went into a bookshop called 'Shakespeare & Company' and I stayed outside in the sun and read messages from a glass-covered noticeboard that was there. *Widower, formerly married to woman with loose dentures, with whom conversation was like water dripping from a stalactite to stalagmite, seeks quiet girl like Emmy in Vanity Fair.* It made me wonder if the whole world was full of widowers in search of ladies to replace their wives? If he saw Marie would he think she looked like Emmy in *Vanity Fair*? In my mind, the defect of the widower's wife was transferred to himself, and I saw him with his rainy teeth, approaching the bookshop in search of his reply. I looked around quickly. There was no one who resembled the squishy-toothed widower but all the same I went and stood guard in the doorway of the bookshop in case he should come along and see Marie and try to claim her.

That night we ate in a restaurant where each dish was covered in a silver dome. Marie was like a fairy princess with her hair done up on top of her head and a dress of something blue and filmy. She and father drank champagne, giving me a little in a glass, so that by the time we went in to dinner I was a bit foolish.

The menu was brought – like a huge birthday card with a picture of wildlife on its cover and each inscription inside an exercise in calligraphy.

'Something light,' Marie suggested. 'A little *pâté* or some *cuisses de grenouilles*.'

'Kwees . . . ?' I giggled.

'*Cuisses de grenouilles* – frogs' legs!' said Marie with her lovely smile.

'I'll have the *pâté*,' I said quickly, hiding my horror. 'I have tasted *pâté*.'

'Not this *pâté*, little one,' she said. 'This is a speciality – very good. *Pâté de grives* – thrush *pâté*.'

'No!' I cried out, horrified. I thought of the family of thrushes in our garden, sunbathing on heaps of mown grass, their wings spread like fans. They swooped into our peach tree and called to one another when the fruit was ripe.

'The boy is . . . fond of animals.' Father looked embarrassed. He shot me a yearning glance.

'Of course he is.' Marie was relieved. 'But these are not pets. These are garden pests – frogs and thrushes.'

'I have a pet thrush,' I told her.

'Aah!' She made a face, considering. 'You must tell me about yourself. Everything!'

'I have a dog and a donkey and six cats.'

Father looked as if he was in pain.

'. . . a pet rat and a snake and a spider.'

Marie was nonplussed. She grinned first and then, seeing that I was serious, she shuddered. 'My God, what a *ménagerie*!' She spoke rapidly to my father in French while I strained to understand but he, seeing my anxiety, gave a little hopeless smile and said for both of us in English:

'I am afraid, my dear, that they are all quite indispensable. They are his family.'

She sipped her wine and swirled the contents of her glass. 'I am afraid of spiders,' she said to herself. 'A donkey! A rat! *Mon Dieu*!'

When a very long time had passed she turned to me with that bright smile of hers. 'May I join your family, Nicholas?' Father and I laughed with relief and we raised our glasses. 'What a *ménagerie*!' she said again.

Marie ordered for us all. 'Do you have pet prawns?' she said. I had had a few sips of wine diluted with water by now and I laughed like a drunk old man.

We ate our prawns and made our plans. Marie was going to come and live with us. When she had got the house in order she would work with my father in his antiques business. Sometimes she spoke to father alone and ignored me as if I was a child, which made me jealous. Sometimes she pretended that father was an old man and that she and I were the same age. 'Have you ever had a pony? Your old papa is too decrepit to ride a horse but you and I, Nicky, will have ponies and will go riding in the fields.'

The argentine domes of our main courses arrived. Marie lifted one and closed her eyes to sniff. 'Now I think I have chosen well,' she said. 'A little crispy duck for your papa and I, and for Nicky, a more delicate fowl.'

'Kentucky Fried Chicken,' I cried cheekily, executing a mock drum roll upon the dome of my dish with my knife and fork and making the adults laugh but retaining enough sense to know that I must not actually allow the cutlery to touch the silver. I swept up the cover from my dish. A tiny bird, no bigger than a robin, it seemed, lay dead and bleeding on a piece of toast. The shock was such that I glanced up quickly to see if the others had noticed but they had lost interest in me and were busy with their plans. 'No!' I said, but silently. I covered it up in its silver coffin. Some chips had come with the main course, and I ate those.

'Have some cheese!' Marie said, when our dishes had been taken away. 'Or would you prefer dessert?'

'No thank you. I'm a bit tired,' I said. 'May I go to bed now, please?' I had seen a table of delicious sweet things near the entrance to the restaurant but they might be hedgehogs covered in whipped cream or chocolate-coated mice. I slid down from my chair and left the room quickly before they could argue. In the doorway I turned and looked back. Their hands were joined across the table, their faces lit with happiness. I had not failed my father. He would not lose her. But as I stood there, feeling small and brave, straining to see them through the teasing filter of woven candle flames, past the wealthy diners eagerly dissecting small birds and fishes and waiters scurrying with mirrored prisons of more slaughtered wildlife, I suffered another shock. It was the realisation that I had not allowed myself that last look to assure myself of my father's salvation but for another glimpse, for myself, of Marie.

In bed that night I had a dream.

I was walking up the path to the *château*. I came across a mass of creatures seeking shelter beneath a large tree from the breeze: furry rabbits, baby deer, lobsters, pheasants and smaller birds, shuddering dreadfully. I went to look for the gamekeeper. 'Look at these creatures,' I rebuked. 'They are so cold! See how they shiver. Why are they not properly housed?' The old keeper pointed to the sunny sky. 'Cold? No, my little man. They are watching the approach of the gourmet. They are terrified.'

In the morning I ran to find Marie. She was on the terrace, having breakfast with my father. She put out her arms and I laid my head on her white angora sweater. 'Marie,' I whispered. 'This is a secret. Don't tell my father. Why do French people eat so many little animals? I don't mind the big ones, but the little ones!'

She dipped her roll into coffee and held it out to me to bite the hot, soggy, buttery mass. 'A secret,' she said. 'Yes. God put the little creatures on the earth for our pleasure. They know this. They are happy to die for me.'

I believed her. I would have died for her too.

For some reason father seemed discontented this morning. He remained silent through most of the breakfast and then he said to me: 'We are going out to lunch. Marie's *maman* will be joining us.' He said it like a challenge, as if he expected me to object. I did not mind. I knew that it was customary for a lady to introduce a prospective husband to her mother and I was surprised my father did not know this.

'If you marry father,' I said to Marie, 'your mother will be a part of our family too. She will be our gran.'

Marie stroked my hair. 'You are an exceptionally nice and clever boy,' she said; and father frowned.

Meeting Marie's mother was as much of a surprise as meeting Marie herself had been. She was dressed in black and she was old, old – the sort of old that seems never to have been young, like a parsnip. I could see that father did not like to think that this ancient root was a source of Marie. Normally when speaking to old people, he made himself seem older to put them at their ease. Now he seemed very young and offhand, a lout. She did not appear to like him either but gave a very insincere little laugh when Marie presented him with breathless pride.

She was put into the back of the car with me and we drove away. For a while she did not say anything but looked out of the window. Then she said to nobody in particular, 'He thinks he is on trial but it is I who am on trial.' She gave me a very bitter little smile and after that she did not speak until we got to the restaurant.

We came into a very pretty place with plates on the walls and thick lace curtains on the windows and, in the centre, a long table covered with tarts. I was put sitting opposite the old woman. My father sat across from Marie, his eyes smiling and his stubborn look gone.

The menu was scrawled in pen on a piece of card. I read it several times over but could find nothing that was not cruel: the oysters eaten live (I once heard that they flinch when you put on the lemon juice), the *foie gras* of force-fed geese, the veal of imprisoned calves, lobsters boiled alive. 'I'll have melon,' I said miserably and ... 'steak'; for at least the cow was large and fed a lot of people.

'No, no, dear little peasant,' Marie said. 'Have some oysters. Have them for me.'

'Melon! Melon and fish and chips.' The old woman spoke out. 'I have no teeth to chew and my stomach prefers plain food. Keep me company.'

'All right,' I said and gave a silent sigh of relief that I would not have to eat anything which was cooked alive.

My father ordered the food and a bottle of wine and some water. He poured wine for himself and Marie while she poured water into her mother's glass and mine. She took the wine from father then and used it to top up our glasses. 'Talk to my *maman* and I will talk to your papa,' she whispered into my ear.

The old woman was looking around the restaurant, tearing pieces of bread from the slices in a basket and chewing on them rapidly.

'I have to talk to you,' I said after a while.

'Well I hope you have something interesting to say.' She lifted up her glass. '*Santé!*' She tasted her diluted drink and then puckered her mouth into an old, savage grin. '*Elle a baptisé le vin,*' she said with a look of contempt for Marie.

I told her about my animals but I did not think she was very interested. She kept looking around her at other guests and seemed most concerned by old ladies of her own age. 'Watch her!' She would jab a finger at a very dainty old woman, dining on her own. 'See her!' She pointed out an ancient creature presiding over a Sunday lunch of several generations. The woman had whiskers and grey hair cut short like a man's and looked almost identical to her old husband who sat beside her.

When the food was brought Marie's mother ate it as a bird eats, her head on one side, considering the tastes. Every so often a jerk of the head towards me and my glass indicated that I should drink the watered wine.

'I'm not very fond ...' I tried to say. She made a rapid movement with her hand to dispose of my argument.

'Good for the stomach!' she said.

Father and Marie leaned across the table so that their faces were close and they talked together in low voices. They seemed indifferent to the food. They ate very little although they drank the wine.

In a strange way, I felt quite comfortable with the old woman. She spoke to herself, sometimes. When her fish was put before her she stared at it sadly. 'Pusspusspusspuss,' she called out hopefully, looking under the table. She pushed the plate aside. '*Des hot dogs*,' she said. '*Et des glaces. Avec des noix.*' She was dreaming. '*Et des cerises*!' Her eyes filled with tears. She looked up then and gave me her sour little grin. I ate a great many chips and drank the Ribena-coloured wine and after a while I got a feeling of exceptional power and peace.

The old woman, I noticed, drained her glass very quickly although each time she drank from it she made a face which suggested she did not like its contents. When her glass was empty, Marie would absent-mindedly attend to the mixing of liquids. Granny kept an eye on Marie and on the bottle. She did not look at her the way my mother used to look at me. It was hard to think of her as Marie's *maman*. She seemed quite removed from her – quite removed from everything, in fact, except the mixture in her glass. When she spoke again it was with a sharp tug at Marie's sleeve. 'The wine is finished!'

Marie gave father an apologetic smile but he looked understanding and signalled at once for more wine. To my astonishment, the old woman winked at me.

Wine was poured. Father filled glasses for himself and Marie and then they raised them and touched them gently and their eyes had a soft burning look with a gentle light like candles. They moved the glasses, still touching, away from their faces and very slowly their faces touched; their lips.

'They haven't ...' I was about to protest that they hadn't put water and wine into our glasses but the old woman put a bony finger to her lips and eyed me severely. I hung my head and sighed in confusion. A touch on my head made me look up. That same finger was on my head. The old woman was smiling at me the way that adults look at each other when they know something that you do not. She lifted her finger from my head in such slow motion that my

158

eyes were forced to follow it. A corner of her eye watched our kissing relatives. The finger swivelled clockwards and stopped upon the wine bottle. With astonishing speed she seized the bottle and filled both our glasses. She made a motion to me that I should drink it up quickly. I did as I was told, too amazed by her boldness to notice the bitter taste. When I had drained my glass I gave a laugh, a hoarse laugh that sounded strange to me and she nodded and gave an ordinary old woman's laugh.

She raised her eyebrows now, with a little smile for her foolish daughter and my entranced father. Father held Marie's face with the tips of his fingers. Once more the old woman's hand moved slowly over the table and made a catlike pounce on the bottle. As she was refilling our glasses, Marie gave a funny little grunt – the sort of noise you would make if cream from an éclair spilled on your chin – and her arm groped sideways and took the bottle from her mother. She held it up to father and gestured sideways with her eyes to let him know what had happened. Father looked quite shocked, but he looked dazed too and when Marie laughed he beamed on us all. The old woman gave him a poisonous smile. Father and Marie returned to their courtship but they kept the bottle on their own side of the table.

'*Merde!*' said the granny.

'That's a curseword!' I said.

She looked at me scornfully. 'I don't suppose you know any cursewords?'

'I do.'

'Go ahead!'

'It's not allowed.'

'*Cul!*' she said provocatively.

'That's a terrible word!' I looked around in case anyone might have heard it. I lowered my voice. 'It means your bum!'

'Bum!' the old woman cackled with delighted wickedness. 'You said a bad word. Bum! Bum!'

'That's not a bad word. I know much worse than that.'

'I don't believe you.'

'Shitehawk!' I shouted out.

Father looked around in alarm and confusion, as one woken from a dream. 'Nicholas!'

'Sorry, father.'

'It's the wine,' Marie giggled.

'Don't worry,' the granny said. 'I can handle him. Pphhh!' – she made a noise to suggest that she was already worn out with handling. 'But not without my medicine!' She held out her glass.

'I don't know!' Marie shook her head; 'two delinquents!' She dealt the glass its watery mixture and left the bottle in the centre of the table.

'That spider of yours,' the old woman said. 'Is it poisonous?'

'Of course.'

'How do you know? Has it ever bitten anyone?'

'No!'

'Is it ... deadly?'

'I think a doctor could save you,' I hazarded.

'Then we must try it out sometime.' She raised her glass to her lips but instead of drinking with it she merely gestured with it and muttered with a grin, *'Du pipi d'âne!'*; and then with a conjurer's flick she emptied the mixture into a plant which was on the edge of our table, in a pot wrapped in red crepe paper.

She filled our glasses deftly with unadulterated wine and raised hers once more but instead of the usual phrase she said in a ladylike and barely audible murmur, *'Salaud!'* I drew in my breath with excitement and admiration. She managed to make it sound like a harmless salute but this was a really strong curse. A boy in school had told me. It meant ... bastard!

I gulped from my glass. 'Arseholes!' I hissed.

'Salope!'

'Horsepiss!'

'Zizi!'

'Ratfort!'

'Trou de balle!'

I drank more wine. It had the colour of cherries, the taste of fruit and fire. It filled my head with wildness and I dared say anything. 'Fff....' I drew out the worst word of all, pressing my teeth down into my lower lip.

'Non!' The old lady looked alarmed.

'That's a really bad word, isn't it?' My eyes were sparkling and my head swam. 'I don't care how bad it is, I'm going to say it.'

'I know your word,' she said. 'It is not so bad. It is a sad word.'

160

'Sad?' I said with a coarse laugh. 'Do you understand it?'

'Do *you* understand it?'

I understood and I did not. 'It's awfully rude. It has to do with men and women.'

'Ah, yes,' she said. '*L'amour.*'

'Love!'

'Love? *Non.* I prefer *l'amour.* Your English love is too noble – too full of expectation and disappointment. Too full of duty to parents and country. *L'amour* is touching and foolish and human.'

She leaned across the table until she was as close to me as father was to Marie. 'It is –'; she tapped the table for emphasis; '– the miracle of creation in the magic of enchantment. Only a sad man would so curse his frustration.'

The moment passed. It was as if it had never happened. The old woman called out for strawberry tart. She dug her spoon into the glistening bumps of fruit and made sounds of appreciation.

She had forgotten me. Worse, Marie had forgotten me. I turned to her in appeal but she was lost to me, far away on some voyage of the heart, safe in the magic of enchantment.

'What are you thinking?' The old woman had finished her tart.

I pretended I had not heard. Her foolishness had cost me Marie's attention.

'You are thinking about *l'amour*. You are thinking you know it all and you are a disillusioned fellow.'

I shook my head crossly.

'You are jealous of my daughter and your father because they have found happiness in each other; because they need no one else.'

'It's true!' I said. 'They're all right. They don't want us.'

'Poor fellow. Have some tart. Already you are a victim.'

I ate the tart. It was glorious.

'There will come a moment in your life,' the woman who looked like a parsnip was saying, 'when you will look at a person the way *they* look at one another and from that moment you will never be free.'

'Then it's a spell! It's a trap!'

'How quickly you are growing up,' she said. 'It is not the spell that is the trap. It is the vanishing of *l'amour* that imprisons us. Where did it go? How can we live without it?'

161

'Well . . . how?'

'There is no answer. Whole lives are spent searching for it, trying to entice it back. Look!' She pointed out a beautifully dressed old lady who was dining on her own. 'Do you know who that lady is? That is the dognapper of Paris. Once she was a respectable woman but she fell in love with a man who was married. Love made her disreputable. When he left her she was so lonely she took to stealing little dogs. She had dozens of them in her apartment. Watch her closely! See her now!' She turned to point out the whiskery old peasant at whom she had earlier been staring. 'That is the richest woman in France. Her husband still loves her.'

Almost as she spoke the old man at her side turned and said something to her and then he kissed her whiskery, horrible mouth and smiled into her eyes.

'Then Marie and my father must be very rich,' I said.

The old woman shrugged. 'They are gamblers. Their fortune depends on the turn of a card. Marie is very young. When she looks at him she sees in his eyes a mirror of her own perfection. Wait until they each discover that the other is not perfect! *Quelle barbe!*'

'But Marie is kind! She is willing to put up with all my animals.'

'She is a clever girl. She has thought to herself: He is growing up. Soon he will be tired of all these rats and spiders. It is not long to wait. Or else she believes she can charm you away from your leggy friends.'

'But my father!' I said. 'What about him? He would do anything for Marie.'

She gave her sour old chuckle. 'We shall see.'

We were all distracted then by a piercing cry. A woman was standing up, shouting for the management, the police. 'Someone has stolen my little dog!' she wailed.

I looked quickly for the old lady in furs but she had vanished. Madame Duclos was smiling at her empty plate.

In the morning father was alone and in a fury. 'Confounded women!' he said, rattling the grey printed wastes of a French newspaper. 'I have been deceived.'

I knew he was not really speaking to me so I spooned jam on to my bread and drank my milky coffee.

'She intended to bring her mother to live with us. That foul-

162

mouthed old drunkard! Good God! That would be nice company for you, Nicholas.'

'I don't mind,' I said, but he did not hear.

'If there is one thing I cannot and will not tolerate it is deceit. She waited until the very last minute, until all our arrangements had been made, before springing that pleasant surprise. What an idea!'

'What else could she do?' I said, but he was not listening.

I did not see Marie again. We left quite soon afterwards, on our own.

I thought, later on, that the old woman had been both wrong and right. Father did not appear to be in a trap. In fact, he was freer than before. For a while he was in a rage and then he brooded and after that he resumed life with the energy that had seemed to die with my mother. After a year he married a plump Miss Windhouse and he often whistled with contentment.

The animals were gone by then. I thought it best to face up to the fact that it was not normal to spend so much time with stupid creatures. Their dumb faces began to annoy me. 'How would you like to be cooked?' I shouted one day when my thrush was making a racket for food.

All of that is in the past now and I am free to think of other things. In a little while I shall be teenage and soon after that I will be a man. Then I can start to plan properly for my return to Paris. I know Marie is waiting for me. We had a promise: to be friends, to ride ponies over the fields. We will drink champagne together and I will eat lobster. For Marie.

THE BLIND MAN EATS
MANY FLIES

by

David Profumo

David Profumo was born in 1955, and read English at Oxford, where he took a First. He taught in schools and at university and now lives and works in London, where he is writing a novel. A former deputy editor of the Fiction Magazine, *his articles, stories and reviews have appeared in a number of magazines, and he is a regular contributor to the* TLS *and the* Literary Review. *He is the co-editor, with Graham Swift, of an anthology of fishing literature to be published later in 1985.*

She was lugging a huge bottle of vodka by its plastic handle.

'You said the check-in counter,' he reprimanded, kissing her on both cheeks.

Marina smiled. 'I got impatient. Here. Carry this.' She swung a squashy leather flight-bag at Simon's chest.

'They'll never let you in with this lot,' he said. 'You'll be gallons over the limit. You'll be shot.'

'I can handle them.' The old assurance. 'Anyway – it's for two.'

Simon raised his eyebrows. From behind the wall of stacked cigarette cartons walked a bearded man cradling a pile of green tobacco tins.

'Meet Simon,' said Marina; her hands made a scissor-like gesture of introduction. 'Neil Adams – Simon Lang.' They shook hands and nodded, unsmiling.

Her note to him in March had read: 'Chris is going to marry that foreigner of his. I think we ought to go. Ring me?' It was over a year since Simon had seen her; but they'd spoken, and had fixed to fly out together. He had been looking forward to the break, but somehow, perhaps arrogantly, he hadn't expected her to have other company.

'Well, you're certainly looking good,' Simon told her, running his eyes appraisingly down her brightly-striped cotton dress. 'I always liked your hair shorter'.

They were queuing at the till. She turned and said, 'Actually, I'm growing it.'

Having missed each other earlier, they were seated in separate parts of the aircraft, which was full. After half an hour of flight, and several miniature bottles of gin, Simon wandered forward, slack-tied, and perched on her arm-rest.

167

'Recognise any other familiar faces?' he asked her. Neil was lounging, his head against her left shoulder, asleep. She pursed her dark mouth and blew out her cheeks, shook her cockerel hair.

'Not that I can see. I've a feeling we may be the full team. Not much of a turn-out. And Neil's never even met him.'

He looked at the other man, in his crumpled linen shirt and canvas jeans flecked with paint. Dishevelled, with gold studs in each lobe, he was not her habitual type. Simon noticed as he breathed that the columnella between his nostrils was slightly eroded.

'Decent of him to come, under the circumstances,' he smiled disarmingly at her. A steward squeezed past him down the aisle with a little dance.

Marina tipped some nuts into her mouth. 'And, you know, his father isn't even coming out. He's refused. They haven't spoken since Chris didn't come back for the funeral. So there'll be none of his family. Just us.'

'His friends.' He nodded. Neil was stirring, swivelling to sit up. 'Nice nap?' enquired Simon, deliberately cheerful. He received a look of irritation.

She had been better than him, more conscientious, about keeping in touch. Since Chris had moved abroad four, five years ago, Simon had not seen him. She'd been out a couple of times, and had maintained a straggly correspondence. Simon hadn't written for over a year. That he disapproved of what Chris was doing with himself was only one reason for this lack of communication.

'What do *you* do in life?' he asked Neil, now successfully surfaced from his slumber.

'I'm a composer,' came the guarded reply.

'Oh.' Simon pointed to the trousers. 'What about the paint?'

'He's also a painter.' Marina looked up imploringly. She knew how difficult Simon could be when he got someone in his sights.

'Should get on famously with old Chris,' he continued, as if genuinely pleased, 'because I gather he now does a bit of painting; isn't that right?'

Marina said yes, he did, among other things.

A stewardess approached trundling a tall metal trolley, and Simon headed back to his own seat. He ordered another drink and wiped his forehead with a perfumed towelette from the sachet provided. The damp little paper oblong came off his body with a blur of city grime on it. He crumpled it up with distaste, and stuffed it in the string compartment in front of him.

He was not a good traveller at the best of times. A glib, rather private person, Simon resented any occasions when he was dependent on others for his movements. He disliked the unsolicited company of other people, also, which meant that his preferred method of transport was his own motor car. His many friends teased him constantly about being unsociable.

The prospect of seeing Chris again, in a few hours' time, was slightly confusing him. It seemed so long since they had last properly spoken, there was now more than geographical distance between them. Simon still felt instinctively that Chris was wasting his time living abroad; he could recognise the faint 'malaise' about being in England that had possessed his friend even when they were at University, that feeling of being hemmed in, but he firmly believed that staying away for good was a mistake. In the event, there was little that anyone could do.

Overhead, the perforated voice of an intercom began to inform him of his height and velocity, and give details of the weather at Kerkyra airport. Corfu: the green limestone beauty, washed by so many cultures, famous and splendid and civilised. A tourist cliché, though: a centre of draught beer and disco-dance, hamburger and scooter-ride. Fun, maybe, to visit – but surely no place to live? Coming up now beneath them, like a dune-fly trailing its long legs westward across the Ionian.

They landed, with those little spurts of smoke, in the dark. As they shuffled their luggage through Customs, Chris clambered past a barrier to greet them, kissing Marina, shaking Neil by the hand and then, turning to Simon, gripping him by the shoulder with cautious affection. He seemed taller; more tanned, of course, than when they had last met, and his hair bleached paler by comparison to the last picture Simon's memory held of him. He had the same, enormous smile.

There was with him another, shorter man. He had dark curly hair and sported a pair of red-rimmed glasses.

'Here, let me,' he drawled at Marina, grasping the handle of her suitcase. 'Marc Lord. Delighted to meet you.'

'Marc's been here three days already,' explained Chris as they made for the glass doors. 'He's rented a jeep.'

The night air fell thickly around them as they went out into the car park. Despite the fumes, there was a distinct fragrance of shrubs. Bags loaded, they bundled into the two vehicles and, Chris in front with Simon, they bumped and veered their way off through the old town, teeming with brightly-dressed tourists, and, more dignified in dress, the residents taking their nightly *volta*.

'This your car?' Simon asked him. Chris laughed and shook his head, leaning on the horn out of bravado.

'No; I don't have one. It belongs to Spyros – my future brother-in-law.' Nevertheless, he was driving with that native confidence that seems so unbelievable to a visitor, especially on arrival, and at night.

Simon decided the best approach was to ask all the questions.

'So – when do we get to meet the lovely Nina? Tonight?' Chris began to explain the arrangements in store for them. By tradition, the bride on such occasions had to stay in with her family for a couple of days prior to the wedding, so they probably wouldn't set eyes on her until the ceremony itself. In the meantime, Chris thought it tactful to stay out of the village as much as possible, and leave the family to themselves.

'They're a traditional lot,' he added, 'and the whole thing's to be Orthodox. Even gave me a dowry!' Simon whistled.

The coastal road swung alarmingly around embankments, through villages bright with bars and clubs, and up towards the northern part of the island. Gouvia, Kalami, Nissaki: the names loomed up.

'What's this – are we taking a short cut through some architectural dig?' asked Simon, as the car jolted through several particularly severe potholes and slewed to one side to avoid a parked lorry.

Kouloura, Kassiopi. They had been on the road for an hour, and talked in little bursts, caught up on unimportant news, mostly

170

about mutual friends. Simon felt they were understandably skirting larger issues for the time being. The blazer was clinging to his back.

'A touch close. I was told it would be fresh in May.'

Chris clicked his tongue. 'Usually is. I'm afraid we may be in for a storm; it's the *maestros* blowing.'

They turned left, and started to climb away from the coast. The road was even worse, and uncomfortably steep.

'Almost there,' said Chris. 'By the way, you and Marc are staying with me. The others will be billeted around the village with friends. We'll be ten in all. Others are flying in tomorrow.'

The headlights described a jerky arc across a dry-stone wall studded with geraniums, and the car tilted perilously down a short driveway.

What Chris was living off nowadays he had no idea, but Simon was pretty certain he'd got funds from somewhere. He looked up admiringly as they entered the farmhouse's large kitchen, with its pink stucco walls and articulation of gnarled beams. There was a long table, and an assortment of electrical gadgetry. It was more elaborate than anything Simon had been expecting.

'I had this done specially for Nina,' Chris told him, unpacking some brown bags of provisions. 'She's a tremendously good cook.'

'It's nice. Very nice indeed.' Simon was sure of one thing: Chris hadn't made that sort of money from dabbling on canvases. It was difficult to take seriously the idea that he was now a painter. Every six months or so, it had been something different – running a bar, starting up a boat-hire business, writing a guide-book too quirky for anyone to publish; he'd tried so many different things. Any money Chris earned he would spend straight away – even at University he'd been like that, and Simon couldn't believe he'd suddenly started to be sensible about it.

'Still drink?' Chris held out a tumbler. 'Scotch?'

'Here's to you – both,' replied Simon over the rim of his glass. There were two smiles, a rustling of ice-cubes, and a pair of satisfied gasps.

'I'll show you to your room,' said Chris, getting up. 'It's already tomorrow.'

He experienced that delicious sensation of waking up somewhere and seeing it for the first time in daylight. Padding to the window, he looked out towards the sea which, from high up where he was, seemed almost solid and hard. Clouds were seeping over like a bruise, lending the distant water a bad colour. In the jumble of olives down the hillside to the coast the breeze was riffling green leaves into silver, the occasional dark finger of a male cypress alone rigid among the activity. The storm did seem to be collecting, away to the right beyond Pantokrator, its peak still smudged with snow. Simon slid the window to, despite the closeness.

It was getting on for ten. He wrapped on his silk dressing gown and went down in search of coffee. As he entered the kitchen, his bare feet making faint sucking sounds on the tiled floor, the rain began, with a crack.

Marina had arrived, a shawl round her shoulders; she and Neil were disembowelling a fat melon at the table.

'Chris is out,' she said, gesturing to the hob. 'He said to help ourselves. Marc hasn't appeared yet. We've got to have our skates on by eleven – going into town to hire more cars, or something.'

Neil lit a cigarette and started to cough. He fished around in the side of his mouth and extracted an oval melon-seed. He looked across at Simon almost accusingly.

They breakfasted quietly in a bright confusion of fruit, jam and honey.

None of them, it seemed, had anticipated anything but gentle sunshine. There was not a waterproof in the party as, cotton jackets stretched uselessly above them, they scuttled to the safety of the cars. Rain was bouncing up a foot above the cobbles, and amber rivulets were coursing down the village gutters as they followed the road down to the sea. The air was sharp with the sapid smell of warm soil split open with the water.

In such a sudden downpour, Kassiopi presented an incongruous spectacle. Beneath the bunting and bright canopies of every *taverna*

172

and bar huddled clutches of surprised tourists in their tee-shirts and shorts, sunburnt limbs shining like frankfurters from the week's previous weather. As the water churned past the kerbs, they blinked resentfully like livestock waiting at a ford.

Marc, who had taken it upon himself to do it, was experiencing difficulty in hiring the extra transport they needed.

'Dzeep, is difficults,' he was assured by the sweating young man at the rental office, who methodically offered each one of them a Marlboro cigarette. 'Tomorrow, maybe possible – but, you know, is besser you take scooter.' Of these he had a long line available. Marc, quite patiently, explained it was raining, and they had to pick up people from the airport.

'You are my friend,' the Corfiote informed him, 'tomorrow we can do business. Okay?' They agreed to try elsewhere. Chris suggested it would be easier, in the long run, to go the whole way into Kerkyra itself, where there would be more to choose from.

On the way there, the rain eased off and the cloud started to lift. Damp leaves gleamed on the road like fish. Men in string vests began to emerge among the olive groves, resuming their work with hoes and baskets among the roped veins of the tree trunks. They stooped to avoid brushing down the rain trapped on the branches and cupped in the whey-coloured flowers. Beneath every tree was its black net: some pegged out roughly on the stony ground, others strung in neat horizontal rows, to catch the falling fruit like acrobats.

The road seemed more dangerous by daytime. The precipitous course was now all too apparent, and its extravagant bends had to be negotiated without the warning benefit of headlights. Where flat enough, the surface was daubed with assorted political slogans.

From where he was sitting in the back, Simon could just see Marina's eyes reflected in the rear-view mirror, a bright little rectangle bouncing and lurching against the oncoming landscape. She looked back at him with her intelligent, challenging gaze. What had happened to her, he wondered, that she could have settled for someone like Neil? It seemed incomprehensible to him. The man had so little to offer a person with her energies; none of her vigour had diminished. But, admitted Simon to himself, perhaps he was not in the best position to judge. It was really no longer any of his

173

business, and, after all, she did look quite happy. He winked affectionately at her reflection.

It seemed that there should be more conversation. Marina said: 'Marc's fun. How do you know him?'

Chris smiled at her in the mirror. 'Met him when I was on the mainland, working in a hotel.'

Simon asked, 'Who was – you or him?'

'Me, of course.' Chris gave a laugh. 'You wouldn't catch Marc doing anything like that. He was a guest. Runs his own antiques business, in New York.'

The others nodded, and they drove on into Kerkyra in silence.

They split up, arranging to meet at two, in the Liston. Neil and Marc declared they needed drinks, so Simon followed Marina shopping. Leaving the square, they ventured down a narrow street between the rows of tall houses with their egg-blue shutters and crumbly balconies. Pitted walls were sprouting with plants and fuse-boxes. The sky between the roofs was webbed with wires and washing lines, onto which, now the rain had passed, women were conjuring damp linen, craning out of their upper windows, calling to one another through teeth full of pegs.

The shops also were starting to hang out their wares once again. Beach-balls stacked like boiled sweets; straw hats and objects of carved olive; *komboloïa*, the colourful local worry-beads; and that other inescapable specialty of the island, the lurid liqueur known as *koum kouat*, all diverted the eye's attention. From their places of dry refuge, tourists once more ventured abroad, ducking their heads into doorways, gliding with a grin into shops, picking things up and displaying them to one another, fingering, pointing. It was something Simon particularly disliked: these dawdling people, many of them his own compatriots, somehow in their innocent enjoyment of holidaymaking brought out an aggressive streak in him. They made him feel claustrophobic, hemmed in. The faintly narcotic expression on their peeling faces irritated him, because they appeared to be free of troubles, and he felt envious, and wanted to shout at them.

174

Remembering how much it made him cringe, Marina decided to play the enthusiastic souvenir-hunter to the full. She rummaged deliberately among baskets and bowls, hunted through necklaces, inspected piles of clothing; he lingered in the street outside, occasionally peering in at her furiously, and reminding her they had to press on. She held up a yellow sweatshirt against him and turned him to look in the mirror: 'What do you think, Si? For Neil – would it suit him?'

Exasperated, he sighed, 'It's ghastly. And, yes, I think it would.'

She opened her blue eyes directly at him, and realising she was winding him up, he managed a pallid smile. As they turned and made their way together to the rendezvous, she asked him if he'd had a chance yet of a proper conversation with Chris, and it struck him that they'd both managed successfully to avoid it.

'How does he seem, to you?' she said.

Simon shrugged. 'Caught up in a world of his own here. He's been away so long he's forgotten most of what we all had in common.'

'Maybe we all have,' Marina said, looking straight ahead. There was a pause, as they walked down some steps.

'It's like staying with a stranger: I don't feel we really know anything about him any more,' Simon concluded. 'For Christ's sake, the man's getting married tomorrow, and we haven't even met his wife.'

'This is a foreign country,' she said, 'and, as from tomorrow, he's going to be one of them.'

Among the surrounding Venetian architecture, the arcade of the Liston looked beautifully out of place, modelled as it was on the colonnade of the rue de Rivoli. House-martins were spilling over the roof and plunging down around the pillars above the heads of those drinking or strolling between the tables.

'Hey, you guys. Over here,' Marc hailed shrilly from the shade. He was drinking vodka, and his eyes looked watery. The waiter dragged up an extra chair; like all Corfiotes, he would do nothing in a hurry, and proceeded to peel over the pages of his notebook, adopting the stance of one about to take evidence.

Marina asked what was good. '*Tzinzerbira*,' came the islander's beaming reply. She looked hopefully at Chris.

'Ginger beer,' he explained, 'it's their speciality. A legacy of the British Empire.' Simon indicated the little cups in front of the others and ordered Turkish coffee. The waiter shook his head as he collected the crumpled menus.

'Nossing here Tur-kish,' he said. 'Only Grik coffees.' He ambled off, between the many crouching cats waiting for scraps.

Neil was hunched over his tobacco tin, rolling a thin cigarette. He was still squinting down at it as he spoke. 'You know, Chris, it seems to me your islanders are bloody tolerant of foreigners, right, considering how constantly they've been invaded. The Ottomans . . . Venice, Britain, Italy . . . and now tourists, if you like. I mean, you'd think they ought to be a race of xenophobes, okay?' He looked up with a certain satisfaction, not at Chris, but at Simon, and planted the cigarette between his lips. This remark was greeted with one of Simon's patronising stares.

'They're still a naturally hospitable people,' Chris said, 'although they have no history of peace.'

Inhaling a blue mass of smoke, Neil went on. 'But doesn't it strike you they're prepared to be tolerant of anyone who's spending money?'

For the first time, it looked as if Chris was growing angry. He assumed an infinitely patient expression, and pointed out to Neil the psychological effect on the Corfiotes of having been so constantly overrun. Not a mile and a half across the channel from Kouloura was Albania; at night, their helicopters patrolling with searchlights could often be heard firing at those trying to drift to the free world on the inner tubes of tyres. But for the grace of God, and St Spyridon, that could have been them.

'They are a thankful, and pacific people,' he concluded, 'at least, on the whole.' He made a circular gesture to the waiter for another round of drinks. 'They're not quite so undiscriminating as Neil thinks, though. Memory is very long here, as it is on all islands, and I'll tell you a quick story that concerns the very village where you're staying. When the Germans annexed Corfu from the Italians during the war, the first thing they did was punish any of the occupying forces suspected of fraternising with the islanders. This was before they deported the Jews, and destroyed half the town.' He sipped some coffee. 'Two Italian officers, billeted for some time in the village, and friendly with the locals, were tied up in sacks and thrown over the cliff into the sea, just where the hill road there joins the coast.'

He paused to clear his throat, and Simon looked at him curiously; it was ages since he had felt his friend exuding such energy. Chris continued, 'About ten years ago or so a retired German couple came and rented a villa on the coast. The place is terribly popular with German tourists, despite everything. Anyway, one morning the man's body was found on the rocks, precisely below that point on the cliff. It was largely hushed up, given out as an accident. But I heard on good authority who was reponsible – old George, whose son runs the *taverna* in the village. He's just one who remembers what happened.'

Chris fingered the car-keys in his hand, and then threw a glance at Neil, who was draining his beer. 'The irony of the business was that this particular old German had never been to Corfu before in his life. Now; I must meet the others at the airport.'

Spyros had masterminded the evening. 'The Fishing Nets', 'Corfu By Night', the inevitable 'Lido' – they had visited several clubs along the coast after eating in the town. His future brother-in-law had made a rousing speech about Chris at several stages of the festive progress, his rudimentary English becoming increasingly broken as drink succeeded drink. He was a compact-looking man in his early thirties, with a beak of a nose and a scrubby moustache. Like most of his countrymen he smoked all through the evening. His party trick was to drink brandy from a tumbler balanced in the crook of his arm while dancing around the table. He was jovial enough company, and they all applauded him wearily.

'Holy Christ,' whooped Marc later as they stumbled into the kitchen, 'it's right on midnight.'

'It's past three,' Chris corrected him, head in the fridge searching for beer, 'that's the kitchen scales.'

177

Marc lolled at the table, exhausted by drink. 'I'm totally fried,' he admitted. 'Christopher, don't you make a point of getting married again too soon; brother, I'm through.' He rested his head on the table.

'Feeling the *ouzo*?' asked Simon, steadying himself against the cupboard.

The American had begun, purringly, to snore. Chris retrieved a leash of beer cans from the fridge and walked to the table with the deliberate gait of someone who is aware he is drunk.

'I'm drunk,' he confessed, peeling the top off the can with a pop.

Simon looked at him out of one eye. 'If you're not, you ought to be.' They nodded sagaciously and tilted the froth into their mouths. It was one of those moments where alcohol was generating a confessional atmosphere that might be regretted at a later date. Simon felt the sensation of looking at things in their proper perspective. He leant forward across the table on his elbows and addressed his friend abruptly, looking first into one eye, then the other.

'Listen, Chris, we used to know each other just like that, right?' He crossed two fingers. 'And tomorrow's going to be a hell of an important day for you. The thing is ... you could still pull out.'

'Why ever should I want to do that?' said Chris cocking his head incredulously. 'You're mad.' A mottled moth shook on the lampshade.

Simon stared down at his can and twiddled it around on the table. He was aware that Chris was staring at him. 'Look; it's nothing to do with Nina,' Simon continued, warily, 'haven't even met her.... Looks very pretty from the photos. Lovely in fact.' There was a pause while he took a deep drink. 'No, I don't mean anything like that,' raising a hand to prevent interruption, 'it's more ... well, this whole island. I mean; it seems to me you're going to be stuck here for the rest of your bloody life. Roots right down, Chris, grafted onto the community. It's a hellish small place ... you'll be stifled. Have you thought of that?' Chris had closed his eyes wearily. 'It's great now, I'm sure,' continued Simon, 'it must be a great place to live, I can see that. But what about when the time comes and you want to move on? You're the footloose type; you'll be stuck. One day you could get fed up just....' He finished with a shrug.

178

Chris stood up a little clumsily.

'Just *what* exactly?' he asked, his jaw jutting in challenge.

'Ach, I knew you wouldn't listen.' Simon rubbed his eyes.

'I'm listening,' said Chris, arms folded, still standing. His friend looked up at him and hesitated.

'Just knocking about on paradise island. You'll be stuck. A wife, maybe kids. . . .'

'Let me worry about that.'

Simon raised his palms vertically, in a defensive gesture. 'Oh, I will, believe me.' He realised as he spoke that he had not meant it to go this far. 'But would you mind telling us what you're planning to do with yourself perched on top of this island for the rest of your life?'

Chris brought his face up very close to the other man's, and said in a whisper: 'Try and be happy. Satisfied?' Simon's gaze lurched. Phrases swam in his head. He wobbled to his feet.

'I've said enough. The others feel it, too. That's all.' He began feeling his way along the wall towards the door. 'I just think you might be making a bloody great mistake. Becoming a foreigner.'

His hand was on the handle of the corrugated glass door when Chris spoke. 'There's a Corfiote saying, and I go by it: the blind man eats many flies.' Simon looked back at him uncomprehendingly. 'You learn to live with things that look like mistakes to other people. Think about that, Simon. It's in the eye of the beholder, eh?'

'I really hope you know what you're doing,' said Simon as he crawled upstairs, leaving him alone with the American breathing like the sea.

He spent a terrible, broken night and, stiflingly hot, he woke just after dawn. To placate his gravelly palate he slouched to the basin for water, eyelids soldered with sleep. On the way back to bed he peered out of the window at a steamy fog stretched over the trees.

When he awoke hours later, the weather had changed. Sun had broken open the mist and out across to the sea the whole air was rigged with light. The drape of the water was trimmed with a rope of surf and the noises of the heat, the crackle of insects and frogs, came up from the garden.

His insides plunged with apprehension about facing Chris; the sensation overrode the pulsing pressure behind his eyes, and the faint sickness fingering his stomach. He felt foolish, though he could not recall precisely how much he had said. On the landing he met Marc, sporting red braces over his white shirt and trousers. He seemed improbably cheerful.

'Catch any sleep?' he asked. 'I woke around five, found Christopher insensible on the couch. You two stay up for long?' Simon made a grimace, and nodded.

They went down to the kitchen together. Chris was poking coffee grounds down the sink. He turned with his wide smile. 'Well. Today's the day. Kick-off in an hour and a half! Nothing much in the way of breakfast, I'm afraid. Nina would kill me. Just coffee, and fruit.'

'Nervous?' asked Marc. 'Or just hungover?'

Chris squeezed out a laugh. 'Both,' he admitted.

Picking a peach off the wooden bowl, Simon nuzzled its velutinous skin. Chris nudged him with his elbow. 'You all right?'

Simon regarded him. 'Fine. I'm sorry. It was unforgivable.' Marc looked at them both inquisitively.

'Forget it.' Chris laid a hand on Simon's shoulder. 'It was a great evening.' His fingers were quivering, very slightly.

It was the first chance they had had of really seeing the village. They trooped up the hill towards the church at eleven o'clock, *bouzouki* music rasping out from the stereo in the *taverna* where, in long rows under the trellis of vines, tables were being arranged for the reception. Inside, on a metal chair, behind a glass of *raki*, sat George, gazing at the foreign guests as they filed past.

The heat threatened to iron everything flat; it was making the roof of the tiny church tremble as they approached it. The bells in its three campanile began their swinging tintinnabulation; the churchyard gate squealed to and fro as the villagers entered, nodding, smirking to one another, children squeaking with laughter

180

and hiding and running in the festive atmosphere.

Inside was a mixture of informality and devotion. Simon stood towards the back of the church, Corfiotes having made a little vacuum for the foreigners. The *papa* in his black stove-pipe hat looked stern and patriarchal, swinging incense by the altar; the congregation milled around the nave, separated from him by an iconostasis let into a stone architrave. There was a representation of the Day of Judgment, the Garden of Eden, Calvary; side altars were clustered with votive marble plaques; thin candles were unwrapped, impaled on spikes and lit. Wherever Simon's eye went, the scene was busy, Ionian and baroque details mingled and clashed. An icon representing the Blessed Virgin Mary *gorgoepicous* – who swiftly answers prayers – hung under a rose window on which there roosted a gesticulating angel carved out of marble.

Standing apart, to the right, Chris was talking in a low voice to Spyros. Both men wore suits and had flowers pinned to their lapels. Simon watched them. He reflected on the image he had instinctively constructed of his friend when they were students – the one from their number most likely to do something original, to be creative, to succeed. It seemed strange to be witnessing him going through such a marriage, to a girl none of them had ever seen except in a photograph. Chris was so much a part of their memories of the not-too-distant past, they were tacitly reluctant to lose him.

Nina's face, when she appeared at the door, decked in flowers and smiling, was far more arresting than Simon had envisaged. She had a proud, glorious look about her: dark, challenging eyes, an aquiline nose, and full, black hair that swept out under her headdress like the neck-feathers of some great bird. As she moved up to take her place next to Chris, they did not look at each other. A choir of children was singing, the *papa* had turned to face them with a large book, and the congregation craned on its feet to watch every move of the lengthy Orthodox ceremony.

It may not have been as his old friends imagined it, but it was now happening. To his astonishment, Simon realised that their evident happiness was making him rather depressed.

★

Lambs had been butchered that morning, various dishes were prepared from them. Between the vines overhead, light ran down the smoke from the grill. The air was pungent with their burning. The long tables, draped in white, surged with bottles and bowls and heaps of flaky white bread. In front of each guest there was a tiny jar of sugared almonds.

Each new lukewarm dish was delivered with a grin of triumph by the waiters, who thrust it between the feeders with a flourish – *choriatiki salata, barbouni, kokoretsi,* there was too much to choose from, as well as the hunks of lamb. Simon was getting steadily drunk, a bottle of Robola wine refreshing and sharp by his left elbow. He fiddled with his food, crumbling the bitter white *feta* cheese onto his tongue, picking from his salad the dark little eyeballs of olives. Neil was walking around taking photographs; Marc was engaged in an animated discussion, sign-language the method, with a Corfiote woman in an apron who happened to be passing, leading a donkey loaded with a mangle.

There were constant toasts – *Panta chara*; *episis* – the infernal stereo launched its own noise over the rest of the clamour, as the children of the village raced between the chairs, chasing the dogs which watched attentively for food to fall from laps as guests rose to make 'impromptu' speeches or to raise their glasses. A mongrel plunged his muzzle up between Simon's knees, his head clustered with ticks, sultana-big. A man in a lime-green shirt stood up on his chair with unsteady solemnity and began to sing in a thin nasal voice. Simon and Marina clapped loudly when it was over.

Making a slow progress around the scene, stopping at each group of guests for embraces, compliments, presentations, Chris and his bride were approaching that part of the table where Simon and Marina were seated. Simon caught his eye with a little mock bow. He shouted over the wash of voices the only Greek word he knew: '*Kalispera!*' He repeated it several times until Marina stuck an elbow in his rib-cage and said he was embarrassing her.

A circle of the other male villagers was beginning to assemble on the hard ground beyond the tables. Jackets off in the heat, grinning, they rolled up their sleeves in readiness, all of them wearing large digital wristwatches. Their faces, tanned with the salt wind, were fruit-like and supple. Cigarettes were pinched out, the dancers were in readiness; as an appropriate tune began to be broadcast over the speakers, they started up to the circular movements of the *kalamatianos*.

Chris ushered his wife towards them, murmuring into her ear. She nodded, and held out a thickish hand to Simon in greeting. He bent over and kissed it with stylish formality. Her other hand fluttered to her mouth in surprise, as he congratulated her on the marriage. 'My dear Mrs Maxwell, I wish you every happiness in your life here together,' he said.

Nina blushed slightly in confusion. '*Den katalaveno*,' she said with a giggle to her husband.

'Something complimentary, I take it?' asked Simon.

'She said, she doesn't understand!'

'Well, you tell your blushing bride that you're both very lucky to have found each other. And here's to the honeymoon.' Simon raised his glass with a flourish and spilt a little wine over his shoulder. The couple glided on their way.

'Pretty, isn't she?' Marina remarked watching them together. Simon said nothing, but splashed more liquid into his glass. She continued, 'Have you noticed how the women tend to lose their hair before the men do?'

He let out a little bark of a laugh. 'Except around the mouth, maybe.'

Marina regarded him, her chin tucked down. 'What's got into you, apart from the alcohol?' Simon gave her a wan smile, and leant forward, confidentially.

'Just jealously,' he said, 'that's all.'

The dancers had been joined by Marc, who was clapping and skipping enthusiastically to some private rhythm of his own. He whirled by quite close to them, slapping his thighs.

'When in Rome...' he called.

'I like the braces,' Marina laughed.

'Suspenders, honey, suspenders.' The man's voice swung away from them.

Slowly, she slipped her arm under Simon's. 'I know what you mean,' she told him. 'But, it's a big old world.'

'Sure,' he said, 'and here we all are, up to our eyes in it.'

The hot wind came through the trees and swept towards the sea.

At five, they waved goodbye to the couple as the ferry pulled away for Brindisi, then they drove to the beach. Towels and mats were laid out on the sugary sand, and Marc produced a bottle of golden Tequila with a cactus-grub preserved at the bottom. They began to doze in the heat.

The water was thick with finely shredded weed for the first couple of feet away from the shore; dark and flimsy. Simon kept away from it, with a childish fear of having his toe grabbed by an unseen creature. There were larger stalks of weed cast up on the sand, stems thick as rhubarb. A fisherman in brightly-striped shorts was unloading his catch from a small dinghy; he carried a speargun, two small scaly fish, and a medium-sized octopus. The falling light slipped off the dull grape of its body.

Later, they gathered up wood and made a bonfire. Simon stretched out on his back, hands clasped under his neck. 'You think she'll make him happy?' he asked Marc, who was half-asleep.

'Sure, why not? She's cute. An ingénue, maybe, kinda short on the old "savoir-vivre", perhaps, but they'll do fine together.'

Simon rolled over onto his elbow. 'You happy in the world, Marc?'

The American closed his eyes with a smile. 'Yup, basically. I guess.' A frying sound was coming off the surf. The horizon's pale mouth was just crimped with red. 'Life's pretty exciting in the Vertical City.'

'Good,' said Simon, 'I'm glad.'

'You?'

'My touble is, I don't get too lucky in love.' Marc gave a grunt of commiseration. Simon went on wryly, 'Now Chris, he was always the one to have luck.'

There was a pause, then Marc sat up slowly. 'You mean he didn't tell you?' He sounded incredulous. His eyes played over Simon's face for his reaction.

'Tell me? What?'

'Uha; so. He did not. But I guess he was going to, if he'd found the right moment. Told me, any rate.' Marc started to rub the back of his neck. He went on, 'It's Nina. She's a primagravida.'

Simon looked blank. 'Pregnant for the first time,' explained Marc. 'It's a technical term; I majored in zoology. You'd call it, I think, a bun in the oven?'

'So; he hadn't much choice after all,' muttered Simon.

'*Philotimo*, dear boy,' Marc said, 'the quiet honour of the islands.'

A cataract of sparks gushed from the wood. The points of light flittered away like insects into the dark. Simon felt suddenly quite exhausted. He closed his eyes, and had a bright after-image of whirling flames, but gradually the colours blurred and ran into each other; and then there was nothing.

They were leaving on the lunch-time flight. The wind spun coin-bright over the houses as he walked through the village up to the churchyard, skin still crusty with salt, sand lodged behind his ear, hair matted into elflocks by his sleep. It was early, but at the window of the *taverna* sat George, his expression passive, a small white cup of coffee beside him.

Simon wondered. Had he done it? Was it in fact him? They did not offer one another any greeting.

He entered the churchyard with a squeak of hinges. From the outcrop where the building sat you could see right down the east side of the island, with Albania beyond. Simon imagined the thousands of people that must be moving between himself and the horizon; yet he could not see one of them. Making their holidays, getting away, meeting up. But here in the heart of the island, something much older was going on. He did not think he would be back. As Marina had said, it was a big enough place, plenty to see elsewhere. Simon wandered through the rows of gravestones like an invigilator.

Plenty of people still to meet, he thought, and things to see.

He breathed deeply into the horizontal distance.

WALKABOUT

by

Nicholas Wollaston

Nicholas Wollaston was born in 1926 in Gloucestershire. He has been a navigator on a minesweeper, jackeroo on an Australian sheep station, manager of a tannery in Kenya, and BBC hack. He is the author of four novels, four travel books, a biography of the explorer August Courtauld, and articles and reviews for many papers. He is a fellow of the Royal Society of Literature, and now lives in Suffolk, in a house owned by the National Trust.

His novel Mr Thistlewood *will be published later this year.*

Some years ago a friend of mine, a man with a melancholy humour, celebrated his second marriage with a party at the London zoo. The marriage was an even worse disaster than his first, though mercifully briefer. All I remember about the party is meeting Professor I. A. Richards, literary pundit and author of a book with the most stunning title I know, *The Meaning of Meaning*. I have never read it and suspect I wouldn't understand a word.

When we were introduced, and through the party noise – through the cries from monkey cage and lion house – the old professor heard my name, he asked if I was the son of Dr Wollaston, the explorer. I am always pleased to meet friends of my father, who died when I was three and became only a shadowy presence in my life, so I picked the professor's memory. He told me something I hadn't heard before, which he had got from my father and which gave a glimpse of him in a strange light – something new and precious to be added to the picture I had always had.

In the early years of the century my father led an expedition to the mountains of New Guinea, which were unexplored and very difficult to reach. The only other white man in the party was a Dutchman, the rest were native porters. For weeks they cut into the interior from the coast, through the jungle towards the foothills. It was exploring in the classic style, with naked savages and poisoned arrows and a whiff of cannibalism. The Dutchman died of fever, the porters mutinied or ran away, and in one of the infested rivers my father's dugout canoe capsized with the loss of scientific instruments, medicines, diaries, guns – everything. He never reached the mountains, never got more than an agonising view of distant snows, and had to turn back.

I knew all that, because it was in the book my father wrote, but to the account of the retreat to the coast – a tough journey over endless ridges of the foothills, along tortuous jungle tracks, down unhealthy streams that backed and meandered for ever – Professor Richards

189

supplied a fresh twist. The party was assailed by fatigue and sickness and the terrible climate, and my father, himself weak with malaria, struggled to bring them out alive. But through the tropical mists and heat haze and rainstorms he was led on by another white man ahead of him, the back view of a stranger in the distance travelling in the same direction, towards the coast. Each time my father topped another ridge the man was already going over the further one, and each time my father turned another bend of a path or river the man was disappearing round the next.

Yet was he really a stranger? He looked maddeningly familiar and even in his feverish state my father thought he recognised him from long ago, but he could never catch him up to make sure. When he got close enough to shout, the man wouldn't stop or turn round to show his face. All my father knew was that another explorer, always pressing on in front, kept him going and rescued the expedition.

At last they reached the coast where the stranger gave him the slip once more and disappeared for good. Though my father tried to settle the mystery, making enquiries about other travellers in the country, he discovered nothing. In time he gave it up, paid off his porters and on the long voyage home forgot all about it, till a year or two later when he went to a London tailor to be measured for a new suit. In the fitting-room he tried on the jacket and watched the tailor in the mirror, marking the front, snipping and pinning, then turning him round to show him the back. There in the glass was the same elusive figure that my father had followed in the New Guinea jungle, who had saved his life.

I liked the professor's story not only for the new, very literary angle it gave to my father's image but because it fitted a suspicion I have about the jungle – a superstition, almost, of its powers. I was aware of it for the first time when I had a British Council job in Africa and once camped in the heart of the Congo basin, and since then I have felt it in Vietnam, Laos, Guyana, the Himalayas – wherever I have been in primeval forest. It isn't too fanciful to detect it, at night or in fog or with a companion who is attuned to such things, in what remains of England's old forests. I even caught it, with happy consequences, early one morning in Epping with a girl whose virginity had been giving us trouble. It is a sense of ancient and infinite life, of dense habitation where the map says

190

'uninhabited'. The jungle is no desert but can seem as crowded, though without the people, as any city. Human beings, as it were, are supplanted by inhuman ones.

Recently I had the feeling intensely in the sort of equatorial scene that my father would have known in New Guinea, but on another island a thousand miles further east. It was the whim of a man living in the Solomon Islands, where I got to know him when I was information officer and editor of the local paper. He was then in the colonial service. He stayed on after independence, reluctant to face the rigours of post-imperial Britain and glad to be useful as adviser to the new rulers, who were just as glad to exploit him. Besides, as he used to say only half-flippantly, his Melanesian 'wife' would put a curse on him that could reach him round the world if he dared abandon their immense family of half- and quarter-castes. His name was Mordaunt Fry.

Last year a commission from an Australian magazine – one of Rupert Murdoch's, I'm afraid – took me to Queensland and left me in Brisbane with a few days to spare and several hundred dollars to lose from my expenses. I hadn't seen Mordaunt for too long and grabbed the chance, but warned him by cable that I would be on the twice-weekly flight to Honiara, capital of the Solomons, in case he chose to leave town and avoid me; he could be a capricious man, liable to annoy people wanting something more predictable from an ex-administrator. But to my relief and delight he was in the little airport hut.

'My dear fellow, what did you expect?' he protested when I said I was surprised to find him there.

I don't know Mordaunt's age, probably not much over sixty, but he had an archaic way of speaking, as if to preserve something of the time when he was agent of the British crown, ruling a district the size of Wales and licensed to sentence the natives to death. Also, talking at home in pidgin English or some local dialect, he was out of practice in anything more up-to-date.

'I've taken a room for you in the Mendana,' he said, snapping his fingers at an airline porter who was carrying my bag cushioned on top of his fuzzy head. 'You'll be very comfortable there, they do one awfully well.'

I might have guessed. Mordaunt wasn't exactly embarrassed

191

when Europeans visited his weird bi-coloured household – he couldn't have felt awkward in his life – but he believed they would prefer to stay in the hotel; and the Mendana, named after the Portuguese navigator who discovered the islands and hoped he had reached the source of Solomon's wealth, must be the nicest in the Pacific.

Mordaunt came into the bar for a drink, then half a dozen more, and stayed for dinner. His family might not have existed, for all he showed, and I told myself that Rupert Murdoch's accountant would never notice how far I had swung off course.

'Try the Barrier Reef prawns,' Mordaunt said, dismissing the elaborate menu, a phoney Franco-Australian affair dressed up with a South Seas garnish. 'They came up on the plane with you. And stick to beer if I were you.' He clipped the wine list shut in the ebony face of a waiter who was rehearsing his blurb for hock or burgundy – this in a country where the nearest thing to a vineyard is one of the biggest coconut plantations in the world.

He didn't want to talk about local politics, thank God, except to chuckle at some of the mumbo-jumbo going on in the capital of the new republic, the 150th member of the United Nations; and he was never much good at gossip. Towards the end of dinner, having learnt that I had a week in hand, he touched on something that must have been in his mind since getting my cable from Brisbane.

'How about going walkabout, Nicholas?'

Whether it's pidgin or aboriginal Australian, I only knew that he didn't mean a stroll after dinner along the Honiara beach. 'Fine,' I said. 'Where?' I was already looking forward to a visit to a lonely planter at the other end of the archipelago, or to one of the very worldly Catholic missions for a night or two of feasting and laughter with the fathers, or even a fishing trip – anything for a holiday at Rupert Murdoch's expense, and perhaps a story. 'When do we start?'

Mordaunt looked at me sharply. 'First let me tell you about my devil-devil.'

'Your what?' I thought he was changing the subject but I should have known better.

'Everyone's got one, who's been here long enough.'

'Your devil-devil?'

192

'Or rather, my devil-devil's wife.' Mordaunt loved to mystify. 'The old man's a friendly fellow, quite harmless. His wife's another story.'

'Have you ever met her?' I wasn't sure what we were talking about.

'Never. Or not yet, I should say. But I know what to expect. In the forest, when everything's absolutely still and there's a sudden rustling of wind in the trees with the smell of a bat – if that happens, that'll be her.' His eyes grew with mock horror, or it could have been genuine. 'And something dire will follow.'

'Mordaunt, really!'

'I thought the same when I first came here thirty-five, forty years ago. All that funny stuff about a devil-devil in a tree or calamity in a heap of sticks or the penalty for disobeying someone in an epileptic fit – now I don't think it's funny any more.'

'What's this to do with going walkabout?'

'I'm coming to that. Something Beaconsfield's been cooking up for years, hoping to take me with him. It might amuse you too, Nicholas. You remember Beaconsfield?'

I remembered him clearly – a small, nimble, pitch-black 'bush boy' – because I had written a piece about him when I lived in the Solomons. Beaconsfield wasn't his original tribal name, but one he took from a brand of cigarettes with a picture of Disraeli on the packet which he admired. The bush boys considered themselves an ancient aristocracy, descended from chiefs who had fled from the coast when white men first arrived and led their people into the forest to preserve their blood from adulteration. Beaconsfield's ancestors were cannibals and possibly he too, long ago, had tasted human flesh. He had once gone through a painful initiation when gongs were banged to drown the boys' screams, and still cherished primitive beliefs and practised secret rites. Though he had briefly been to a mission school, the war came and much of his childhood was spent under Japanese occupation. But he slipped out of his father's house and acted as a runner in the forest, carrying information to the coast-watchers, Europeans who stayed behind and lived in hiding to report on the enemy by radio. Mordaunt, who had arrived in the Solomons as a young district officer on his first appointment only a few months ahead of the Japanese, was one of

193

those coast-watchers. It was a dangerous game and anyone captured was beheaded.

After the war Beaconsfield never went home to his village in the forest, but got caught up in the 'Cargo Cult'. Ships from America would come sailing over the horizon laden with all the good things that anyone could want and there was no need to work ever again. It suited the native temperament and disillusion was a long time coming. Beaconsfield was rescued in the end when Mordaunt found him scavenging under the Honiara jetty, picking over the empty tins and bottles, and took him on as houseboy.

It was another ten years before Beaconsfield saw his home again, when Mordaunt was posted to his island. Together they went on a journey, black man and white master cutting through the forest for a week, sleeping in villages, telling each other stories of their childhood, till they came to Beaconsfield's father's house. The old man, who for all those years had been spinning a ball of twine with a knot in it for every day of Beaconsfield's absence, was overwhelmed: 'You have brought back my son,' he said to Mordaunt. 'Now he is your brother.' And in a mysterious ceremony he bound the two together with his twine.

It was a chance, back among his own people, for Beaconsfield to take a wife. And why shouldn't his master, who had proved to be no ordinary white man, have one too? The next few days, the last in which the two bridegrooms could enjoy the status of unmarried men, were given up to ritual while suitable girls were found. To the sound of sacred flutes and bullroarers a pig was sacrificed for Mordaunt's and Beaconsfield's protection from female contamination – women being an inferior race, impure though necessary. On the night of the double wedding, under the old man's eye, pods from a rare tree were boiled to extract the oil, for a virgin's cunt is hot and will damage a man unless he first pours oil over it – a trick, I imagine, that might be useful in Epping Forest too. In time, after solemnity had broken down in ribaldry which turned into mass copulation, the two men came out of the forest with their wives. Mordaunt's, I suspect without ever having asked, was Beaconsfield's sister.

'Yes, I remember Beaconsfield,' I told him, finishing off the **Mendana prawns**.

'There's a set of huge boulders that he keeps worrying me about, the Stones of Bau, far up in the forest on one of the islands, a sort of sacred ring. . . .'

'Sculpture? The local Henry Moore?' I could see it, a jungle one-man show.

'More of a Stonehenge, I gather,' Mordaunt said, 'from what he can remember. He went there once as a child with his father, who's been dead for years, and now he wants to take his own son there. Passing on the magic or whatever, down the generations.'

'Could he find his way?'

'Trust Beaconsfield. Drop him blindfold in the forest anywhere, give him a leaf or two to feel, and he'll lead you home.'

'By the sounds?'

'Something more private – signals, a sense of waves. . . .'

'How do we get there?' It sounded a good idea; it sounded as if Mordaunt had fixed everything.

'Take the Western Solomons plane the day after tomorrow. Three hours' island-hopping and get off at Munda. A night in the rest house there, time to find a canoe to take us over the lagoon, then two days' walkabout, another night at Munda on the return, back here with two days to recover before your flight to Brisbane. . . .' He looked at my clothes. 'It'll be warm in the forest, even in the rain. Get yourself some sneakers and a cotton hat.'

It was settled and next morning I did my shopping; Rupert Murdoch never spent his money better.

After lunch, defying the heat, I walked through the somnolent, scruffy town – Honiara must be the world's least noble capital – and across the creek to the European cemetery. I'm not sentimental, but I had liked Michael very much – a rich young renegade from the Guards and Chelsea who had joined the crew of a trading schooner and become one of the brightest memories of my time in the Solomons, too high-spirited to survive there. After a party one night he decided to swim back to the schooner, but never reached it. Later, the bits left by the crocodiles were found in the mangroves. It touched a nasty chord in me; I had known another man who died the same way in Uganda, a hunter called Sam whose boat was upset by a rogue hippo in the Semliki river. Because he couldn't swim the crocodiles had got him too. It says something, I don't know what,

195

about being a friend of mine; or about the fragility of life in the tropics and the likelihood of its sudden, macabre end. But I couldn't find Michael's grave, it was too hot to search and I think he laughed, in the shimmering afternoon, when I went back to my air-conditioned room at the Mendana.

Mordaunt picked me up to take me to the airport with Beaconsfield and two boys of twelve or fourteen. Beaconsfield was more shrivelled than I remembered and if possible even blacker, like a half-burnt stick pulled from the ashes of a fire. One of the boys, just as darkly charred, must have been his son. I guessed that the other, much paler as if milk had been poured into him at birth, was one of Mordaunt's own.

'They've got names of some sort – I forget what,' Mordaunt said. 'We'll call them Black and Tan.'

We were the only passengers in the six-seater plane and the boys, who had never flown, darted about the cabin, shouting at the view, rubbing each other to make sure it was true. Mordaunt caught the excitement and became a child again, while Beaconsfield went to sleep; his time would come tomorrow in the forest. When the pilot let Black and Tan take the controls they were in heaven, silent at last and as sublime as angels.

We flew past Savo, a conical island where Mordaunt had lived as coast-watcher in the war: 'The most extraordinary night in my life – one of the great sea battles,' he said, looking down at the pyramid of forest growing on the water. 'I was in the grandstand with cruisers dodging round me and heavy guns tearing into the dark, bangs and flashes going off like fireworks – you'd pay a lot for a seat like that. The bottom of the sea must be strewn with bones.'

We flew on into the west, past islands bigger than Corsica or Long Island sweltering under their coat of trees, lifting it above us in ancient humps and untrodden ridges – untrodden because there were no paths to tread and nobody to tread them anyway. We flew past islands that were mere patches of greenery afloat on the water down there, with a ring of bright surf; and submarine islands that had never surfaced, like huge jellyfish swimming in the translucent sea. We came down near a plantation where we opened the door and got the hot blast of copra scent, and lines of palm trees marched for miles in all directions – so much soap and margarine. We stopped at

196

a mission station where an astonishing black bishop, in robes and purple stock, came galloping down the grass runway to shake Mordaunt's hand and bless us all. And at midday we reached Munda.

That afternoon Mordaunt and Beaconsfield went to find a boatman who could take us next day to the start of our walkabout. Black and Tan collared a pair of little dugout canoes and splashed till sunset in a water jousting match. I sat on the concrete verandah of the rest house, toying with one of Jack London's stories of the Solomons. Perhaps his imagination had wilted in the reality. Perhaps my own could do no better, but it was good enough for me.

Chickens and pigs and children rootled through the tiny village. Some boys kicked a football across a patch of powdered coral, but gave up and vanished into the shade. A lizard plopped from the roof and landed in surprise between my feet. Half a verse of a hymn, 'Jesus loves me, that I know', drifted out of nowhere, then was stifled by the heat. A brief explosion of laughter reached me; or was it a scream and a girl was being raped? Sometimes a canoe sliced across the indigo lagoon, gently flickering the water. Otherwise it was an unshattered sheet of glass, the details of every palm and islet doubled in its surface. When a fish jumped it was a surprise that it didn't tinkle among broken pieces as it fell back, and leave a hole. When the sun dropped it was quickly dark and Mordaunt appeared, followed by Beaconsfield with beer and peanuts.

We started at sunrise in a vast scooped-out tree that must have stood in the forest for two or three centuries. The boatman was just as fine, a trunk of human mahogany that could have picked up Beaconsfield and snapped him like a fishbone. Black and Tan were subdued by the effect and sat up in the bows where they were told. The boatman pulled the cord of his outboard and we sprang away from the shore, unfolding two wings of spray and dividing the lagoon with a smooth white furrow.

'Thirty Japanese horse-power!' Mordaunt shouted above the motor. 'Not such fun as it used to be, with thirty warriors paddling into battle, but a lot faster.'

Across this lovely inland sea, among a thousand islands, our boatman ripped and twisted through the early morning. Now the channel narrowed to a track between the trees, now it opened to

197

wide horizons. On one island a man had cleared the bush for a leaf house, ridiculously pretty, and planted coconuts; a feather of smoke waved over the palms from his copra drier. Thick mangroves lined the shores, standing on their infinite stalks – nature's special torture, a device for shipwrecked sailors. Behind grew trees; no land was visible, only trees, though there must be something solid for them to put their roots in. Far away – or were they clouds? – the mountains faintly steamed. I could see them at the beginning of the world when they were all exploding.

We left the lagoon by a deep cut in the reef where the current ran fast, taking us at speed between two strips of brilliant sand painted on the sea, and out into open water. A long swell came rolling from Australia – or Japan, Hawaii, America – with hundreds of yards between each approaching hump, but not a ripple. The dugout climbed a slope for half a minute, then slid down the other side. All round us the world rose and fell in a vast rocking seesaw. A leaping school of porpoises swam over to laugh at us, and Black and Tan laughed back. A man alone in a canoe, far from anywhere, paddling to somewhere, waved and was lost in the swell.

A sudden storm attacked us, a blizzard of rain shutting out the day, hissing on the sea and filling the bottom of the dugout. When it cleared we were close to our island. The sea bed rose below us, patches of sand and coral, and the boatman stopped the motor. With a pole he stood up on the prow, one bare foot on each gunwale, toes gripping the edge, and punted us over the reef. Soon it was shallow enough for him to wade; he dropped over the side and strode like a sea god through the water, an Olympian straining on a rope. Black and Tan dived in and swam alongside; Mordaunt and Beaconsfield and I were towed. Inside the reef the boatman started the motor again and steered along the shore. Now it was up to Beaconsfield.

'Pretty solid in there,' Mordaunt said, watching the forest edge. 'It'll be a tight squeeze.'

Beaconsfield was searching for a chink. 'There!' he said suddenly, pointing at a red-leafed tree, hardly the obvious way in.

The boatman swung into the beach and landed us. His part was over, he belonged down by the sea and could no more cut his way up into the forest than Beaconsfield could catch and skin a turtle. He

198

would wait for us – build a fire, hunt for crabs, go fishing – and expect us back tomorrow.

Beaconsfield opened a small cotton sack, took out a bush knife, slung the sack over his shoulder and looked up at the morning sun – to tell the time or say goodbye.

It was like going indoors on a hot day, plunging up into the darkness, into the dim comfort of an alien religion. At first I was confident and felt safe; they wouldn't go too fast for me. Mordaunt was twenty years older, Beaconsfield not much less – small and frail and growing bald – and Black and Tan would soon get tired. But it was a lesson in human decadence. Beaconsfield the houseboy, expert with vacuum cleaner or bottle opener, moved with the utmost economy, his energy as spare as his figure. He hardly seemed to breathe, just glided at the same steady speed up and down the foothills, through the forest all day. With his knife he snicked and swiped, clearing a way for the rest of us and perhaps, I thought, for his own future use or his descendants'. Mordaunt crashed along behind him through sheer force, and Black and Tan scampered round our legs like puppies. I struggled miserably to keep up.

Sometimes we travelled easily along a forest ridge between deep valleys that fell on either side. Sometimes we dropped into a gulch, slipping down steep mud flanks, wading up a stream, the cool water a relief on blistered feet and bleeding legs, then climbing out on the far bank, up the valley side, clutching, slithering, grabbing. There were awful spiky things – it was like holding a rope of needles; and fallen trees to climb over or duck under or balance along – a bridge across the undergrowth; and wild yams with prickles like a shark's jaw; and orchids, ferns, mistletoes growing high above the ground; and whistles and cackles, the crash of an animal, the clamour of insects, the ancient noises of fear and protest; and immense trunks rising from the squelch of roots, supported by thin buttresses, their tops out of sight with a ropework of lianas, rattans, vines hanging loose like the rigging of some crazy giant ship, and we were mice or beetles creeping through its wreckage.

'Bush pig!' Beaconsfield whispered and stopped dead, frozen to his own footprints. But there was nothing that I saw or heard.

Later Mordaunt said, 'Look at him!' and pointed to a ridiculous

199

bird, between a parrot and a chicken, that couldn't fly. Though it managed to glide down from a branch on its silly ungrown wings it had to get back by climbing a vine in pathetic hops and flaps, using its beak and claws. It belonged to a different stage of evolution, forgotten in the forest here, and enhanced the feeling of anachronism. We were excluded from the world we came from, the sky as remote as in a prison cell, the ground unlike anything I had trodden on before – soggy, matted, rotten with burrowing streams. Virgin forest indeed! I thought of Epping with regret.

About noon the rain began again, falling solidly through the foliage, becoming part of it. Leaves were battered, branches tossed, and the noise grew to a roar of fury. My sodden clothes were an extra weight to carry, but Mordaunt hardly noticed it – he seemed driven by defiance and purposefulness – and the boys became water puppies, sloshing upwards and always chattering. Beaconsfield cut a bunch of fronds to hold over his head and kept perfectly dry. After the storm the forest dripped for hours, with the odour of decay enriched by rain. And there was plenty to drink, cupped in our hands from the enormous leaves.

Climbing always higher, by late afternoon we reached a rim in the ground where it fell away in front of us.

'Must be an old volcano,' Mordaunt said.

I hoped for a pause, though the forest was too dense for any view, but Beaconsfield wouldn't wait. He slithered down into the steep crater where the fire and vapours had been plugged a million years ago, and we followed, crashing and tripping behind him to the bottom.

'Bau! Bau!' he cried with demoniac excitement and fell headlong at the foot of an enormous block of granite. There were dozens more of them, upright or lying flat among the trees.

'The Stones of Bau!' Mordaunt cried too, and prostrated himself beside his houseboy, I wasn't sure whether in prayer or from fatigue.

They were the size of coffins, some rectangular, some six-sided, irregular but too smooth to have been cut by nature.

'Bau! Bau!' Black and Tan cried, as if it was El Dorado or Xanadu or at least Disneyland, and tumbled beside the men – their fathers.

'Jesus Christ, at last!' I found myself crying, invoking God incarnate – a thing I never do – and collapsed with them on the sopping ground. I had made it, I hadn't disgraced myself on the walkabout, but I couldn't go a step further.

From his sack Beaconsfield got out some bread and bananas and a tin of tuna fish, and we picnicked among the Stones.

'I've never seen rock like this round here,' Mordaunt said. 'It's not the usual volcanic stuff. Probably from another island. They must have built a raft of canoes to carry them.'

'Who are *they*?' I asked.

'Who indeed? People with a lot more energy than anyone now, who wanted a pile of rocks up here.'

'They dragged them up through the forest? The way we've come? What the hell for?'

'What for?' Mordaunt repeated to Beaconsfield. 'A sacrifice? Something nasty going on?'

'Don't go into the woods tonight,' I sang to the tune of 'The Teddy Bears' Picnic', and caught a touch of scorn on Beaconsfield's charcoal face. 'But what are they *for*? – a heap of rocks as big as refrigerators. It's not a castle.'

Beaconsfield said, 'Not a castle,' with a look of indignation. 'And not refrigerators.'

'Come on Beaconsfield, old man,' Mordaunt said to his houseboy – to his tribal brother. 'Don't be frightened, we're on your side – you can trust us to keep it dark.' It was an odd word to choose.

'You see,' the black man began, then looked round into the forest as if for help. 'One time there was a big-big feast here – plenty people, plenty food. . . .'

'Cannibals?' I suggested, and wished I hadn't.

Beaconsfield looked at me with contempt, Mordaunt with a scowl that told me not to be frivolous. Black and Tan nudged each other for support or safety.

'The people at the feast were told . . .' Beaconsfield stopped, afraid that he had gone too far.

'Told what?' Mordaunt asked quietly.

'They must be silent, they must make no noise. They had to swear.'

'We'll do the same, old man. It's a promise – don't worry.'

'So the people were all silent. They had sworn it, so they kept it.

201

But there was one woman who was a number one bad woman because she didn't obey. She broke it. She laughed. Loudly, when she was wrong to make a noise – she made a big-big laugh.'

'What happened?' the four of us wanted to ask, but didn't.

'You see, she laughed – and while she did it . . .' Beaconsfield was saying something very solemn but quite simple, something old and true that he had known all his life and wanted us to keep for the rest of ours. 'Her ear dropped on the ground.'

'My God!' Mordaunt uttered in a hollow tone, empty of obvious meaning but oddly convincing. I couldn't tell if he was serious. 'Her ear fell off – my God, my God!' His voice went on echoing inside him after the words had come out. He put his fist to his chest as if to stop it, and stared hard at Black and Tan like someone telling a fairy tale, half-believing it himself and challenging their disbelief. But he needn't have worried, they were hushed and waiting for more.

'You see,' Beaconsfield said, 'more people laughed when the woman's ear fell off and so their ears fell off the same as hers and then their noses and it was a sickness that the people caught, all were laughing and their parts were falling off because they must be silent and they had sworn it but they didn't obey, so their arms and legs and heads dropped on the ground and there was nothing except their bodies which turned to stone.' Beaconsfield surveyed the Stones of Bau in triumph and reproof. He knew no more, or wouldn't tell.

There was silence. I must have looked sceptical, though trying not to laugh or even smile, and caught another flash of Beaconsfield's contempt. He packed up the rest of the food and put it in his sack. The boys sucked their bananas like lollipops. Mordaunt seemed troubled and restless, stumbling over the granite blocks, feeling their texture, examining the shapes and positions; then he turned to me and I thought he was going to speak about them – more with pity than ridicule, from the look on his face – but he only said, 'My God!' once more and nothing else.

'Well,' I said after a while, feeling a need to be practical and lift, or lower, the mood from this uncomfortable state. 'It'll take a long time to get back, won't it?'

'Not a hope, old fellow,' Mordaunt said, with an effort to recover his good temper. 'Too late to think of it tonight – we'd never make it and the boatman will have pushed off somewhere, he's not expecting us till tomorrow. We'll have to camp up here. Safe enough, so long as we don't laugh.'

'You're sure?' I asked him, playing along.

'Beaconsfield will take care of us, or else his friends.' Mordaunt tossed a glance round the Stones. 'Treat them with respect, that's all, the way you'd treat the tombstones in a church, only more so. There's a lot we'll never get to the bottom of – you'd be amazed.'

In the tropical way the night arrived swiftly in the crater. Flying foxes came over in the brief dusk, squadrons of them hunting for fruit, wheeling like ghosts between the trees. Before it was quite dark, with a few swipes of his bush knife and the help of Black and Tan, Beaconsfield cut some canes from the undergrowth and built a shelter for us, thatched with leaves. It took ten minutes and looked absurdly easy. Mordaunt and I tried to get a fire going, but nothing was dry enough to kindle and it only smoked. The boys made a bed of foliage inside the shelter and fell instantly, puppyishly, asleep on it. Later, having given up the fire, Beaconsfield and Mordaunt and I crept in to join them.

There wasn't a whisper of wind or the least crackle of twigs; not even a moon, still less a firefly. The world might have stopped, or been suspended. The only disturbance was the breathing of my companions, and even that was as quiet as they could make it. My body was stiff and full of aches and I longed to ease it, but to move at all, unless for some ritual purpose, would have been a sort of profanity. I have never known such a dark, still night.

I lay awake for two hours or more, waiting not so much for sleep or for the dawn as for the plane back to Brisbane. I had spent a night in other forests but none so oppressive as this. I was choked with airlessness, suffocated by impatience, clammy with the wish to be anywhere else, with anyone but these sleeping forms of men and boys beside me. I wanted a woman, but love would be a sticky business here without much fun or comfort for either of us. When my hip at last found a hole to sink into, something hard stuck up to pierce my kidneys. The damp that seeped into me could equally be from the ground under me or my own sweat. Whatever it was that tickled my cheek, before I could scratch it, ran away. Two nights ago I had been in an air-conditioned room at the Mendana, naked in clean sheets, and in two nights' time I should be back there. In the end, after midnight, I slept in a desultory way, worried by dreams.

Dreams? Was that a scream? Or a laugh? I woke up – or was I still asleep? It was the heart of the night, the pit, the deepest black, and though I could make out nothing in the shelter I knew I was alone. My first feeling was anger, then fright. They shouldn't have left me. I would have shouted, 'Bugger you all!' but was stopped. By fear, I admit. Then by something else. Nothing visible, but a quick rustling in the forest. A squall blowing through the dark. In the desert it would have been one of those dust devils, a vortex of sand and rubbish lurching and twisting through the heat. Here it was only the air spinning across the crater, picking up no leaves but quivering suddenly in the trees. A tremble in my blood. And a quite unmistakable smell. I remembered it from the temples of Angkor in the forest of Cambodia, and I used to catch it sometimes in my house in Africa where the roof was full of bats. But this was flying foxes, of course, which are a giant kind of bat.

Probably I slept again, I can't be sure. I was very tired. I believe I had a dream but afterwards I couldn't remember it. When I opened my eyes it was already light and I was still alone. Bugger them all, again. Now I would have to find my own way back to the sea, and the thought defeated me. I would lie a little longer before making a start, putting it off.

But they hadn't left me, as I found when I crawled from the shelter. The sun was up, though not high enough to filter through the trees and fall into the crater. The thinnest mist lay on the ground like a cobweb left carelessly by the night, soon to be taken away. I saw Black and Tan first, sitting on one of the Stones – two boys of different colours wrapped in the same sullen air of having suffered. This morning the puppies were meek and dispirited. One of them gave a shiver when he saw me and the other caught it, but neither spoke. Beyond them stood Beaconsfield. He was framed between two trees, dwarfed by the trunks, but his slender figure defied their size. It exuded power. He turned stiffly and blinked at me. In the burnt black eyes, far inside, an unholy spark glinted, transmitting a message that might have been either victory or terror.

In a moment I knew why.

'My God!' It was my own voice this time, not Mordaunt's.

At the same moment my dream came back. I had heard Mordaunt's cry, 'Oh God!' and I laughed at him, knowing it was fatal, and then he shouted, like a command, 'Nicholas!' It wasn't an appeal, more of a reprimand, and it worked instantly, cutting off my laugh at source. Long ago as a district officer he had ordered men to be hanged; he hadn't lost the knack, he still knew how to throttle them.

'My God, Mordaunt – what happened?' The dream had already gone again.

He was sitting propped against one of the Stones, arms dangling on the ground, head tilted, eyes fixed on nothing. A faint grey colour lay under his cheeks, a trickle of dry saliva issued from his mouth. I had never seen anyone who had died of a heart attack, and thought they might be bruised with purple or horribly contorted. Perhaps it wasn't a heart attack. I touched his shoulder and felt only the sardonic mockery of a corpse.

'What happened?'

'Him fellow dead long time.' Beaconsfield, standing by me, was lost for an English way to show his feelings and settled for pidgin. 'Now him all same father and father's father and father's father's father.' Mordaunt, in other words, the ones he might have used himself, had gone to join his ancestors.

'But how?'

'Heart belong him finish.'

It was useless to get angry. Uselessness, in fact, was what filled the morning. Useless to ask questions, to shout or weep, to expect anyone to tell us what to do. We could make a stretcher – Beaconsfield would knock it up as easily as his shelter last night – and somehow get Mordaunt down to the sea, then back to Munda in the dugout and to Honiara by plane, to be buried with Michael in the European cemetery. It would be a daunting job; the two boys wouldn't be much help and Beaconsfield, though supreme at moving in the forest, was hardly muscular. I myself was weak with shock, and glad when Beaconsfield took charge of his tribal brother's death, as he once had of his marriage. He began hacking a grave with his bush knife in the soft, decaying ground. In that stuff a body would quickly moulder and we poured it back on top, then tore down the shelter to cover everything, to keep wild animals off. I wondered if my father on his expedition to New Guinea had buried the Dutchman like this – I had never thought of it before. Afterwards we stood there in silence, praying or cursing or just remembering.

'Mordaunt, old friend,' I said, but not aloud, 'I believe you're not too sorry about this, are you? And it's a funny thing – I feel a sort of privilege, I'll never have another walkabout like ours.'

Later we followed Beaconsfield down through the forest. Yesterday's trail seemed to be overgrown already, or else he led us by another route. None of us could have found the way out, down to the beach where the boatman was waiting, without the little old bush boy in front. Black and Tan were very quiet and I didn't care to interrogate them on the night's happenings. Truly, I didn't want to know. Curiosity was irrelevant, overlaid with sadness, and I was tired and hungry, dizzy with heat or my emotions. I must have become delirious, as confused about the events as about the forest track. I might have been anywhere, at any time. Once, when I stumbled, Beaconsfield looked round and for an instant in my stupefied eyes, though his face was as black as ever, it was my father's, which I only know from photographs.

Next day in Honiara I went to the police to make a deposition. They could go back and recover the body if they wanted, but nobody would find it unless Beaconsfield showed them and after a few days in that climate there wouldn't be much to take away. I told the police officer, a shiny young Solomon islander, that I thought it should be left.

'Please, sir, write that above your signature,' he said, giving me the feeling that a white man's request still counted, though no doubt it was what he intended anyway; and a black man's interest couldn't be suppressed: 'I'd like to ask, sir – how many are the Stones of Bau?' Perhaps he thought there might be an extra one now, but he must have taken my perplexity for disapproval and quickly said, 'From the police I thank you for your respect to Mr Mordaunt Fry – he was our most favourite Englishman, more than Princess Diana.'

As Mordaunt had arranged, I had time to recover before my flight to Brisbane. A week later, with nothing left of Rupert Murdoch's expenses, I was back in London. Among my letters was an invitation from the friend with a melancholy humour who had once had a wedding party at the zoo. He was getting married again, for the third time, and there was to be a celebration at the Royal Asiatic Society. Professor Richards of course was dead, but without reading it – without understanding why – I gave my friend a copy of *The Meaning of Meaning*.

AU PAIR

by

Fay Weldon

Fay Weldon is married, a mother of four, and at present lives in Somerset. She is a novelist and dramatist, for the stage as well as the screen, and has recently completed dramatising her latest novel Life and Loves of a She Devil *for BBC Television. A new volume of her short stories* Polaris and Other Stories *was published recently. Her work is read and produced not only in the English speaking world but has been translated, to date, into fourteen languages including Russian.*

'It's all a matter of landscape,' Bente's mother Greta wrote to her daughter from her apartment in the outer suburbs of Copenhagen, there where the land tilts gently and gracefully towards a flat Northern sea, and the birch trees in Spring are an almost unbearably brilliant green, and at nights the lights of Sweden glitter across the water, with their promise of sombre wooded crags, and dark ravines, and steeper, more difficult shores altogether. 'The English are dirty because they are so comparatively unobserved. They can hide behind hills from their neighbours. Dirt is normal, Bente, all over the world. It's we in the clean flat lands who are out of step.'

Bente's mother was fanciful. It was one of her many charms: men loved her absurdities. Her folly made men feel strong and sane. Greta had wide grey eyes and flaxen hair and a good strong figure and a frivolous nature. Her daughter had inherited her mother's looks, but not, alas, her nature. Bente's father had been Swedish born. He had passed on to his daughter, Greta feared, his deep Swedish seriousness, his lofty Swedish standards. He had been killed in action towards the end of the war. Whereupon, at least according to the neighbours, the girl Greta had slept with enough German soldiers to man a landing raft. She was lucky, all agreed, including Bente, to be accepted back into the community. Greta, of course, maintained that she had only done these things on the instructions of the Resistance, the better to gain the enemy's secrets. Be that as it may, there was no arguing but that Greta had gained a taste for sex, somewhere along the line; and Bente had not, even by the age of 23, and with her mother's cheerful example before her. Bente was glad to get away from Copenhagen and the tread of male footsteps on her mother's stair, and to come as an au pair in London, to the Beavers' household.

But within a week Bente rang in tears to say that the Beavers' household was dirty, the food was uneatable, she was expected to

211

sleep in a damp dark basement room, that she was overworked and underpaid, and the two children were unruly, unkempt, and objected to taking baths.

'Then clean the house,' said Greta firmly, 'take over the cooking, and the accounts, move a mattress to a better room, and bath the children by force if necessary, or better still, get in the bath with them. The English are too afraid of nakedness.'

Bente sobbed on the other end of the line, and Greta's sailor lover, Mogens, moved an impatient hand up her thigh. Greta had told Mogens she'd had Bente when she was seventeen. 'But I want to come home,' said Bente, and Greta said sharply that surely Bente could put up with a little dirt and discomfort. Adrian Beaver was a Marxist sociologist/journalist with an international reputation and Bente should think herself lucky to be in so interesting a household and not abuse her employers' hospitality by making too many long distance calls on their telephone. Greta put down the phone and turned her attention to Mogens. Lovers come and go: children go on for ever!

There was silence for a month or so, during which time Greta, feeling just a little guilty, sent Bente a leather mini-skirt and a recipe for steak au poivre using green pepper and a letter explaining her theories on dirt and landscape.

Bente's next letter home was cheerful enough: she asked Greta to send her some root ginger, since this was unobtainable in the outer London suburbs where she lived and she had only four hours off a week, and that on Sundays, and could not easily get into central London where more exotic ingredients were available. Mrs Beaver had objected to her wearing the mini-skirt, so she only put it on in her absence. Mr Beaver worked at home: life was much easier now that Mrs Beaver had a full-time job. She, Bente, could take over. The house was spick and span. When she, Bente, had children, she, Bente, would never leave them in a stranger's care. But she, Bente, liked to think the children were fond of her. She got into the bath with them, these days, and there was no trouble at all at bath time. Mr Beaver, Adrian, said she was a better mother to the boys than his wife was. She was certainly a better cook!

Greta's new lover, Andy, from the Caribbean, posted off the ginger without a covering letter. Silence seemed, at the time, golden. Greta knew Bente would just hate Andy, who was probably not yet twenty, and wonderfully black and shiny. Greta told him she'd had Bente when she was sixteen.

Bente rang in tears to say Mr Beaver kept touching her breasts in the kitchen and embarrassing her and she thought he wanted to sleep with her and could she come home at once?

Greta said what nonsense, sex is a free and wonderful thing; just sleep with him and get it over. There was silence the other end of the line. Andy's hot breath stirred the hairs on Greta's neck. She knew the flax was beginning to streak with grey. How short life is!

'But what about his wife?' asked Bente, doubtfully, presently.

'Knowing the English as I do,' said Greta, 'they've probably worked it out between them just to stop you from handing in your notice.'

'So you don't think she'd mind?'

Andy's sharp white teeth nibbled Greta's ear and his arm lay black and thick across her silky white breasts.

'Of course not,' said Greta. 'What are you getting so worked up about? Sex is just fun. It's not to be taken seriously.'

'I'm not so sure,' said Bente, primly.

'Bente,' said Greta, 'pillow talk is the best way to learn a foreign language, and that's what you're in England for. Do just be practical, even if you don't know how to enjoy yourself.'

Andy's teeth dug sharply into Greta's ear lobe and she uttered the husky little scream which so entranced and interested men. After she had replaced the receiver, it occurred to Greta that her daughter was still a virgin, and she almost picked up the phone for a longer talk, but then the time was past and Andy's red red tongue was importuning her and she forgot all about Bente for at least a week. Out of sight, out of mind! Many mothers feel it: few acknowledge it!

Bente wrote within the month to ask if she should tell Mrs Beaver that she and Mr Beaver were having an affair, since she didn't like to be deceitful. Adrian himself was reluctant to do it, saying it might upset the children and it should be kept secret. What did Greta think?

Greta wrote back to say, with feeling, that children should not begrudge their parents a sex life; you had to take sex calmly and openly, not get hysterical. Sex is like a wasp, wrote Greta. You must just sit still and let it take its course. It's when you try and brush it away the trouble comes. Fanciful Greta!

Bente wrote to say that Mrs Beaver had moved out of the house: simply abandoned the children and left! What sort of mother was that? She, Bente, would never do such a thing. Mrs Beaver was hopelessly neurotic. (Didn't Greta think her, Bente's, English had improved? Greta had been quite right about pillow talk!) Mr Beaver had told his wife she could continue living in the spare room and have her own lovers quite freely, but Mrs Beaver hadn't been at all grateful and had made the most dreadful scenes before finally going and had even tried to knife her, Bente, and Mr Beaver had lost half a stone in weight. Could Greta send her the pickled herring recipe? She enclosed a photograph of herself and Adrian and the boys. She and Adrian were to be married as soon as he was free. Wasn't love wonderful? Wasn't fate an extraordinary thing? Supposing she and Adrian had never met? Supposing this, supposing that!

Greta studied the photograph with a magnifying glass. Adrian Beaver, she was surprised to see, was at least fifty and running to fat, and plain in a peculiarly English, intellectual, chinless way, and the Beaver sons were not little, as she had supposed, but in their late adolescence and ungainly too. Her daughter stood next to Mr Beaver, twice his size, big-busted, bovine, with the sweet inexorable smile of a flaxen doll. Greta did not want to have grandchildren, especially not these grandchildren. Greta, one way and another, was in a fix.

Greta had fallen in love, in a peculiarly high, pure, almost sexless way – who'd have thought it! But life goes this way, now that! – with a doctor from Odense, who wanted to marry her, Greta, save her from herself and build her a house in glass and steel where she could live happily ever after. (Perhaps she was in love with the house, not him, but what could it matter? Love is love, even if it's for glass and steel!) The doctor was thirty-five. Greta, alas, on first meeting him, had given her age as thirty-four. Unless she had given birth to Bente when she was ten, how now could Bente be her daughter?

'You are no daughter of mine,' she wrote back to Bente. 'Sex is one thing, love quite another. Sex may be a wasp, but love is a

214

swarm of bees! You have broken up a marriage, done a dreadful thing! I never wish to hear from you again.'

And nor she did, and both lived happily ever after: the mother in the flat, clean, cheerful land: the daughter in her dirty, hilly, troubled one across the sea, where fate had taken her. How full the world is of bees and wasps! In the autumn the birch trees of Denmark turn russet red and glorious, and the lights which shine across from Sweden seem hard and resolute and the air chilly, and the wasps and the bees move slowly and sleepily amongst the red, red leaves and how lucky you are if you escape a sting!

Also available in ABACUS paperback:

FICTION

FOREIGN EXCHANGE	Ed. Julian Evans	£3.50 ☐
THE HOUSE ON THE EMBANKMENT	Yuri Trifonov	£2.50 ☐
BILGEWATER	Jane Gardam	£2.50 ☐
THE SEIZURE OF POWER	Czeslaw Milosz	£2.75 ☐
THE ISSA VALLEY	Czeslaw Milosz	£3.25 ☐
IN COLD BLOOD	Truman Capote	£2.95 ☐
THE WAPSHOT SCANDAL	John Cheever	£2.50 ☐
THE LAST TESTAMENT OF OSCAR WILDE	Peter Ackroyd	£2.50 ☐

NON-FICTION

BEYOND THE CHAINS OF ILLUSION	Erich Fromm	£2.50 ☐
IRISH JOURNAL	Heinrich Boll	£1.95 ☐
THE AGE OF CAPITAL	E. J. Hobsbawn	£3.95 ☐
THE AGE OF REVOLUTION	E. J. Hobsbawn	£3.95 ☐
THE PRIMAL SCREAM	Arthur Janov	£3.95 ☐
BLACK AND WHITE	Shiva Naipaul	£2.95 ☐
MRS. HARRIS	Diana Trilling	£2.95 ☐

All Abacus books are available at your local bookshop or newsagent, or can be ordered direct from the publisher. Just tick the titles you want and fill in the form below.

Name _____

Address _____

_____

Write to Abacus Books, Cash Sales Department, P.O. Box 11 Falmouth, Cornwall TR10 9EN

Please enclose cheque or postal order to the value of the cover price plus:

UK: 55p for the first book plus 22p for the second book and 14p for each additional book ordered to a maximum charge of £1.75.

OVERSEAS: £1.00 for the first book plus 25p per copy for each additional book.

BFPO & EIRE: 55p for the first book, 22p for the second book plus 14p per copy for the next 7 books, thereafter 8p per book.

Abacus Books reserve the right to show new retail prices on covers which may differ from those previously advertised in the text or elsewhere, and to increase postal rates in accordance with the PO.